PRAISE FOR *EYES WIDE OPEN*

"Raine is a masterful wordsmith, and once more her ability to balance impeccably developed characters with a solid plot in *Eyes Wide Open* makes her a force to be reckoned with."

—NATASHA IS A BOOK JUNKIE

"*Eyes Wide Open* is a jaw-dropping, heart-palpitating, pulse-racing thrill ride of emotion, romance, lust, and ultimately the most unconditional and unforgettable love."

—KATIE ASHLEY, AUTHOR OF THE *NEW YORK TIMES* BESTSELLER *THE PROPOSITION*

"Fans of The Blackstone Affair will not be disappointed. The conclusion to the series with *Eyes Wide Open* is pure perfection."

—BECCA THE BIBLIOPHILE

"It's all there! Heat, passion, intrigue and a thrilling ride of emotions . . . *Eyes Wide Open* delivers!"

—TOTALLYBOOKEDBLOG

"5 AMAZING stars! One of my most highly anticipated books of the year. It was PERFECT. Intense. Emotional. Simply beautiful. And Ethan is one of the best book boyfriends of all time!"

—R. K. LILLEY, BESTSELLING AUTHOR OF THE *UP IN THE AIR* SERIES

"*Eyes Wide Open*—by far the best book of 2013; beautifully written, intense, remarkable, superb."

—DONNA, MY STICKY PAGES

"I can't put into words how completely *Eyes Wide Open* consumed me with love for Ethan and Brynne and their powerful love story. By far the best Blackstone Affair novel yet!"

"Sexy, alluring and seductive! *Eyes Wide Open* is an addictive tale of love, passion, and mystery that will sweep you away from the start."

"Raine delivers yet another 5 star read in *Eyes Wide Open* that will leave you glued to your seat and unable to put the book down. The sexual tension will melt your panties off and leave you begging for more. A must-read!!"

"*Eyes Wide Open* had everything: wonderful character development, hair-raising tension, scintillating sex scenes, and sad, poignant moments dashed with clever splashes of humor at just the right moments."

"Everyone loves a hot guy, it's a fact of life. In Ethan Blackstone, Raine Miller has not only given us a hot guy but a thoughtful, dependable . . . REAL guy too! I'll admit in *Naked* and *All In* I fell in lust with Ethan Blackstone, but in *Eyes Wide Open*? Now that's when I fell in love."

Eyes Wide Open

THE BLACKSTONE AFFAIR
BOOK III

RAINE MILLER

ATRIA PAPERBACK

New York • London • Toronto • Sydney • New Delhi

ATRIA PAPERBACK
A Division of Simon & Schuster, Inc.
1230 Avenue of the Americas
New York, NY 10020

First Atria Paperback edition August 2013

ATRIA PAPERBACK and colophon are trademarks of Simon & Schuster, Inc.

For information about special discounts for bulk purchases, please contact Simon & Schuster Special Sales at 1-866-506-1949 or business@simonandschuster.com.

The Simon & Schuster Speakers Bureau can bring authors to your live event. For more information or to book an event contact the Simon & Schuster Speakers Bureau at 1-866-248-3049 or visit our website at www.simonspeakers.com.

Manufactured in the United States of America

10   9   8   7   6   5   4   3   2   1

Library of Congress Cataloging-in-Publication Data

Miller, Raine.
Eyes wide open : the Blackstone Affair, book 3 / Raine Miller. — First Atria Books trade paperback edition.
    p. cm. — (Blackstone Affair ; 2)
    1. Romantic suspense fiction. I. Title.
    PS3613.I547N35 2013
    813'.6—dc23   2012049352

ISBN 978-1-4767-3560-3
ISBN 978-1-4767-3561-0 (ebook)

For my parents,

Who still see into each other's soul

The eye sees a thing more clearly in dreams than the imagination awake.

—Leonardo da Vinci

Acknowledgments

There are so many I have to thank, and the first goes out to my family, my prince of a husband, and my boys, who accepted the lack of a proper wife and mom for weeks while I was deep in my writing cave and not coming out much. Thank you for your patience, guys. I could not be more blessed and I never forget it.

To the most wonderful agent on earth, Jane Dystel, THANK YOU for all you do and have done for me. Again, I am blessed to have found you on that Friday in October when I needed the guiding hand of somebody much wiser than me. To Atria Books, for taking on the Blackstone Affair and helping me achieve something I never dreamed would be a reality. To my lovely and charming editor, Johanna Castillo, for guiding me through this process every step of the way, and in the kindest way possible.

Behind the scenes there are so many people I am indebted to for their unwavering support and sharing of the books on Facebook and Twitter, but mostly just in their conversations with me; the simple sharing of daily events and the trials and tribulations of life. That's true friendship, and it means the world to me. Becca, Jena, Franzi, Muna, Karen, and Martha, you are angels sent down from heaven I am sure, and I hardly have words to express how appreciative I am of each of you.

To my peers who are some of the most amazing and creative people I will ever know, thank you for the friendship and the inspiration of your hard work and dedication to keep on writing the stuff that people today want to read. Katie Ashley, you were a blessing from our very first meeting, and I knew I'd found a lifelong friend that day. Thank you for all the late-night chats about this crazy writers' world we now find ourselves in. To the other writers who blow me away with their talents and just for being my friend—Rebecca, Jasinda, Tara, CC, Jenn, Belinda, Tina, Georgia, Amy, and a ton more—you make my job the best one in the world.

And finally to the fans and bloggers who read my books. I say it all the time and I mean it every time. I have the best fans on the planet. Thank you for loving Ethan and Brynne and embracing these stories with all of your heart. I am forever in your debt for that.

My very best,
Raine ♥

Prologue

I watch. I remember what she felt like. How she moved and sounded. All of it—everything about her.

She doesn't see me, though. It bothered me at first, but now I know it doesn't matter because she will. Soon enough she *will* see me.

Fate came along and put her in my path all those years ago and fate made another appearance when that plane went down. I never forgot about sweet Brynne Bennett. Never. I've thought about her for years, I just never imagined we'd meet again. I knew she left the States and moved to London, but it wasn't until I saw her modeling photographs that I realized just how much I wanted to find her again.

Now I have.

The fates have aligned. Everything has come together. I can get my due and have her in the process. Brynne deserves this. She's a treasure. A rare jewel in the crown. Something to savor and enjoy for as long as I want.

We are all pawns. She as much as I. Pawns in a game I did not invent, but one I can certainly play. I'm fighting for equity. This is my opportunity of a lifetime and I won't let it, or her, slip through my hands. Brynne just comes as a value added, and I look forward to the time when I can show her just how much I've missed her and our time together.

In my defense, I did try to get her to help me directly. I would have wooed her and been nice. She would have been happy to see me again. I know she would have been. Those assholes didn't deserve her, and they certainly earned what they got. Doesn't matter now, though. They're out of the equation and that makes it better for me. In the end I'll be the sole beneficiary anyway.

Now, Blackstone is another story. That bastard came along and swooped her up and into his life. I know he turned her head with his good looks and money, and it's a damn shame too, because without him it all would have gone off without a hitch.

Blackstone ruined my initial plans, but not everything. He's got good instincts, though, I'll give him that. I thought I had her in the bag when he went out to have a smoke behind the building at that charity gala. I couldn't believe my luck. He was outside. She was inside. Alarm goes off like clockwork. My only mistake was that I didn't expect him to have her cell phone. That was a definite surprise. But still, I wanted him to know about me. He should know. I had her years before he did.

Then something happened that must have worked in his favor. I'm not sure why, but Brynne wasn't where she should have been and she didn't come out like she was supposed to. If she'd had her cell when my message came through I'm certain we'd be together right now, picking up where we left off seven years ago.

I lost her in the mayhem . . . and in the process, my golden opportunity. This is very displeasing to me. Some punishment will have to be delivered in order to restore the balance of things to their rightful place in the world. It's not a problem, though. Everything will all come around to my way in time.

Blackstone has her well protected now, but I'm working on him too. He doesn't have all the answers, and I'll be sure to throw a few more tidbits his way to confuse him. My specialty.

No, I'm not giving up. I've got a few tricks up my sleeve yet, and I can be very patient. There is still plenty of time to make my move, and I'm getting closer all the time.

Closer.

I didn't know it at the time, but when those fools chose that song they were dead on. It *is* perfect. Just perfect.

1

♥

Ethan's eyes held on to me as he mastered my body, his grip firm on my hips, his thick flesh filling me up and moving inside me, his mouth all over me, his teeth on my skin.

All of this from the man who had broken though the walls I'd built and captured me. They were demonstrations of touch and pleasure, a means of cementing the connection between us, of keeping me close to him. It was his way. He didn't need to worry, though.

Ethan had me.

Despite the whole mess tonight, he had me in his arms and underneath him, his commanding strength taking charge in the way it'd been from the beginning. Holding me safe. That night on the street when he'd coaxed me into his car and the later phone calls demanding I acknowledge him were just the start of my understanding of Ethan Blackstone. There was so much more to the man than I ever imagined back then.

I wasn't going anywhere. I was in love with him.

"I want my cock in you all night long," he rasped, his blue eyes flashing against the moonlight as he moved. Looming over me, he plied my body in every which way as the light shone on our naked flesh through the balcony window. Hands, mouth, cock, tongue, teeth, fingers—he used them all.

Ethan said things to me like that during sex. Shocking stuff that made me hotter than hell, nourishing my confidence, and showing me how much he wanted me. It was precisely what I needed. Ethan was my answer, and he knew exactly what I craved. I don't know how he understood me so well, but he did without a doubt. Tonight had confirmed that message loud and clear. I guess I could finally admit that I was in need of another person in order to be happy.

That other person was Ethan.

I'd let someone in. The hard shell around my heart had been compromised, and very thoroughly too. Ethan had done it. He'd worked on me, and pushed me and demanded my attention. He never gave up on me and loved me in spite of my cavern of emotional issues. Ethan did all that for me. And now I could revel in the fact that I was loved by a man whom I loved in return.

"Eyes on me, baby," he commanded on a harsh breath. "You know I have to have your eyes when I take you!" His hand had moved up to grip my hair and he tugged. He never hurt me when he pulled it, though. Ethan knew just how much pressure to exert and was fully aware it sent me over the edge. I did know about his need for my eyes being on him and I held onto his fiery blues with everything I had.

But Ethan knew more about me than I knew about him.

"You're going to come first!" he gritted out, thrusting deep and hard, finding the sensitive spot within me needed to accomplish his directive.

As I felt the pressure build I let myself go to that perfect place of ecstasy, pinned beneath Ethan's body, which was burrowed in mine, his blue eyes just inches above me. He took my mouth as the orgasm ripped into me, filling another part of me, making me accept more of him, binding us together more deeply.

His orgasm followed mine within seconds. I could always tell he was close from how he tightened to inhuman hardness right as he was about to come. The feeling was out of this world and intensely empowering. That I could pull such a reaction from him and elicit such feeling in another person did something to me. Something that healed me a little bit each time it happened—I kept getting better inside my head because of Ethan and the ways he showed his love for me. I had some hope about myself that I could be happy and live a normal life.

Ethan had given me that.

"Tell me, baby," he exhaled in a harsh whisper, but I could hear the vulnerability that accompanied the boldness. Ethan wasn't without his own insecurities, he was just a mortal like the rest of us.

"Always yours!" I truly meant my words as I felt him let go inside me.

When I opened my eyes sometime later, I realized I must have dozed a bit. Ethan had rearranged us halfway on our sides, but we were still joined together. He liked to stay buried inside me for a while afterward. I didn't mind, because it was something he desired and I loved making him happy.

I just wish he'd tell me more about his dark place. He was afraid to share, and while it bothered me, I mostly understood his fear. I often wondered if his reasons for needing to touch me all the time and possess me so thoroughly during sex, and afterward too, had something to do with his time as a prisoner. *They tortured him and scarred him and hurt him.* It pained me just remembering how he'd been that night when his dreams woke him up in a panic.

I trailed my fingers over his shoulder and back. I imagined the angel wings of his tattoo and the words below them. And I felt the scars too. Ethan flicked his eyes open and pegged me hard. "Why wings? They're beautiful, you know."

"The wings reminded me of my mum," he said after a moment or two of silence, "and they covered over many of the scars."

I leaned forward, kissing his lips with a soft touch. I cupped his jaw and decided to take the plunge. I didn't want to scare Ethan away from talking to me if he was in a mood, but figured I had to try again at some point. "And the quote? Why that one?"

He shrugged and whispered, "I think I died a little tonight."

So much for him opening up and sharing. He wasn't up for any more delving into his past. I could tell. "What do you mean you died a little?"

"When I couldn't find you after that message came

in on your mobile." He traced my cheek and then my lips with his finger—just the lightest touch, and I felt a shiver roll through me.

"Well, you did find me eventually, and no dying allowed, mister. That would be a real major buzzkill." I tried to tease him into a lighter mood, but it didn't seem to be working. When Ethan was in a serious frame of mind, he didn't just switch out of it easily.

"I'm glad you feel better," he paused and thrust his hips with a renewed erection, sinking in deep, "because I needed this with you, badly."

"I'm here and you have me," I murmured against his lips as he draped my legs over his shoulders and took charge of another round of pleasure. Once was rarely enough for him.

Ethan made me feel desirable. He made me feel beautiful and sexy, from the words that came out of his mouth to the touch of his body in mine when he made love to me. And afterward, when he held me against him like I was precious.

Somebody wanted me, despite all that had gone down in my past. Someone was willing to fight for me. I was important to another person. To Ethan I was. The power in that knowledge was life-changing.

Ethan's particular brand of attention was intense and a lot to accept at first, but it worked for me. Ethan worked for me. He could show me how much he wanted me, and for the first time I had some hope that we could really make this relationship work. The "let's go slow" part hadn't happened at all like we'd agreed when we first met. But if we had gone slowly, I very much doubt I'd be naked in bed with him at the Somerset coast, in an English manor fit for a king, which happened to be owned by his sister, and being fucked to the brink of another magnificent orgasm right now. A girl has to take things as they come.

It took a bit for me to rouse myself after the second round of sheet-clawing sex, but I managed to wriggle out of his hold to head for the bathroom so I could clean up and prepare for sleep. I loved how he touched me all the time. I needed it, plain and simple, and Ethan knew that. It was just another way in which we were emotionally compatible.

I filled a glass of water and took the pill Dr. Roswell had prescribed for my night terrors. I had a routine. Birth control and vitamins in the morning, sleeping pill at night, once I was ready to actually sleep. I smirked into the elegant bathroom mirror that looked like something out of Buckingham Palace, realizing that bed and sleep were never synonymous when sharing with Ethan. We spent a great deal of time together in bed *not* sleeping, but I wasn't complaining.

I didn't expect to find him awake when I came out of the bathroom, but his eyes were open, tracking my every movement as I settled back into bed. He reached for me and held my face, something he did often when we were close like this.

"How come you're still awake? You must be exhausted after that long drive," I paused for emphasis, "and all that superb shagging—"

"I love you and I never want to let you go," he interrupted.

"So don't." I looked into his blue eyes, which seared me in the dim light.

"I never will." He said it with some hardness and I felt that he really meant it.

"I love you too, and I'm not going anywhere." I leaned in to kiss his lips, the rasp of his beard stubble well familiar to me now. He kissed me back, but I could tell he had more to say and could feel the edge in him, which was surprising considering the orgasms he'd just pounded into me.

"The thing is I—I need something more permanent with us. I need you with me all the time so I can protect you and we can be together every day . . . and night."

I felt my heart begin to thud rapidly, whispers of panic taking hold. Just when I got comfortable with one aspect of us, Ethan pushed for more.

He's always been that way . . .

"But we are together every day now," I told him.

He furrowed his brow and narrowed his eyes a fraction. "It's not enough, Brynne. Not after what happened tonight and that fucked-up message from God knows whom. I have Neil working on your mobile trace right now and we'll get to the bottom of it, but I need something more formal that tells the world you are off limits and untouchable by whatever designs they might have on you."

I swallowed hard, feeling his thumbs start to move over my jaw as I tried to imagine where he was going with this. "What do you mean when you say *'formal'*? How formal are we talking?" Man, my voice was thready, and my heart felt like it would leap out of my chest the next moment.

He smiled at me and leaned in for a soft, slow kiss that calmed me some. Ethan had always calmed me, though. If I was unsettled or scared, he had a way of comforting me and easing the stress of the moment. "Ethan?" I asked when he finally pulled back.

"It's okay, baby," he said soothingly, "everything will be all right and I'll take care of you, but I know what we need to do—what needs to happen."

"You do?"

"Mmm-hmm." He rolled us over and held my face again, propped on his elbows and trapping me beneath his sculpted limbs, hard and smooth against my softer parts. "I'm sure of it, in fact." His lips dropped to my neck and kissed up to my ear and then down my jaw, over my throat, and back to the other ear. "Very, very sure," he whispered between gentle kisses. "I realized it tonight as soon as we got here and I saw that you were wearing this." He kissed the spot where the amethyst pendant he'd given me lay in the hollow of my throat.

"What are you so sure about?" My voice was faint, but every word rang out clear as a bell in the short distance between us, as if I'd shouted my question.

"Do you trust me, Brynne?"

"Yes."

"And you love me?"

"Yes, of course. You know that I do."

He smiled down at me again. "Then it's settled."

"What is settled?" I implored against his gorgeous face,

which had mesmerized me from the first, one side of his beautiful mouth turned up confidently, holding me firmly beneath him in a possessive hold so typical of my Ethan.

"We'll get married."

I stared at him, sure the words that just came out of his mouth were out of a scene from a romance novel. Maybe I was having a dream. I hoped.

Ethan shifted on top of me and shot that idea to hell. *Holy fucking shit!*

"It makes perfect sense," he said with a slow grin, "we make an announcement that goes out big, have you move in with me officially, and let everyone know your fiancé is in the security business—"

"Are you insane?" I cut him off and saw his eyes moving over my face, studying my reaction to his words. "Ethan, I can't get married. I don't want to. I'm just getting used to being in a relationship. It's way, way too soon to even consider something like that for us . . ."

He grinned down at me, utterly calm and confident. "I know, baby. It is far too soon, but the world doesn't have to know that. To them it looks like you're about to be the wife of the former-SF, high-profile CEO of Blackstone Inc. To whoever is out there with an agenda, they get a message loud and clear. That they need to keep the hell away from you; that they won't be able to touch you in any way, shape or form, and that they won't get close enough to even blink at you, let alone deliver threats like that fucked-up shit from last night." He kissed me softly, looking very proud of himself. "It's a brilliant plan."

I just kept staring at him, sure he was a figment of

some fantastical dream I was having. "It's also dishonest, Ethan. Have you even considered what you are asking me to do? To lie? To mislead our families and friends into believing some fiction that we met two months ago and now we're getting married?"

He stiffened above me, and his jaw got that stubborn set to it. "When it comes to protecting you, I'll do whatever I need to do. I'm not taking the risk with you—it's too late for that. I told you I was all in, and that's not changed in the last hours."

His glaring expression was more than a little intimidating, even in the dim light. I tried to explain myself. "Well, no, my feelings haven't changed either, but that doesn't mean we can ..."

My words trailed off as I tried to process what he'd just so confidently declared—that getting married would be a good idea—just like eating more vegetables or wearing sunscreen was a good idea. I had to wonder if the stomach bug that had got to me tonight was making me hallucinate.

"There's no reason we can't." Ethan looked a little wounded as he studied me carefully, and it gave me a pang of regret, but only for about two seconds. What he was proposing was absolutely insane. I could barely wrap my head around being in love with a man who'd stormed his way into my life, audaciously and without apology, a mere two months ago. How in the hell could I agree to a marriage based on my protection from some mysterious threat of unknown motivations by unnamed people?

"I—I'm—you're absolutely out-of-your-mind crazy

right now! Ethan, do you realize what you are proposing here?"

He nodded at me, his face just inches from mine. I couldn't really tell what he was thinking right now either. He wanted his way, I could guess, but his motives were what surprised me more. I knew he loved me. He made sure to tell me often. And I know my feelings for him were the same . . . but . . . *marriage*?! I was sure he couldn't have suggested anything more of a shock to my fragile emotional grid than this. Surely Ethan didn't want a wife. This was way too soon.

"Yes, Brynne, I very much know what I just said to you." He kept his face neutral but firm, giving away nothing.

"You want to marry me, a woman you just met eight weeks ago, who has relationship phobias and—and a fucked-up past—"

He shut me up with a dominating kiss, the kind that left no doubts about the seriousness of his proposal. *God! Am I in Bizarro World here?* I let his mouth plunder mine for a moment, then brought my hand up to the back of his head. I tugged him back and cupped his cheek, seeking his eyes again.

"Baby . . . that thing tonight spooked me," he whispered. "I didn't plan this out; I just know what feels right. I want you with me. You won't need a work visa any more. You can live here and work in London somewhere in your field. You'll have time to find the perfect job without pressure to wrangle the immigration laws, and most important, we can be together. It's what I want. I can shield you as your husband. I can make sure you're always protected.

There's nothing I wouldn't do to keep you safe. I love you. You love me, yeah? What's the problem? It's the perfect solution." He tilted his head at me and squinted his eyes like I was being illogically stupid.

"I'm not anywhere close to being ready for that, Ethan, despite how I feel about you."

"I'm not either, and the timing is horrible, but I think it's our only good option." He softly brushed my hair back from my face with a gentle touch. "I'm willing . . . and I think you should at least consider it." He gave me the eyebrow look. "I'm not enduring another episode like we had tonight at the National."

I started to protest but he shushed me with another demanding kiss that was so very typical of him. He held me beneath him, pressing me into the soft mattress and stroking into my mouth with a skilled tongue. I let him kiss me and just floated along for a bit, trying my best to process what he'd shared.

"Before you get all feisty and worried, I want you to just think about it for now. We could have a long engagement, but the announcement is what will make people sit up and take notice. We had a tough night and there's a ton of shit to be sorted, but in the end, we're together and that won't be changing." He kissed me on the forehead. "And you're moving in with me."

I just stared at him and took in his words.

"That last part is not a request, Brynne. What went down tonight was utter madness and we cannot be living in two places."

"God, what am I going to do with you?" I stifled a

yawn and realized the pill was making me sleepy. I knew I wouldn't be able to continue this conversation much longer. The idea flashed through my mind that he might have used that fact to his advantage. Ethan wasn't good at poker for nothing.

"You're exhausted, and quite frankly I am too."

I yawned again and agreed with him. "I am . . . but I still don't know what to even say about what you're suggesting," I told him, speaking into his eyes, which were just inches from mine.

He snuggled me against his body in preparation for sleep and buried his face in my neck. "You're going to go to sleep right now, and think about it . . . and trust me . . . and move in with me officially."

"Just like that?" I asked.

"Yeah, just like that." His lips moved against the back of my neck. "It's simply the way things have to be." I felt his stubble graze my skin as he pressed close. "I love you, baby. Now go to sleep."

Ethan's strong arms folded around me did feel magnificent, despite the fact that I thought he was out of his ever-loving mind. But knowing that he would do something so drastic for me just to keep me protected, that he loved me that much, made the small smile on my face feel quite *fucking fabulous*, to quote my soldier-mouthed lover.

I did sleep then, safe in his arms.

2

♠

Out on patrols we saw all kinds of horrifying shit. Democracy is something most people never really have the opportunity to appreciate. I suppose that's a lucky thing for much of the world, but still food for thought for those who don't even know how good they have it. The thing that bothered me the most was the incredible waste of potential. People suppressed and terrorized have very little potential—just the way third-world dictators like them to be.

We'd seen her around begging on the streets of Kabul before, but never with the boy. Servicemen were restricted from interaction with the Afghan women. It was far too dangerous, and not just for the troops, but horny men are the most predictable, stupid creatures on the planet. They'll go looking for pussy and find trouble just about every time. It was fair to assume she was a prostitute. Although not common, brothels did exist in Kabul, not that I'd ever be caught dead in one. But some of the men took the risk, morons that they are, thinking with their cocks. I made do with porn and the

18

occasional secret shag with a "fellow" enlisted when it could be managed on the sly. I had a fair bit of interest and enough offers from women in the army. Discretion was key for any sex on base. Female troops had reason to be wary when they were so vastly outnumbered by men.

The woman's name was Leyya and she died an inhumane death. The Taliban executed her in the town square for her crimes. The crime of working to feed her child. The bawling boy alerted us of the situation. He was about three years old and sitting in his mother's blood in the middle of the street. I later wondered if anyone in the town would have ever picked him up, or if they would've left him to die right there with his mother's desecrated body. In the end the point was moot.

It made me insane leaving him there while the possibility of a suicide bomb was ruled out. Took fucking hours. I was the one who set out to go get him off her corpse. I went in quickly and scooped him up. He didn't want to leave her and clutched at her burka, dragging it away from her face as I lifted him up. Her throat had been slit from ear to ear, her head mostly severed. I dearly hoped he was too young to remember seeing his mother like that.

I got a terrible feeling almost immediately. A coldness swept through me as I ran him out of there. And then his crying stopped abruptly. A whoosh of air passed my ear and then . . . blood. So much blood for such a tiny little body. A moment later all hell broke loose . . .

"Baby, you're dreaming," a voice said gently in my ear.

I turned toward the voice, straining hard to find it. The sound soothed like nothing else before. I wanted that voice.

And then again, "Ethan, baby, you're dreaming."

I opened my eyes, sucking in a breath as I saw her, and took in her words. "I was?"

"Yeah, just some mumbling and moving around." She reached a hand up behind my head and held my eyes to hers. "I woke you because I didn't want you to dream anything terrible."

"Fuck, I'm sorry. I woke you up?" I still felt disoriented, but was coming out of it quickly.

"It's all right. I wanted to wake you up before it got . . . bad." She sounded sad to me and I could only imagine that she'd try to get me to talk about this dream like she had the last time.

"Sorry," I repeated, feeling shamed for doing this shit again and disturbing her with it.

"You don't have to be sorry for having a dream, Ethan," she said firmly. "But I'd really love it if you told me what it was about."

"Oh, baby." I drew her close and smoothed over her head and hair with my hand. I pressed my lips to her forehead and inhaled. Just breathing in her scent helped me immensely, as did the feel of her breasts against my thudding heart as I held her close to me. She was real, right here, right now. Safe with me.

I was hard. Hot and hard against her soft skin. "I'm still sorry for waking you up," I said tightly as my lips found hers. I plundered her mouth with my tongue, pressing in deep and forceful, determined to have more. Nothing could help me right now but Brynne. She was the only cure.

And I *was* sorry, but I'd been like this with her before. Waking in the night and needing sex to bring myself down from the hyperanxiety of wherever I'd been in my dreams tonight.

"It's okay," she rasped against my mouth.

Her response emboldened me. Most everything she did turned me on. I liked to be dominant, but it thrilled me when Brynne assured me that she was willing, and desired me in the same way I did her. I instinctively knew she wanted me. It was just another form of the communication we shared. I wished all aspects of our relationship were so easy. The sex part we had figured out quickly, from the very first. Yeah, the fucking had always been hot and wickedly good for us.

I rolled her under me and split her legs wide with my knees, opening her up and dropping my head. I tossed off the covers and drew my eyes down over the gorgeous, willing body I would be buried deep inside of in another moment. *Thank sweet Christ.*

"Good, because I need to fuck you until you come, saying my name," he said in typical fashion. "Then I'm going to take my cock out of your divine cunt and fuck your beautiful mouth with it. And watch your lovely lips wrap around it and suck me dry." His eyes flared and his sculpted chest moved from the heavy breathing as he moved into position. "Yes, baby, I'm going to do all of that."

Ethan and his filthy mouth. It was crazy as hell, but that dirty talk did something to me.

Tensing in anticipation of what he would do, I moaned when he plunged into me hard and deep, filling me so full, bringing us so close together, my mind flashing back to what he'd said to me earlier in the night. *We'll get married.* Not a question posed, but a directive as only Ethan could state and get away with, just as he'd done so many other times since we'd met.

Ethan held my wrists in one hand and roamed with the other as he rode me hard. In and out at a furious pace, almost angry in his method. I knew he wasn't angry with me, though. It was the dream he battled. He needed to get the thing out of his head. I totally understood what was going on. Didn't matter to me. I was a completely willing participant in his form of self-discipline.

He pushed me open wider and worked my sweet spot with his cock so perfectly it didn't take very long before I was striving for an orgasm, feeling the tightening of my muscles readying for the blast that would take me to heaven on a supernova of heat and light.

He pinched my nipple, much more sensitive than usual, and the pain blinded me for an instant. I cried out as the climax started to roll through my body. He soothed the tender flesh with his tongue and spoke: "Say my name! I have to hear it."

"Ethan, Ethan, Ethan!" I chanted against his lips as he plunged his tongue into my mouth and swallowed my words. I shuddered and clenched my inner muscles around his cock, pinned down and fully taken. And never more satisfied than I was in this moment. He took charge of my pleasure and never let me down.

But he wasn't done. I remembered what he'd said to me before.

Ethan growled a very primal sound and pulled out of me. I protested the loss, but welcomed the jerk down the bed and the hot head of his penis filling my mouth as he readjusted his point of penetration. I could taste myself mixed with the taste of him and the eroticism was blatantly explosive. Gripping his hips, I pulled him deeper and sucked him to the back of my throat. Just a few strokes of my lips along the shaft before I felt the spurt of semen splash down. The sounds he made were carnal and oddly vulnerable for such a dominant act. It always made me feel powerful when Ethan came. *I made it happen.*

He was staring at me, watching the whole thing as he liked to do, our eyes connecting us deeply beyond just the physical act.

"Oh, God," he whispered as he slid out of my mouth and drew back down my body to press us close. He covered me again, gently this time, sliding inside me in a perfect fit of his body to mine before his erection faded. I could feel the thudding of his heart blending with mine.

I held on to him and let him have his way. For a long time he kissed and touched me, needing to be inside me for a while longer, telling me he loved me and making me feel cherished. I understood so much about this man and what made him tick. So much . . . except for the one thing I wanted to know, and didn't know at all.

Ethan's dark place was still as mysterious to me as it had ever been.

"I love that you brought me here." I felt myself start

to slip away into drowsiness again, determined to talk to him tomorrow about the nightmares, knowing that he wouldn't like it, but screw it, I was going to anyway. I wondered if he sensed what I would do. Ethan had the uncanny ability to predict my intentions. "And I love you."

He settled me in his arms and stroked my hair. I breathed in his spicy scent mixed with all the sex and his cologne and let myself go, knowing I was in the arms of the only man who had ever gotten me to stay there.

As morning dawned I disentangled myself very carefully from the body wrapped around me. Ethan just sighed into his pillow and rolled deeper into the blankets. He had to be worn out from last night's stressful show at the National Gallery and then the three hour drive up the coast late afterward. I couldn't discount the time spent on sex once we got here either. Or his bad dream. And the fucking after that. The look in his eyes and the silent domination was a replay of his nightmare that other time. I knew what I knew. The resulting encounter had not been as intense as before, but I sensed Ethan had been working very hard to control his response so he didn't lose it quite as badly as last time. My poor baby. I'd never tell him that, but it pained me to see him hurting; even more so that I couldn't do anything about it because he refused to share it with me. Men were frustrating as hell.

With the soap in the shower, I scrubbed at my skin in annoyance and hurried to finish, determined to be dressed and out of the room without waking Ethan from his much-needed sleep in.

I tucked my phone into my jeans pocket and tiptoed

out of the room, closing the door softly behind me. I just stood and looked down the hall from the wing where our room was situated at one corner of the estate. This place was something else all right, shades of Mr. Darcy's Pemberley with a dash of Mr. Rochester's Thornfield Hall thrown in. I couldn't wait to get an official tour, still enthralled with the fact that Ethan's sister and her husband owned this place.

I took the stairs halfway down, stopping on a dramatic landing. There on the wall was the most stunning painting. Larger than life and most definitely an artist I knew well. A portrait created by none other than the hand of Sir Tristan Mallerton hanging on the wall in a private home. *Wow. I'm so out of my league with this family.*

I pulled out my phone and dialed Gaby. "You won't believe what I'm staring at," I spoke to a thick sounding "hello" that could only be my roommate but didn't sound at all like her usual confident self.

"Oh? What would that be? And it's a little early, isn't it?"

"Sorry, Gab, but I couldn't resist. You would be drooling if you could see this . . . oh . . . midcentury *Mallerton* looming not a foot from me. I could rub my hands all over it if I wanted to."

"Better not do that, Bree. Tell me," she demanded, sounding a bit more like herself.

"Well, it's probably about seven feet by four, and gorgeous as hell. A family portrait of a blond woman and her husband, and their two children, a boy and a girl. She's wearing a pink gown and pearls that look like they belong in the Tower's crown jewels collection. He looks like he's in love with his wife. God, it's beautiful."

"Hmmm, I can't place it offhand. Can you ask if it's all right to take a photo so I can see?"

"I will, as soon as I meet someone I can ask."

"Can you make out his signature?"

"Of course. It was the first thing I looked for. Bottom right, *T. Mallerton* in those distinctive block letters of his. It is, without a doubt, the real deal."

"Wow," Gaby said, in a very unwowed voice.

"Is everything okay with you? Last night was insane and I never saw you after that alarm went off. I wasn't feeling well and Ethan was in high stress mode from some other stuff that happened."

"Like what?"

"Umm, not really sure yet. Some weird message on my old phone came through, and Ethan had it on him. The person sent a crazy text and the song from . . . ah . . . that video they made of me."

"Shit, are you serious?"

"Yep. I am afraid so." Just telling her made my stomach flip a little. I just didn't want to deal with it right now. Avoidance had worked well in the past for me, and would again I was certain.

"No wonder Ethan was stressed, Bree. Why aren't you?"

"I don't know. I just want to believe that nobody is after me and that this is just some kind of blip on the radar that will go away when the election is over. Trust me, Ethan is all over it."

"Yeah, well, it's good that someone is," she grumbled. I decided right then that I wouldn't share Ethan's "proposal" of the previous night. I needed some coffee before

I tackled anything of that magnitude. Better wait about telling her of Ethan's ultimatum to move in with him too. Gaby had no trouble giving her opinion on things. And at the moment I didn't need to hear the resulting noise it would bring.

"Hey," I asked her, "you didn't answer my question. Are you okay? Last night was so messed up. I know we exchanged texts and no damage done, but still . . ."

Silence.

"Gabrielle?" I asked again, notching up the intensity by using her full name.

"I'm fine." Her voice sounded flat and I knew she was holding back.

"Where did you go? I wanted to introduce you to Ethan's cousin, but that obviously never happened."

"I got distracted . . . and then that alarm went off and I had to get out just like everyone else. I waited outside on the street for a while until I got your text. Once I knew you were safe, I found a cab and went home. I just wanted a shower and a bed. It was a weird night." She sounded more like herself, but I had to wonder if she was feeding me a line. "Benny called too. He saw it on the news and was worried about us. I talked to him for a long time."

"Okay . . . if you say so." Gaby was stubborn and if she wasn't in the mood to talk about stuff, then over the phone would not cut it. I'd have to get her in person.

"I do want to meet Ethan's cousin with the houseful of Mallertons someday, though. Maybe you can arrange it," she said in what seemed like a peace offering.

"Yeah, maybe. I'll work on that with Ethan."

As soon as I said the words, I sensed I was not alone anymore. I turned and met the solemn face of the most beautiful little girl, her blue eyes reminding me so very much of another pair I knew well. "I gotta go, Gab. I'll talk to you later, and I'll see what I can do about sending a pic of the painting. Love ya."

I hung up and slipped my phone back in my pocket. My serious companion just kept staring. I smiled at her. She smiled back, her long dark curls framing a face that I predicted would someday evolve into a great beauty. I couldn't wait to see Ethan with her.

"I'm Brynne." I stuck out my hand. "What's your name?" I asked, although I had a pretty good idea.

"Zara." She took my hand with hers and tugged. "I know who you are. Uncle Ethan loves you and drinks Mexican beers now because of you. I heard Mummy tell Daddy that."

I couldn't help the giggle that escaped. "I know about you too, Zara. Ethan told me how much he admires your smarts in handling your brothers."

"He did?"

"Uh-huh." I nodded as she looked up in wonder. "Where are we going?"

Zara did not share that information, but I let her pull me along anyway, weaving through rooms and corridors until the lights of a warm kitchen became clear and what was most certainly the smell of heavenly coffee found my nose.

"Mummy, I have her," Zara announced as she pulled me into the room.

"Ahh, I see that, love," said the dark beauty who could

only be Ethan's sister, Hannah. She smiled at me as she answered her daughter, and I got an impression of Ethan for just a moment in her expression. There was a resemblance for sure, but she favored their father more, I thought, than Ethan did. Hannah had the same dark hair and coloring, but her eyes weren't blue like Ethan's eyes. Her eyes were gray. And she was petite, whereas Ethan was muscular and tall. Genetics were interesting in the way that they managed to mix the genes of male and female to create combinations that made perfect sense.

"Welcome, Brynne. It's lovely to meet you," she said, moving forward, her eyes making a swift assessment. "Hannah Greymont, mum of your small captor there, and big sis of a man I never imagined would put me in this situation. There are plenty of surprises from him yet, I have realized."

I laughed at what she said, liking her honesty immediately as we shook hands warmly. "Same to you, Hannah. I've been looking forward to this trip for a long time. Ethan speaks so affectionately of you. I met your father. He's quite the charmer, as I am sure you know."

"Yes indeed. That would be my dad." She handed me a mug of coffee and pointed toward the table where the cream and sugar were sitting. "E told me about your coffee habit." She grinned and winked at Zara.

"Thank you." I breathed in a lungful of the delicious smell and gave my own wink to Zara. "Your daughter informed me that Ethan drinks Mexican beer now, and it's entirely my fault."

She opened her mouth in mock horror at Zara. "She did not!"

Zara giggled.

"My brother is nearly unrecognizable, Brynne. How on earth did you do it, and where is he, by the way?"

I started doctoring my coffee with sugar and cream. "Well, I can say in all honesty that I have absolutely no idea. Ethan is quite . . . ah . . . single-minded much of the time. Except for right now." I laughed. "He's pretty out of it, and I left him sleeping. Long drive last night and the evening ended . . . weirdly." I looked over at Zara, who was soaking up every word of our conversation, and figured less said was better. Little ears can be very big, and I really did not know these people, despite how charming they were being toward me right now.

"Yeah, I heard about that when he rang me." She shrugged and shook her head. "Crazy people out there for sure. As for E's single-mindedness, that's nothing new. He's always been that way. Bossy, stubborn—very annoying as a boy."

I just smiled and leaned against the counter opposite from where she appeared to be making bread. So, Hannah was a cook.

"The house—it's amazing. I was just on the phone to my roommate gushing about the Mallerton that's hanging on your stairs."

"You found Sir Jeremy Greymont and his Georgina. Freddy's ancestors . . . and you're correct, Mallerton was the artist."

I nodded at her and took a sip of coffee. "I study art conservancy at University of London."

"I know. Ethan's told us all about you," Hannah paused before adding, "much to our surprise."

I tilted my head in question and accepted the challenge head-on. "Surprised that he told you about me?"

She nodded slowly with a slight smirk. "Oh, yes. My brother has never talked about a girl, or ever brought anyone to my house for the weekend. This is all," she gestured with her hands, "very *different* for Ethan."

"Hmmm, well it's pretty *different* for me too. From the first time I met him, he was very difficult to turn down." I took another sip. "Impossible, really."

She grinned at me. "Well, I'm glad for him, and glad to finally meet you, Brynne. I'm sensing there is more to come for you two?"

Hannah worded it as a question, and I had to give her props for being so intuitive, but I absolutely was not going to share the crazy lunatic proposal of marriage Ethan had dropped on me during the night. No way. We still needed a good long discussion about that little suggestion. I shrugged instead. "Ethan is very . . . confident about what he wants. He's never had any trouble telling me. I think I have more trouble hearing stuff than he has with saying it. Your brother can be as blunt as a wooden plank."

She laughed at my assessment. "I know that too. *Subtlety* is not in his lexicon."

"You can say that again—" My eyes caught a picture on a cabinet shelf. A mother with two children—a girl and a boy. *I wonder* . . . I stepped closer and got a good long look at what I was sure was Ethan and Hannah with their young and beautiful mother, sitting on a stone wall looking almost posed, but possibly just serendipity in capturing a perfect moment. "This is the two of you with your mother?"

"It is," Hannah said softly. "Taken shortly before she was gone."

The moment felt odd to me. I was so curious as I soaked up the image of a four-year-old Ethan and the woman who had given him life, but I didn't want to be rude and bring up sad memories. Still, my curiosity kept me from looking away. Mrs. Blackstone was unbelievably beautiful in an aristocratic way, elegant yet with warmth in her smile. Her hair was up and she had on a very fitted burgundy coat dress and tall black boots. She had amazing style for the period. I didn't want to stop looking. In the photograph Ethan was leaning back against her body, snuggled into her arm, his hand on her lap. Hannah sat beside her on the other side, her head tilted in toward her mom's shoulder. It was a sweet, loving moment captured in time. There were so many questions I wanted to ask, but I didn't dare. To do so felt gauche and intrusive. "She was lovely. I can see a close resemblance between the two of you." And Hannah did indeed look like the woman in the picture, but it was baby Ethan I wanted to stare at for a long, long time. His rounded, innocent face and little body in short pants and a white sweater made me want to wrap my arms around him.

"Thank you. I love to hear people say that to me. I never get tired of hearing it."

"You both look like her," I said, still staring at the photograph, wishing I could hold it in my hand but I was far too unsure to risk asking.

"Our dad gave us each a copy of that picture." Hannah looked at me questioningly. "You've never seen it before?"

I shook my head. "No, it's not out on display at his flat. I never saw it when I went to his office either time."

I got a pang when I mentioned his office; the last time I'd set foot in the place had not ended well for us. I'd gotten angry and left him, unwilling to listen to anything he had to say to me. *Including "I love you."* I could remember the look on his stricken face from just outside the elevator as the doors closed between us. *Painful, unpleasant memories.* Ethan had not asked me to stop in since we'd gotten back together and I'd not offered to come by either. It was weird. Like the two of us being in his office was something a little too raw to sift through at the moment. Ah, well, maybe in time we'd get back to finding a comfort zone with the offices of Blackstone Security International, Ltd.

"Hmmm . . . interesting . . . I wonder where it is." Hannah turned back to her breadmaking project and lifted a cloth from a bowl.

I sipped my coffee and continued to study the photograph.

"Ethan didn't speak for almost a year after her death. He just stopped talking one day. I think he was in shock when she didn't come back . . . and it took him some time to accept it, even in his four-year-old mind," Hannah said softly as she worked her dough.

Wow. My poor Ethan. It hurt me just to hear this story. The sadness in Hannah's words was pretty intense and I struggled with any kind of response that didn't sound ignorant. I wish I knew how their mother had died.

"I can't even begin to imagine how hard that must

have been for everyone. Ethan speaks so kindly of you and his father, though. He told me you all got closer and hung together once your mother passed."

Hannah nodded as she worked. "We did, it's true." She punched the ball of dough and covered the bowl with the cloth again to allow a second rising. "I think the suddenness was a good thing in the end. There was no long illness or sad dwellings on what could not be changed, and in time Ethan adjusted and began talking again. Our grandmother was wonderful." She smiled sadly over at Zara. "She's been gone about six years now."

I didn't know what to say, so I just stayed quiet and sipped my coffee and hoped she would share more of the family history.

"Car crash. Late at night. Mum and my aunt Rebecca were headed home from their grandfather's funeral." Hannah turned to Zara, who had gotten down from her chair and was heading out of the kitchen. "Don't wake up Uncle Ethan, my love. He's very tired."

"I won't." Zara answered her mother but looked at me and gave a little wave.

My heart melted as I waved back and gave her a wink.

"That is one adorable child you have. So independent. I love it."

"Thank you. She is a handful sometimes, and more curious than is good for her. I know she'll be trying to get Ethan up out of bed and getting her sweets."

I laughed at the image of that scene. I hoped I got to witness it. "And you have two other children too—both boys, I heard. I don't know how you manage everything."

She smiled as if the thought of her kids gave her a good feeling inside. I could tell Hannah was a great mom and I admired her for it.

"I'm pretty lucky with my man and I enjoy having guests here. We meet a great deal of interesting people. Some we'd like to never meet again, but on the whole, it's good," she said jokingly. "And some days I don't know how I'd manage without Freddy. He took the boys to volunteer at a charity breakfast for the Boy Scouts. They'll be home in a bit, and you can meet the rest of the clan."

"You don't have other guests staying here?"

"Not this weekend. You and my brother are it. By the way, what can I get you for breakfast?"

I came closer and peered at her breadmaking mission. "Oh, I'm fine with the coffee for now. I'll wait for Ethan. In the meantime, could you use some help with the bread? I love to bake. It would be therapy for me after the insanity of last night."

She grinned and pushed a lock of hair away from her face with a bent wrist. "You're hired, Brynne. Aprons are on the back of the pantry door and I want to hear all about the insanity of last night."

"That was easy," I said as I went for the apron.

"I'm not stupid. I've learned over the years that help is a good thing." She pegged me with warm gray eyes. "And you never have to ask me twice."

3

♠

I don't know what compelled me to open my eyes. Probably the breathing on my face smelling faintly of jam, but regardless, I now understand why horror movies with children in them are, without a doubt, the most terrifying films of all. There is nothing quite like a silent child staring at you while you're sleeping, or even worse, to wake up to.

Some questions come to mind pretty fuckin' quick. Like how long have you been standing there watching over me like one of the ill-fated Grady sisters in *The Shining*?

Scared the ever-living shit out of me for about two seconds.

And then she smiled.

"Uncle Ethan is awake!" she yelled at the top of her lungs as she ran to the door, flinging it wide open.

"Zara! Shut the door behind you, please." I sat up carefully, well aware I was nude and taking care to keep the blankets arranged. I was also alone in the bed, so I leaned around and looked toward the bathroom to try and catch sight of Brynne.

No Brynne.

"She's downstairs talking to Mummy. They're having coffees." Zara poked her head back in.

"Is that so?" I said, wondering why on earth I sleep like the dead now and how long my niece had been hovering over me. Creep factor? About a twelve.

Zara nodded solemnly. "She came down ages ago."

"What do you think of her?"

She ignored my question and tilted her head at me. "Did you get married, Uncle Ethan?"

I am sure my eyes bulged out, because Zara gave me a thorough looking over as she waited for a response. "Um . . . no. Brynne is my girlfriend."

"Mummy and Daddy are married."

"Yes they are. I was at the wedding." I smiled and wished I could get out of bed and into some clothes, but she had me good and truly trapped.

"Why do you sleep naked?"

"Excuse me? Zara, I need to get dressed—"

"Daddy doesn't sleep naked like you do. Brynne is nice. Will you take me to get an ice cream with Rags? He loves ice cream and I let him lick it and Mummy says that's dirty but I let him anyway. Mummy said not to come in here, but I got tired of waiting for you to wake up. You're the only person that's still sleeping."

Unbelievable. A five-year-old held me captive in a bed where I could do nothing but listen, mesmerized by her litany of observations, opinions, and requests, and praying for some way to escape. She gave me quite the disgusted look too with that last bit. Sort of along the lines of, *"What in the hell is wrong with you, Uncle Ethan?"* And really, I had to agree with her five-year-old logic too. A hell of a lot was wrong with me.

"Okay. I'll tell you what, Miss Zara. I'll see what I can do about the ice cream with Rags if you go on out so I can get up and get dressed." I gave her my best eyebrow quirk. "Deal?"

"What about Mummy?" she fired off with absolutely no change of expression. This one could play poker with the big shots some day, no doubt about it. My niece was magnificent.

"What Mummy doesn't know about ice creams won't hurt her, I always say." I wondered how long it would be before that declaration came back to haunt me. Probably about as long as it took for her to make her way downstairs, but hell, if it worked to get some immediate privacy . . .

"Deal." She gave me a thorough perusal before going to the door and backing out, her blue eyes tracking me with a certain message. *You better get your arse downstairs in the allotted time or I'll be back in here.*

"I'll be down straightaway," I insisted with a wink.

I waited a good long minute after she left before getting up. I used a pillow to cover my front and made a dash, clicking the bathroom lock before I hit the shower. The last thing I needed was to get caught by a child with everything hanging out. So Brynne was down talking to Hannah . . . I wondered what they were saying about me and hurried to finish.

The shower felt good. The hot water helped clear the cobwebs out of my head. *Fuck that dream last night, though.* The fact that I'd had another nightmare with Brynne right there to witness it really pissed me off. And while I was relieved it wasn't as bad as the last time, I still hated the resurfacing of shit I so did not need to be dealing with at the moment. She would want to talk about it again . . . *I'm not ready.*

My hand brushed over my cock as I washed, reminding me what I'd done to her after that nightmare. She took everything I wanted to give her when it came to the sex, with no protest, no complaint, just willing and generous with her body every time, helping me to come down from the terror. *She does it because she loves you.* I had to wonder if her reaction had something to do with her past—the things she'd told me about her assault and how she had felt about herself when she was younger. Brynne seemed so confident to me most of the time, it was hard to imagine her feeling broken and vulnerable. My position was simple, really. I didn't care about her past. It changed nothing in my feelings for her. She was the one—the one person I needed to be with. Now it was just a matter of convincing her of this fact. *And I will . . . because I love her.* I snapped down a plush towel for drying off as I stepped out of the shower.

I grinned into the mirror as I trimmed up my beard. The look on her face when I told her we should get married. Priceless. I should have used my mobile and taken a video. My smirk turned into a frown at the thought of the video sent to her last night. It reminded me I should touch base with Neil sometime today. I wanted details on the motherfucker toying with her. He wouldn't be doing it for long, I vowed.

It nearly hurt to put myself back in the moment of last night. So many images flashed through my head—Brynne's periwinkle dress, the pendant I'd given her around her neck, the disturbing text messages and video, the bomb threat, searching for her in a panic, and then her being ill on the side of the road. Christ! The whole thing was absolute madness. We needed a little peace and some rest. I was determined to get that for us this weekend if it killed me.

I immediately felt guilty for being so demanding with her in bed last night. Not a lot of peace and rest for my girl in there with me. I remembered the desperation to be inside her again . . . after that dream. *Fuck!* I was thankful I'd been less strung out than the last time, but still worried it was just too much. That *I* was too much.

On second thought, Brynne didn't give off that vibe even after I'd told her about my plan for us to announce our engagement. She told me I was insane, true, but she wasn't upset with me in any way as far as I could tell. In fact, she still took care of me *after* that—when I was wrecked from another twisted dream mixing all the bad from Afghanistan with worry about her. *Totally. Fucked. Up. Shit.* She'd said she woke me up because she didn't want my nightmare to escalate. And what did I do for my sweet girl in thanks?

I fucked her again.

I'd taken her hard, and yet she accepted what I did to

her and accepted me. She said it was okay. *Yeah, she loves me all right.*

I was well aware of how Brynne's touch soothed me like nothing else had before. She was the only lifeline that I wanted to grab on to when I found myself in that state.

Just remembering how our session ended got my blood humming and my mind taking off. I went to find clothes and realized I thought about sex way too much now. A diversion was definitely a good idea. For now. When I got her alone again, well, then all bets were off that I could keep my hands off her. Highly doubtful. It was just another testament of how well we worked together and why I was going in all the way with my American girl. I'd never needed anyone like I needed her.

A long workout was definitely on the menu for me today, I decided. Some time just doing normal things with Brynne and my family away from jobs and other problems would be a nice change. I also wanted Brynne to have a good visit here. Maybe she would be up for a run along the sea path. I hoped she felt well this morning. I slipped into joggers and trainers and grabbed my mobile.

I decided to check in with Neil before I went down. It would ease my mind to ring him. Sometimes talking through a case was cathartic.

"You're up late today, boss," Neil announced after the first ring.

I grunted at him. "Maybe I've been up for hours, how would you know?"

"Doubtful, that. I'm surprised you didn't call as soon as you got in last night."

"I might have . . . if I wasn't so exhausted from a long drive and less-than-restful sleep," I retorted. "Oh, and Brynne was ill and had to be let out on the side of the road to be sick."

"Christ, that's unpleasant."

"Agreed. The whole night was pretty unpleasant."

"What's wrong with her?"

"Don't know. Stomach bug or something? She was sick at the gallery too."

"You don't suppose somebody tainted her food or drink, do you?"

I pondered the idea, even though it made me see red. "I can't rule it out completely. Paul Langley needs a checking into. He does have her old mobile number and he was there at the gala, but he uses her new number now. You know, on second thought, he handed her a glass of water." I wanted to get that prick in a room alone. I could find out all kinds of things, I'm sure. I tried to focus on my conversation with Neil. "The thing is, whoever sent the text message was there. Maybe not inside at the event, but he was watching me have a smoke. And that alarm was set off just a moment or two after the music video was sent."

"Langley checked out when you looked into him before."

"Don't remind me, please." If that motherfucker was involved, I swear he was a dead man. Brynne and I needed to talk about her history with Langley, a prospect that felt even more unpleasant than last night's fiasco. "Just see what you can find out. Any luck on the caller location to Brynne's mobile?" I'd left it for Neil to investigate, determined to have a weekend without focusing on her situation or my job.

"Some. The call was made from inside the UK. Whoever called her mobile was most likely watching you in real time and not on web cam from the States. I'm guessing you were thinking that was a possibility?"

"Fuck." A smoke was sounding very appealing right about now. "A long shot, but I hoped. Well, it's not Oakley then, he's active duty in Iraq. Lurking around London would be a stretch when he's dodging missiles in the desert. It's not Montrose either, because he's taking a well-deserved dirt nap. So that leaves the third in the video. That cocksucker is next on my list. We've got nothing on him yet. The file is accessible on the Q drive. His vitals are all there. Can you do a bit of digging on him? Find out what he's been up to lately? Make sure he's not been using his passport. Um . . . name is Fielding. Justin Fielding, twenty-seven, living in Los Angeles, if memory serves. I want to know if he went to the funeral for Montrose too. I'm betting he made scarce—"

"I got this, E," Neil interrupted. "Have your weekend and try to let all this shit lie for a bit. I'll get into it for you. Right now you have her safe and out of the loop. Nothing's going to happen from Somerset."

"Thanks. Appreciate it. Oh, yeah, can you toss some feed in for Simba?"

"He doesn't like me," Neil said dryly.

"He doesn't like me either, but he does like being fed. And if you don't he'll start eating his tankmates."

"All right. I'll feed your surly and poisonous fish."

"You don't have to cuddle him, just throw in some krill."

"Easier said than done. That creature is part piranha, I am sure."

I laughed at that image. "Thank you, brave soldier, for going into battle for me by feeding my fish."

"You're welcome."

"Hold down the fort for us, and you know how to reach me. We'll be back in town Monday evening."

I ended the call and headed out of the bedroom, eager to find Brynne. Time to face my girl and see what trouble I was in this morning from all of my bad behavior last night. I wasn't really worried, though. *My baby loves me, and I know how to give her what she needs . . .*

I smirked to myself at my smug thoughts, opened the bedroom door and nearly stepped on my niece.

Zara was sitting on the floor, her back against the wall, waiting for me apparently. I caught my balance and crouched down to meet her at face level.

"Finally, you've come out," she said disgustedly.

"Sorry. I had to make a telephone call, but I'm done now."

She looked up at me hopefully. "Can we go get ice creams now? You said you would."

"It's morning still. Ice cream is for the afternoons, I'm sure."

She wrinkled her cute little nose at me in response. I guess she didn't share that pragmatic view.

I pointed to my cheek. "I did not get a nice welcome yet from my favorite princess."

She reached up, put her little arms around my neck and kissed my cheek.

"That's better," I said. "Would you like a ride?" I gestured to my back.

"Yes!" She brightened her expression.

"Well, climb aboard then," I told her.

She attached herself and hung her arms around my neck as I held her little legs tucked under my arms. I groaned, pretending to struggle to rise to my feet. I stumbled into the wall with exaggerated movements, being careful of her head. "God, you weigh a lot. Been eating a lot of ice creams, have you?"

She giggled and dug her heels into my sides. "Go, Uncle Ethan!"

"I'm trying to!" I grunted, pretending to crash into the walls as I stumbled along. "Feels like I have an elephant back there! Did you change from a princess into an elephant?"

"No!" she laughed at my antics and poked me harder. "Go faster than this!"

"Hold on tight," I said, as we whooped and yelled our way down the grand staircase and into the family area.

My sister and Brynne were both waiting for us when we ducked into the homey kitchen. I'm sure all the screeching laughter preceded our arrival, but it was the look on Brynne's face that gave me a kick. Her eyes widened at the sight of us, probably shocked to see me playing around like this.

"Hello, Han," I said, going forward to kiss her cheek, Zara still clinging to my back and slightly choking at my neck.

"E." She embraced me, her small form reaching to

just under my chin as comforting as she had been for my whole life. For a boy who had lost his mum so young, I'd substituted for my older sister in some ways. She'd always mothered me anyway and we'd just adjusted our relationship in the only way we knew how to. I looked over at Brynne and winked at her. Zara giggled and bounced like she wanted her "horsey" to keep on going.

"Zara, did you wake up Uncle Ethan?" she asked her daughter with a raised brow.

I could feel Zara shake her head back and forth vigorously and had to bite back the incriminating grin threatening to spread over my face.

"He opened his eyes all by himself, Mummy," she announced.

Brynne laughed. "That must have been interesting, I'm sorry I missed it."

"Zara," Hannah scolded gently, "I told you to let him sleep."

"It's all right," I told my sister. "I didn't lose more than a year or two off my life span, I'm sure." I mock shuddered. "Remember those little girls in *The Shining*?"

Hannah laughed and delivered a punch to my shoulder. I turned to Brynne. "Morning, baby. I seem to have a little monkey on my back." It felt good to be playful for a change.

"Oh, I'm sorry but we've not met before. I wonder if you might've seen my boyfriend around?" she asked. "Name's Ethan Blackstone. A very serious fellow, rarely smiles and most certainly doesn't tear around historic mansions shouting and crashing into walls with little monkeys on his back." She tickled Zara's ear and made her giggle some more.

"Nope. That bloke's not around here. We left him back in London."

She held her hand out. "I'm Brynne, nice to meet you," she said with a straight face.

Hannah snorted behind me and peeled the still bouncing Zara off my back while I caught Brynne's offered hand to my lips for a kiss. I glanced at her expression and saw a glassy look in her eyes as she smiled and rolled her lips together. Those lips. She did magical things with those lips . . . *Mine.*

Hannah tapped me on the shoulder from behind. "You look like my brother, and your voice sounds the same, but you're definitely not him." She held out her hand. "Hannah Greymont. Who are you?"

I laughed at her and rolled my eyes. *"You need to have some fun, E. Go out more and meet people. Relax and enjoy life a little,"* I said, mocking the words I'd heard from my sister on more than one occasion.

"Don't get me wrong, I like seeing you horsing around and laughing like this." Hannah held up a hand and gestured at me. "Just give me a minute to take it all in."

"You'll get used to it," I said to Hannah while drawing an arm around Brynne and kissing her temple, breathing in the flowery scent of her shampoo. She always smelled so good to me. "How are you feeling this morning, baby?"

"I feel great." She shook her head. "I don't know what that was last night, but I feel totally fine today." She took a drink from her mug. "Hannah makes a mean cup of coffee."

"Yes she does," I said, going over to pour myself some. "Have you eaten?"

"No. I waited for you." Her eyes looked more brown than anything this morning. And she had a look in them that told me she wanted to discuss things. Fine with me. We had a lot to talk about. I had some convincing to do. *Bring it.*

"You didn't have to wait for me . . . but I have an idea, if you're interested," I said, returning to her side with my mug of coffee, from which delicious-smelling steam was rising.

"What's that, strange-man-who-resembles-my-boy-friend-but-can't-possibly-be-him?" She teased me in a way that made me want to throw her over my shoulder and head back upstairs to our bedroom.

"Such funny ladies you all are this morning," I said, giving each of them a look, including the five-year-old. "Where are all the men? I am seriously outnumbered here."

"Scout thing. They'll be home after lunch," Hannah told me.

"Ahh, I see." I turned back to Brynne. "You fancy a run along the sea path? It's really beautiful and there's a café down there where we can get something after."

Her whole face changed into something indescribable, a mixture of beauty and happiness.

"Sounds perfect. I'll just go change quickly." She backed up and sailed out of the room with a grin. I loved when she was happy, and especially when I did something that made her that way.

"I want to come," Zara said.

"Oh, princess, we're running too far for you to come with us this morning." I crouched down to face her again.

"You promised we could take Rags and get—" Zara did not look happy with her Uncle Ethan. Not at all. It did funny things to my insides too. Unhappy little girls were frightening as hell. Big girls too, for that matter.

"I know," I cut her off and peeked up at Hannah, who rolled her eyes at me with arms folded. "We're going in the afternoon. Remember I told you . . ." I whispered in her ear, "Ice creams are for the afternoon time, princess. Mummy's watching us. You better go play with your dollies or something so she doesn't get suspicious."

"Okay," she whispered back loudly, "I won't say you're taking me and Rags to get an ice cream in the afternoon time."

I laughed silently and kissed her on the forehead. "Good girl." I felt pretty proud of myself for handling that little problem so well. Zara waved good-bye as she went off to play and I gave her a big wink. I leaned back on my heels and looked up into the mocking gaze of my sister.

"You are nearly unrecognizable to me, Ethan. You have it bad, don't you?"

I pushed up to my feet and reconnected with my coffee mug, talking a hot gulp before I addressed her comment. "It's just ice cream, Han."

"I'm not talking about you sneaking sweets to Zara, and you know it."

I pegged her in the eye and told my sister, "Yeah. I have it bad."

Hannah smiled sweetly at me. "I'm happy for you, E. Hell, I'm thrilled to see you like this. Happy . . . you're happy with her." Hannah's gray eyes got watery.

"Hey, what's this?" I pulled her into a hug.

She embraced me hard. "Happy tears. You deserve it, E. I wish Mum were here to see you like this . . ." Hannah trailed off, obviously choked up.

I looked over at the photograph on the shelf of the three of us together, Hannah, me and Mum sitting on the stone wall at my grandparents' place. "She is right here," I said.

4

♥

Ethan led me along a high coastal path that overlooked the sea at the Bay of Bristol with its sparkling blue water winking a million shiny breaks due to the wind. We followed that for a good while until the trail turned back inland. The sun was shining and the air was fresh. You'd think all the physical exertion would clear out my scattered thoughts, putting them into some semblance of order, but no such luck on that one. Nope. My mind just kept whirling. *Engagement announcement? Moving in together? Marriage?!* I so needed to schedule an appointment with Dr. Roswell for the moment we got back to London.

As I watched Ethan ahead of me, the way he moved, his natural agility and stealth, his physique of ripped muscles propelling his body forward, I still appreciated the view. *My guy, my view.* Yep, the scenery *and* my man were both mighty fine.

I did indeed love it here and was happy he'd brought me,

in spite of the turn our conversation took last night. Ethan had come downstairs this morning cheerful and affectionate, as if we'd never discussed a thing of importance last night. It was truly infuriating as hell to me that he could just blow off something like getting married as if it was nothing more complicated than getting a license to drive a car!

I liked when he ran with me, though. We went together in the city when I stayed over and if it didn't rain in the mornings. Ethan kept a competitive pace and I hoped he wasn't going easy on me just because he could.

As the path wound along the coast it began to descend down to the shore and the beach below until we came out into a rocky headland. Ethan turned back and gave me a cover model smile that never ceased to affect me when he did it. He had a magnificent smile that made my insides gooey. It meant he was happy.

"You hungry?" he asked as I pulled up.

"Yes I am. Where are we going?"

He pointed to a tiny gazebo-shaped building perched right on the rocks. "The Sea Bird. Great breakfasts served up in that little place."

"Sounds like a plan to me." He took my hand in his and brought it up to his lips, kissing the top quickly.

I smiled up at him and studied his handsome face. Ethan was easy on the eye, but it was funny to me that he didn't seem to think much of it. I wanted to know about that woman, Priscilla, from the night before. I know he had hooked up with her at some point in the past; he said as much: *We went out one time together.* It didn't take a genius to figure he'd taken her up on some freely offered sex. She had her paws all over him at the bar. I didn't like the looks of her at all. Too predatory. Paul seemed interested, though. I saw them outside on the curb together after the National was evacuated.

"What's on your mind, my beauty?" Ethan tapped me on the tip of my nose. "I can see the cogs turning under here." He kissed my forehead.

"A lot of things."

"Want to talk about it?"

"I think we should." I nodded. "I think we don't have any other choice, Ethan."

"Yeah," he answered, his eyes losing the happy spark that had just been in them.

The red-haired waitress eyeballed him thoroughly as she seated us by a window, something I had grown used to when out with Ethan. Females didn't hide their appreciation very well, and I was always left wondering how the person would act or what they would say to him if I wasn't there. Hah! *Here's my number if you want to come over to my place and have some quick and dirty sex. I'll do anything you want.* Gag.

He waited until she left and then got right to it. "So . . . back to our conversation last night. Are you feeling any more receptive to the idea?"

I took a sip of water first. "I think I'm still in shock that you want to . . ." I hesitated.

"You don't have to be afraid to say the words, Brynne," he bit back, no longer looking so happy with me.

"Fine. I can't believe you are willing to '*marry*' me." I made air quotes and saw his jaw twitch.

"Why does it surprise you?"

"It's way too soon and we're just starting out together, Ethan. Can't we just keep going like we have been?"

His expression hardened. "We are continuing on like we have been. I don't know where you think we're headed, but I can assure you it'll be somewhere where we are together." He narrowed his eyes and glared a little. "All in, Brynne, or did you forget so soon? You said you wanted the same thing last night."

I could tell he was more than a little frustrated with me. "I didn't forget," I whispered and looked over the menu in front of me.

"Good." He picked up his own menu and didn't say anything for a minute or two. The waitress came back over eventually and made the ordering of our breakfasts pretty sickening as she flirted with Ethan throughout the whole torturous process.

I rolled my eyes when she turned and sauntered off.

Ethan kept his eyes on me, never wavering as he spoke. "When are you going to understand that I don't care about women like that waitress and how she just tried flirting with me while you were sitting right here? It was in poor taste and I loathe it. Stuff like that has been happening all my adult life and I can tell you truthfully that it's annoying as hell." He reached across the table and picked up my hand. "I only want one woman to flirt with me now, and you know who she is."

"But how can you be so sure about something as important as marriage?" I went right back to our topic.

He started rubbing his thumb over the top of my

hand—touching me in more ways than just the sensual gesture. "I've decided what I want with you, baby, and my mind's not changing."

"You know this. You know you'll never change your mind about me or wanting to be with me." I said them as slightly mocking statements, but they were really questions posed to him. Hell, if he was offering then I had to hear the *why* of things. "I don't have any good examples to draw on. My parent's marriage was a joke."

"I won't change *my* mind, Brynne." He narrowed his eyes and I could see some hurt there. "You're everything I want and need. I'm sure of that. I just want to make it official to the world so I can protect you in the best way I know how to. People have married for much less." He looked down at our hands and then up at me again. "I *love* you."

My heart melted under the blast of intensity coming off him, and I felt like a mean bitch again. Here he was baring his feelings, telling me how much I meant to him, and I was giving him a hard time.

"I know you do and I love you too." I nodded and twisted my hand to hold on to his, meaning my words with all my heart. "I do. Nobody else has ever got that out of me before . . . but you."

"Good."

He looked vulnerable then, and I wanted to reassure him, make him feel that he mattered to me. Because the truth was, Ethan did matter. So very much. I stroked the top of his hand with a finger, brushing it back and forth.

The past twenty-four hours had been so insane, I was merely trying to keep up. What Ethan was suggesting did make me feel pressured, but he also made me feel loved. He was a good man willing to make a commitment to me, and only asking for the same in return. Why was I having so much trouble with it? The truth was something I pretty much understood even if I hated to acknowledge it by digging down deep into my psyche. Being with Ethan forced me to examine my demons.

"I'll move in with you. How's that for a start?"

"It's just that—a start," he said dryly. "I told you that part wasn't negotiable anyway."

"I know. You tell me a lot of things, Ethan." I couldn't keep the sarcasm out of my voice but I smiled at him sitting across from me in all his male beauty, so confident and assured.

He grinned back at me. "And I mean every word of what I say."

The waitress appeared with our food just then, giggling and leaning over the table in a disgusting display that made my stomach turn. Literally. The eggs and bacon set out in front of me suddenly didn't look so appealing either. I reached for the toast first.

I couldn't help rolling my eyes again as she strutted off, hips swinging for maximum effect. Ethan gave me a soft laugh and an air kiss.

"Let's talk some more about this plan of yours when we get back to London, okay? I want to enjoy our time here together this weekend and forget about that message last night, and have some fun." I couldn't resist adding in just a little snark: "Not that watching women throw themselves at you is fun for me or anything."

He laughed a little harder. "Welcome to my world, baby. Hell, if it helps my cause to make you jealous, maybe I should encourage the admiring females a little more." He gestured in the waitress's direction.

I glared at him. "Don't even think about it, Blackstone." I nodded toward his crotch. "It so won't help your cause or even get you more of what you like."

He bit off the end of a piece of bacon and ignored my threat, sweeping over me with sexy, slow eyes. "I like the jealous you *very* much. It turns me on," he said in a low tone.

What doesn't *turn you on?* I felt the tingle of arousal flutter through me as he raked me over with another look. Ethan could get me hot for him with just the slightest gesture. I noticed how his muscles flexed under his shirt and I wanted to tear it off and proceed with licking down his beautiful carved chest, down farther over his stomach and that V cut that ended in that most magnificent—

"What are you thinking about now?" he asked with a brow twist, interrupting my wicked fantasies.

"How much I like to go running with you," I countered, proud of my pithy comeback when I'd so obviously been caught shamelessly ogling him worse than the redhead who'd served our meal had done.

"Right," he said, totally unconvinced. "I think you were dreaming about getting me naked and having a shag."

I was horrified and stared down at my food, wondering why I was so sexed out these days. My hormones must be wacky again. All. His. Fault.

"Speaking of dreams . . ." I figured this was a good time

to change the subject and let my comment hang in the air between us for a moment.

His eyes turned dark and he frowned. "Yeah, I had another one. I'm very sorry for disturbing you in your sleep. I really am. I don't know why I've started having them after all this time."

"I want to know what those dreams are about, Ethan."

He tried his own brand of distraction by changing the conversation again. "But you're right, baby, I shouldn't have brought up the let's-get-married thing like I did on the fly. It wasn't nice to unload that on you in the middle of the night, even if I am still convinced it's our best option. We can talk some more about it when we get back to town and you've moved into the flat. I already told you the whole scene last night at the National Gallery freaked me out." He shook his head slowly. "When I couldn't find you . . . it was the worst, Brynne. I can't go through that again. My heart can't take it."

I stared at him, frustrated by being shut down again, and stiffened my stance. "Why won't you talk to me about your nightmares? *My* heart can't take *that.*"

His gaze flickered down and then back up. He whispered with pleading eyes, "When we get back home. Promise." He played with my hand, tracing my knuckles ever so gently. "Let's just have nice time together for the weekend like you said, without bringing any of the ugly stuff into it. Please?"

How could I say no? The look of dread all over him was enough for me to give him a reprieve. A few more days wouldn't matter without knowing. I did know this much, though, whatever events Ethan had suffered through had been truly horrible, and it pained me to even imagine it. He said it was from his time in the war and I remembered Neil's words to me once: *"E's a walking miracle, Brynne."*

Yeah, he's a miracle all right. My miracle.

Our return to the house took a different path, as Ethan wanted to show me around. This way was far less strenuous, for which I was grateful; for some reason I was feeling tired again. I felt a flush as I realized why. Lots of sex action last night. Another miracle considering I'd begun and ended the evening by barfing. Ugh. Ethan had been so good to me, though. He really was a considerate and attentive man, with very fine manners for not having grown up with a mother. I'd have to thank his father, Jonathan, for doing such a good job when I saw him again.

The area turned more wooded as we shifted away from the coast. Leaves of green filtered the sun through the branches to make patterns of shadows and light on the ground. The whole place was so peaceful, the little graveyard tucked away under some very old oak trees felt like a good place to stop for a while. The cemetery looked like something out of a gothic novel, all overhanging branches and ornate headstones.

Ethan waited for me to catch up at the gate and extended his hand. As soon as I touched him, he drew me up close against his body, enfolding me. "You want to look around in there and have a bit of a break? I figured you might because you like history so much."

"I'd love to. It's so beautiful in here." I looked around. "So peaceful and serene."

We walked through the plots, reading names on the stones of the people who'd lived and died in the area. A marble crypt marked the resting place of the Greymont family, the ancestors of Hannah's husband, Freddy. I made out the names Jeremy and Georgina and remembered them as the people Hannah had named in the gorgeous portrait I'd discovered this morning on the stairway. The Mallerton. I knew without a shadow of a doubt that the painting of Sir Jeremy and his beautiful Georgina was the real deal and hoped the family would allow some pictures just for cataloguing purposes. Maybe I could get Benny up here to take some good photos. Gaby would want to see it and the Mallerton Society would be very interested in anything to do with the painting's current status. My mind was churning with possibilities as we left the private cemetery and continued inland on the forest path.

We came up to an imposing iron gate, the kind you see in movies that win Academy Awards for cinematography. Secured to the metal was a sales agency sign advertising the place as Stonewell Court.

"Do you know the house back there?" I asked.

He shook his head. "I've never been down that drive. It looks like the property is for sale, though." He tried the gate latch and much to our surprise it opened with a grating squeak. "Let's take a look. You want to?"

"Do you think it's okay?"

He shrugged and looked at the posted sign. "Yeah, probably."

"Then yes." I stepped forward to follow him in. The rusty gate swung shut with a clang behind us. I reached for Ethan's hand, moving closer beside him as we walked down the curved gravel road. It felt like we were moving back toward the coast.

He chuckled softly. "Are you scared we'll get in trouble or something?"

"Not at all," I lied. "If somebody comes after us for trespassing, I plan on letting them know that it was all your idea and you said it was okay." I gave him my best bland face, hoping I could hold the laugh in for more than a couple seconds.

He stopped us on the path and gave me a mocking look of outrage. "Nice. You're going to throw me over to save your own precious little arse!"

"Well, I'll be sure to come and visit your hot, sexy *arse* in prison," I said sweetly, emphasizing the British pronunciation of *ass*, thinking it sounded so much more elegant when he said it. I sucked at trying to do an English accent.

He snaked his hand down to goose me with one hand and tickled my side with the other. "Oh, will you now?" he drawled, easily breaking my composure with his relentless tickling.

"Yes!" I yelled, twisting out of his grip and running for the trees. He was right behind me, though, laughing all the way. I could feel him closing in and I pushed harder to keep a distance, eating up the length of the driveway with every stride.

Ethan caught me just as we rounded the bend in the drive and managed to take us down gently on the soft grass, rolling on top of me and tickling me madly. I twisted and bucked, doing my best to escape, but it was a pointless exercise against his strength.

"No escape for you, my beauty," he breathed, effortlessly pinning my wrists with one hand and holding my chin with the other.

"Of course not," I whispered back, already feeling the flush of heat and getting wildly aroused. Ethan made all kinds of things happen with my body. I was used to it by now.

His eyes flared with passion as he dropped his mouth to mine, opening wide to cover my lips and devour them. I moaned in pleasure and let him in. Ethan could kiss. I didn't like to imagine how much practice he'd had, but I appreciated his skill as his tongue explored me thoroughly. The weight of him pressing down upon me just got me more in the mood.

He sucked on my bottom lip, nibbling and licking, before pulling off with a soft suctioned *pop*. "You ran from me," he scolded, his mouth hovering just above mine.

"You goosed me in the ass," I said in an indignant tone, "which induces running, by the way! Don't think I'm going to forget this either, Blackstone."

"I can't resist your *ass*, ever. There, I said it like you." He licked my earlobe. "You liked my kisses, though."

"Honestly, I could go either way on the kissing," I lied, going for a straight face that I had no chance of holding longer than two seconds.

"Okay . . . so you won't mind if I never kiss you again?" he teased, his forehead bending down to touch mine when I turned my head. Then my eyes caught view of the house and I could do nothing but stare. Ethan followed my lead and whispered, "Holy hell."

We both stared at the magnificent stone façade of an absolutely gorgeous Georgian house of gray stone perched right on the coast ledge overlooking the sea. It took my breath away with its solid rows of paned windows, and tall, narrow, pointed rooftops. It wasn't a huge mansion, but just so perfectly situated in its space and so elegantly designed. I bet the view from the many windows facing the sea was breathtaking.

Ethan pushed away to stand up first and then helped me to my feet. "Wow." I had no other words to say in the moment.

"It's secreted back here so privately. I had no idea this is what it looked like . . . or even that it existed." He entwined his hand with mine. "Let's go check it out. I want to see the view off the back."

"You read my mind," I said, giving his ass a playful smack with my other hand.

"And you are very, very naughty today." He grabbed my spanking hand and brought it up to his lips for a kiss as he had done many, many times with me in the past, but something I never grew tired of and doubted I ever would. Ethan possessed a skill set that combined hot, bad-boy sex god with mannerly, romantic gentleman; something so rare and captivating, I didn't have a chance of resisting the pull. I smiled up at him and said nothing.

"I think I'll have to come up with a good punishment to fit your crimes."

"Suit yourself," I told him saucily as we headed around

the side of the house to the gardens in back. The rear grounds were something else, all right. I could imagine the former inhabitants having garden parties out here on a nice day with their view of the coast of Wales across the bay. I guessed many an hour was spent painting this very scene I was looking at right now. I'd bet my bank account on it.

I strolled farther out across the green that met the rocks of the coast. There, set in the foundation, was an angel statue—no, wait; it wasn't just an angel, but rather a mermaid with angel wings, very finely detailed and serene in the buffeting wind. On the base of the statue was carved a single name. *Jonathan.*

Ethan came up behind me and wrapped himself up against me close, his chin resting on the top of my head. "Your dad's name," I said softly. "The statue is so haunting. A mermaid angel. It's amazing, and I've never seen anything like it. I wonder who Jonathan was to them."

"Who knows. This place is at least two hundred fifty years old and I don't think it was occupied even if it wasn't up for sale these last years. Hannah and Freddy would know if people were living here."

"Who wouldn't want to live in such a beautiful house?" I turned around to face him.

"I don't know, baby. Don't get me wrong, I love the city, but there's something to be said about the country." He nodded admiringly at the house again. "Maybe someone died or they were elderly and couldn't keep it up."

"Probably right. Sad to see something like that fall out of a family legacy, though. Imagine if Hallborough was lost to Hannah and Freddy."

"That would be tragic. She loves that house, and it's a perfect place to raise the kids."

"This whole area is truly amazing. I'm so glad we walked this way and discovered this path today. It's like finding a secret hiding place." I pushed up on tiptoes to kiss him. "Thanks again for bringing me here. It's really lovely being away with you."

Ethan wrapped me up in his arms and kissed me just below my ear. "Yes it is," he whispered.

We started back for Hallborough, Ethan's arm around me loosely. I leaned my head on him, content to rely on the strength he offered. Suddenly something flashed through my brain. It was this image of us, as we were right here in the moment, Ethan's big arm hanging off my shoulders, holding me close to him. I knew then that he would get his way in the end. He'd have everything he'd told me he wanted. Me moving in with him, the engagement announcement, and probably even the marriage.

My. God.

Ethan really was an ace at playing his hand.

5

♠

"That's the third time you've yawned. Are you going to make it back to the house, or do I need to carry you before you collapse?"

"Oh, right," she scoffed. "We both know why I'm so tired today." She gave me a sassy smirk that made me want to do naughty things to those pretty lips of hers.

Well, yeah, you kept her up half the night fucking, what do you expect her to be? I wanted to smile at the remembrance, though. My girl never turned me down, even when I was the freakiest. I'm a lucky, lucky man for sure. But then that's not news and it hasn't been for a while now.

"Sorry, baby. You'll be happy to hear I enjoyed every single minute of keeping you awake." I reached down and gave a squeeze to her lovely bum and watched her jump.

"You are crazy!" she yelped, shoving me off her.

"Crazy for you," I said, wrapping my arm back around her and bringing her in close to me. "We're almost there anyway. I hope Fred and the boys are home so you can meet them."

"I can't wait," she said, trying to stifle another yawn.

"That's it! I'm putting you to bed for a nap when we get back!"

She laughed at me. "That's not a bad idea. I'm starting to love naps."

The sounds of male voices and the smell of fresh bread met us at the door when we arrived. That and Zara's older monkey brothers rushing me in a chaotic blast of shouting.

"The lads! God, you've gotten huge, Jordon. And, Colin, how many dates have you been on this week?"

They both ignored me and stared at Brynne. I think I was witness to a love-at-first-sight moment from Jordon while Colin just turned red in the face. "Lads, this is Brynne Bennett, my . . . girlfriend." I grinned at her. "Brynne, the rest of my sister's spawn—I mean, my nephews, Jordon and Colin Greymont."

"Nice to meet you, Miss Bennett." Jordan stuck out his hand.

Colin looked at me like I'd grown a second head. "You really do have a girlfriend now," he said in awe.

Brynne took Jordan's hand and gave him a killer smile. "I see you've taken some lessons from your Uncle Ethan or maybe even your grandpa," she told him after he plunked a kiss on her hand. "Nice form you've got, Jordan." She winked at him and then turned to Colin next. "You don't have to kiss my hand, Colin, but it's very nice to meet you too."

Colin nodded, his red face getting even redder. "A pleasure," he muttered with a quick shake.

"And that handsome bloke over there fathered the

spawn—I mean, all these children mobbing me." Little Zara had come up and attached herself to my side like glue so as not to be left out. "Freddy Greymont, my brother-in-law, brilliant country doctor, love of my sister's life, and to blame for all of this." I held up my palms.

Fred came forward to greet Brynne and flashed me a look that meant he'd want details later, man to man. "Brynne, it is my great pleasure to finally meet you in person. We've heard so much about you." Freddy narrowed his eyes at me. "Nearly all of it from Hannah's dad, mind you; Ethan tells me nothing." He turned up the charm for Brynne, something he was good at, being a doctor and all.

"Thank you for this weekend at your lovely home. It's really been perfect so far," Brynne said to him. "You have a beautiful family." The poor bloke was probably in shock seeing me with someone. I'd known Freddy for more than fifteen years, and I don't remember ever introducing a girlfriend to him. So I supposed I could count on some form of interrogation coming from him. Here was another one who knew a lot of my secrets, but not all. Maybe I should talk to Fred about the dreams and nightmares. *But I just can't.* I quickly shut down that unpleasant thought and watched Brynne charm my family into devoted fans instead.

"That bread smells so wonderful, Hannah." Brynne walked over and checked out the fresh loaves on the kitchen counter. "I haven't baked bread in a long time. That was fun this morning."

"It was for me too," Hannah said. "Would you like some? I was just getting ready to do an early tea for Freddy and the kids. Fresh bread and homemade strawberry jam."

"It sounds divine, but a shower is calling my name after that long run and walk back here." She tried to hold in another yawn, but it was impossible. She covered her mouth with a graceful hand and murmured, "I really apologize. I don't know why I'm so tired. Must be all the fresh air making me sleepy."

I caught the smirking little glance between my sister and Freddy as we started to leave. I just shook my head at them both and followed Brynne back upstairs. I'm sure they started laughing at me the second we were out of the room. Fun times with family sticking their noses into every private detail of my life now, I thought. *I guess you'd better get used to it.*

Brynne headed for the shower, and I checked my mobile for messages. My assistant, Frances, had promised to forward anything potentially pressing, but I was pleased to see it was minor stuff that could wait. Right now I needed to get clean and Brynne was naked in the shower.

"You're well aware there's a water shortage in England, right?" I asked as I stepped in behind her, all slick with body wash and hot water, and making me crazed as usual.

She turned, reaching for the shampoo, and gave me a thorough looking over. "I think I've seen the reports on the news, yes."

"So I figure we should share the water whenever it's convenient."

"I see," she said slowly, trailing her eyes downward to my awakening cock. "And you think right now is convenient?"

"Extremely convenient."

"Then by all means, be my guest." She moved out of the spray so I could move under it.

"Oh, I'm going to need you closer than that if we're to get the full benefit of sharing the water, baby."

"Is this close enough?" She took a step, the sight of her flushed wet skin making my mouth water in anticipation of getting a taste.

"No." I shook my head. "You're miles away from me still."

"I thought you liked to look at me," she said coyly.

"Oh, I do, baby. Very much." I nodded. "But I like to look at you and touch you at the same time best of all."

She took another step, which brought her within a couple inches, our bodies aligned but still not touching, the hot water streaming down in the small space that separated our skin.

I savored the moment of erotic heat that swirled between us—the anticipation of what was coming, because I knew I'd be devouring her with all of my senses very soon.

"But you're only looking at me and not touching," she whispered. "How come?"

"Oh, I will, baby. I will." I brought my mouth to her neck and inhaled the scent of her skin, the soap and the water all mixed together in a heady elixir that only got me hotter. "How badly do you want to be touched?"

"Very badly."

I could hear the need in her tone, and it cranked me higher. There was nothing headier than knowing she wanted this with me. I pressed my lips to the spot just below her ear and felt a delicious shiver from her. "Here?" I asked.

"Yes." She arched backward slightly, causing the tips of her hard nipples to graze the skin just below my chest.

"Or maybe here is better?" I licked down from her neck, dragging my tongue over her delicious skin, trailing lower to meet one of those hardened nipples just begging to be sucked.

"Ahhh yes," she shuddered, pushing up on her toes, bringing that beautiful, soft, pink flesh to the edge of my lips.

I flicked out my tongue and licked just the tip and heard her moan the softest sound in response. She started to lift her arms to me and I quickly backed off. "No." I shook my head. "No touching me, baby. This is all for you. Put your hands out and press back against the tile, and stay like that for me."

I could see the rise and fall of her breasts as she breathed at me, her eyes sparking a grayish-green that reminded me of the color of the sea on our run that morning. She moved into position and tilted her head back as well, waiting on me for the next command. Watching her submit to my direction did something to me. These games we played were like nothing I'd ever experienced before with another person. They also pushed me into realms of emotion I'd never desired before with anyone else either. Just her. Only Brynne got me to this place.

"You're so fucking sexy right now."

She shivered and tensed her hips when I said the words, flaring her eyes at me with more than a little frustration. I moved back toward her again and watched her shake a little more and breathe heavier. "Please . . ."

"Please what, baby?" I asked before flicking the tip of her other nipple with my tongue.

"I need you to touch me," she whimpered softly.

I licked her nipple again, this time swirling around the dark tip in a circle. "Like that?"

"More than that," she panted, fighting to keep her hands flat to the shower tile.

I moved to the other breast and plucked it hard into my mouth, finishing with a little pinch of teeth over her nipple. She went rigid underneath my touch and gasped out the loveliest sexual cry I'd ever heard, soft and abandoned and beautiful. "That's a sound I like to hear out of your sweet mouth, baby. I want to hear that from you again and again and again. Can you make that sound for me one more time?" I clamped down onto the other nipple in the same way with my mouth and slid my free hand right in between her legs. "Oh, fuck, you're so slippery, baby. Let me hear you!" I worked over her slick cleft, sliding back and forth on her clit until she melted there against the shower wall for me in perfect sexual submission.

She made the sound for me again too.

I kept my hand on her pussy and my eyes on her face, watching every exquisite flutter and undulation of her body as I made her orgasm. After a moment she lifted slow eyes to mine and kept them there. "That was fucking beautiful to watch," I said.

"I want this now," she whispered, gripping around my cock and bringing it to slide against all that slippery, hot heaven between her legs.

"Say it with words." I pulled my hips back.

"I want your cock inside me, deep."

"You do, hmmm?" I pressed inward, sliding my length

back and forth along her pussy lips, working up a nice friction for me and round two for her.

"Yes! Please!" she begged.

"But you were a bad girl and took your hands off the wall. I told you to leave them there," I said, still stroking in and out through her slick folds.

"Sorry . . . I just couldn't wait . . ."

"You're so impatient, baby."

"I know!"

"What do you want from me now?" I asked, my mouth at her neck and my cock still moving slowly down below.

"I want you to fuck me and make me come again." She said it so soft, so pleading, like she really would be hurting if I didn't fuck her. It flipped a switch in me when she said it like that. Gave me permission to take her further than we'd done before, to get more out of her. It was the best feeling ever. In the whole goddamn fucking world.

"Put your arms around my neck and hold on." I gripped under each of her thighs and lifted her up. "Wrap 'em around me, baby, so I can give you what you want!"

She pressed her legs around my hips and her back up against the tile. She said my name. "Ethan . . ."

"Yes, my beauty?" She panted at me. "You look so beautiful waiting for me to fuck you up against this shower wall. You love to be fucked on walls, don't you?"

Her eyes flared and she rocked her spread hips against me in frustration. "Yes!"

"I'll tell you a little secret, baby."

"What?!" she protested, totally out of patience with me.

I positioned the bell end right at the gate of her sex and buried myself to the balls.

"Oh my God!" she yelped as she took me inside, her eyes rolling back for an instant.

"I love fucking you on walls." I pounded her hard, the tight squeeze of her cunt pulsing around my cock, sending me reeling in a haze of instant pleasure so intense I didn't know how long I could hold on. I wanted to last forever. "Remember the night I fucked you on the wall in your flat?" I gritted out. "You felt so good then and you feel so good now."

"Yesssssssss," she shuddered through the hard drilling, her hands gripping tightly for leverage. "I wanted you to. I loved it. I hated when you left afterward."

She was nearly sobbing now as we worked ourselves into a frenzy together, totally merged in body and in mind. Brynne was right there with me the whole way. We connected so perfectly it almost hurt to feel it. Not almost—it totally *did*!

Fucking Brynne hurt so good. It always had and I knew it always would.

"And what did I tell you to say to me that night, baby? It was the first time you told me."

Her flashing eyes, hooded with pleasure, stabbed me hard, like my cock was stabbing into her pussy right now. "That I'm yours," she breathed.

"Yes. You. Are." I started adding a little circular twist to my strokes and felt her inner muscles grip tighter. "And now you're gonna come all over me. One. More. Time!"

Brynne tensed hard and I felt spasms start within her depths, milking my cock for everything she could. *Oh fuck yes!* She shuddered beneath me and began to make those soft sounds I loved to hear out of her—the ones that made me soar. Just like that, she came utterly undone in my arms as I speared into her with hot water streaming over us both.

Sent me to the outer reaches of the goddamn solar system and then some.

And thank holy fuck she did come then because if I'd had to hold on a second longer, I think I would've died. I watched her eyes widen as the climax hit her, loving the knowledge I'd made it happen, and then the glorious rise and crash of my own release as it blasted out of me and into her . . .

My teeth were nipping at her neck and my cock still twitching inside her when I became aware of us. I don't know what kept me on my feet, really. Just an automatic reaction, probably, because I was holding her up and didn't want to drop her, but I wasn't conscious of much beyond that. I was immersed in the complete and total sensual haze of Brynne and my love for her. The way I always felt afterward.

I grazed over her neck with my tongue and rocked the last bit of pleasure out between us, finding her mouth and kissing her deep. If there was a way to crawl up inside her, then I was there. I don't know why it was that way with her and nobody else. It just was.

She opened her eyes slowly, so beautiful in her post-orgasm haze, giving me a sleepy smile.

"There she is," I said.

She swallowed, making her throat move, bringing my eyes to the red mark I'd made on her neck with my teeth. I did that a lot, and I always felt guilty for marking her afterward. She never complained about it, though. Not once did she ever say anything to me in protest about what I did to her when we fucked. Sometimes she hardly seemed real.

"I'm going to set you down, okay?"

She nodded.

I pulled out of Brynne slowly, relishing even that final slide of sensation, feeling the pang of loss because it was so good being inside her. She settled on her feet and wrapped her arms around me. We stood under the spray for a couple of minutes before washing off all the sex. *Too bad.* I know it made me a caveman, but I loved having my spunk all up in her.

I turned off the water and stepped out to grab towels. She let me dry her off, something I loved to do when we had time to spare, like now.

"I need to blow-dry my hair," she said with a sigh.

I wrapped a towel around my waist and reached for the creamy yellow satin robe she'd brought. I helped her into it and tied the belt, pouting that she was no longer naked. "So sad having to cover these up. Tragic, really." I cupped both of her gorgeous tits and squeezed them over the silky material.

She flinched.

"Did that hurt?"

"Not really, they're just sensitive." She yawned, bringing the top of her wrist up to her mouth to stifle it.

"You really do need a nap now. I've worn you out completely. Sorry, baby, I just can't help myself. Forgive me?" I held her chin and brushed my thumb over her lips.

"Forgive you for what? That shower shag? No way, Blackstone." She shook her head sharply.

"So you're mad at me now?" Doubt crept in and I hated the feeling.

"Not at all. I loved revisiting the wall with you." She laughed at me and erased all my dread.

"Okay, my beautiful tease, have a seat and let me comb out your hair." I smacked her bum lightly and chuckled at her little bounce over to the vanity bench.

"Watch it, Blackstone," she warned.

"Or what?" I challenged.

"I'll cut you off from future wall shags. I can do that, you know . . . if I want to." She narrowed her eyes at me in the mirror.

I worked the comb carefully through a section of hair and moved on to another tangled portion. "Ahh, yes you could, but why on earth would you do that, baby? You love my wall shagging almost as much as you love me combing out your hair. More, probably."

She sighed at me. "I really hate it when you're right, Blackstone."

Fifteen minutes later, Brynne even sleepier and her hair dry, I tucked her into bed. She watched me dress and looked sexy as fuck twirling a lock of hair around her finger.

"What are you going to tell them?" she asked.

I came over and kissed her on the forehead. "That I shagged you to the point of sleep."

Her eyes widened. "You wouldn't . . ."

It was my turn to laugh. "Not a moron, baby," I said pointing a thumb at my chest. "What do you think I'd tell them? That you're taking a nap." I shook my head.

"They're going to think I'm a lightweight for crashing."

"No they won't. You're exhausted and you were ill yesterday and I still don't think you're at your best. I noticed you didn't eat much breakfast and you were lagging on the run."

She sputtered and glared at me. "I was *not* lagging on the run, you ass!"

One thing about Brynne? She's as competitive as they come. I swear she could hold her own in drive and determination with some of the blokes I knew in the SF. And *never* insinuate she's weak physically. It makes her spitting mad.

Damn, but she's beautiful when she's riled.

I bit my lip to keep from laughing outright and held up my hands in surrender. "Okay, you only lagged the tiniest little bit," I soothed with kisses. "There's nothing wrong with that when you were sick last night, baby. Your body needs to recover. Have a rest and feel better." I nodded. "I want you to."

She looked down at the blanket and plucked at it distractedly. "What are you going to do while I'm sleeping?"

"I have a date with a local beauty." I shrugged. "She's a real heartbreaker. Dark hair, big blue eyes, absolutely stunning. Very short, though." I gestured with my palm. "Has a particular taste for ice creams."

She laughed through yet another yawn. "I'm sorry I'll miss seeing you on your date eating ice cream with the local beauty. She's adorable. Take a picture with your phone for me?"

"I will, baby." Another kiss. "Now go to sleep."

My girl was already out like a light when I left the room.

6

♠

"Why are fish so smart?" Zara asked me.

I shrugged exaggeratedly. "I have no idea why fish are so smart. Do you know why?"

She nodded seriously. "Because they are always in schools."

I laughed at her smug little face, smudged with strawberry ice cream, and tackling a new angle on her melting cone.

"Want some, Rags?" She offered her treat to the golden retriever sitting loyally beneath the outdoor table.

Rags took a couple of healthy licks with his long pink tongue and I scowled. Zara looked up at me to see what I would say, the little demon that she was. I shrugged at her. "I don't care if you want slobbery dog germs on your ice cream. Do what you want."

She giggled at me and kicked her dangling legs in the chair. "Brynne talks funny."

"I know. I've been telling her that for a long time, but she doesn't listen." I shook my head sadly. "Still does it."

I pulled out my mobile to take some pictures of her and got canned poses the instant she understood what I was doing. Zara cracked me up something fierce. Her parents were in for it once she became a teenager. *Good. God.*

More giggling. "She talks like the words on *SpongeBob SquarePants*."

My mouth fell open in mock surprise. "You know, you're right! Will you tell her?"

She shrugged. "She's nice and I think she can't help it." Zara gave me a look of censure and went back to her strawberry ice cream. Something along the lines of: *Only a real dickhead would make fun of how someone talks, you idiot.* She was so her mother's daughter.

"Nice one, E. Letting your niece share with the dog. I saw the whole thing from the window of the shop." Hannah looked disgusted with us both as she joined us. "I step away for two minutes—"

"He said he didn't care, Mummy," Zara interrupted, selling me out with no trouble at all.

"Oh, Raggsey is pretty disease-free, I think." I gave the dog a nice pat on the head. "And you are a little traitor!" I pointed a finger at Zara. "So sue me, Han. I'm just the uncle here. Letting them run amuck in wild abandon is my role."

"Yeah, well, I haven't had the indulgent auntie role . . . yet."

I shot her a look and discerned something in her expression. Not sure what, but I knew suspicious in my sister when I saw it. Her mind was busy.

"What does that cryptic comment mean?"

"You and Brynne." She shook her head a little. "This is really serious isn't it? I've never seen you like this."

I looked out at the sea with its millions of reflecting ripples and adjusted my sunglasses. "I want to marry her."

"I thought so. . . . Well, I guessed you were heading there with her. Talking to her this morning pretty much confirmed it, and then today when she needed a nap I started putting it all together."

What does Brynne having a nap have to do with anything? "So you approve?" I asked.

Hannah looked at me curiously. "Approve of you and Brynne getting married? Of course we support you. I want you to be happy and if you love her and she loves you . . . well then, it's meant to be." She reached for my hand over the table. "It happens that way sometimes. Nobody's perfect. Fred and I started out the same way, E, and I wouldn't change a thing about us or when the babies came. They are a blessing."

I picked up her hand and kissed it. "They really are, and someday maybe, but a family is not anywhere in the equation right now. I'm just trying to get her used to the idea of getting shackled first."

Hannah looked relieved. "Oh, good. I like her even more now. I must admit I was worried you might be trapped into it and I hated to think of that for you, little brother. I'm glad for you if it's something you want."

I snorted. "Right . . . *she's* the one that needs trapping. Brynne's hard to pin down and having a relationship is scary for her. I'll be lucky to get her to the altar in a year from now. I'm trying to convince her that a long engagement will work best."

Hannah nodded slowly like she was absorbing it. "So

you'll wait until after to have the wedding? That's one option, but Dad's going to hate it. Remember how he was when Freddy and I jumped the gun with Jordan. Dad had us married within a month." She mocked my father's words at the time, "'No grandchild of mine will be born a bastard! Your poor mother would be heartbroken if she were here to see—'"

"What?!" I gaped at her. "Brynne's not . . . I mean, you're greatly mistaken if that's what you're suggesting." I glared at Hannah, shocked at her speculations. "You thought . . ." I shook my head vigorously. "No, Han! My girl is not preggers. No way. She's been very careful with her pills. I see her take them every morning. Hell, I'm sure I heard her in the bathroom this morning getting her pills."

Hannah shook her head slowly at me, her gray eyes looking sympathetic and strangely wise, but even so, I wasn't buying it.

"You think she's pregnant? And that's why I want to marry her?" I was truly shocked and more than a little insulted that my sister would imagine us so irresponsible. "You couldn't be more off the mark, Han. God! O ye of little faith," I said scornfully, reaching for my coffee.

"Maybe you two should talk to Freddy, then," she said, "because I would bet my house that Brynne is very preggers and that the two of you are going to be parents whether you like it or not."

I choked on my coffee, startling the dog, who banged into the small table and made it rattle on the cobbled patio.

Hannah looked down at Zara, who for all intents and

purposes appeared to be listening to every word of our conversation. "Be a love and take Rags over to the grass for a roll around, okay?"

Zara pondered for a moment before deciding that battling her mum was a no-win and left with Rags as requested, melting ice cream in hand.

My heart rate sped up instantly and I felt fear coupled with anxiety and excitement all at once. "We're not talking to Freddy—wait just one goddamn minute, Hannah! What the fucking hell?! I want to know just what makes you willing to bet your magnificent house that she is." I was shouting now. "Tell me!" I dragged my hand over my beard, feeling a sweat break out as I glared at my sister and waited for her to shake off her misguided attempt at a joke.

Hannah looked around the courtyard area of the sweets shop and smiled pleasantly at a few of the other patrons who were now staring rudely at us. "Ease up, brother. How about we take a walk instead." She gathered her shopping bags and stood up, offering me a patient look that spelled out clearly, *Listen to your big sister, you enormous arsehole.*

I thought about leaving my sister and niece, both of them right there in the village center, running back to the house to get Brynne, putting her in the Rover and driving back to London. We could get away from here and pretend this was all some weird, impossible dream or misunderstanding. I seriously did. For about five seconds.

I somehow got to my feet despite the sudden weakness in my knees, picked up my purchase from an earlier stop at an antiques shop, and followed my sister instead.

"How late is she?" Hannah asked as we walked.

"Late? Fuck, I don't know about this stuff! She said the pills she takes makes her periods skip out sometimes."

"Ahh, so she wouldn't know if she was late. Makes sense. She told me all about being sick last night. Said you had to pull over on the side of the road. She also mentioned being lightheaded last night as well."

"Yeah, so?" I said defensively. "Maybe it was something she ate."

Hannah bumped me in the shoulder. "Stop being an arse. I've had three children, E, I know the symptoms of pregnancy, and my husband is a doctor. I know what I'm talking about."

I felt a line of sweat trickle down my back. "But . . . this can't be possible."

"Oh, stop moaning and tell me facts. I assure you it can be very possible. What happened when Brynne felt lightheaded?"

"She had to sit down and said she was thirsty."

"Thirst is a symptom," Hannah said in singsong.

"Fuck, and after that she had to puke. Oh, God."

"Some women get morning sickness in the *evenings*," she announced, "Fred will even tell you it's very common."

"What else happens to you?"

"I got very moody and emotional. It's the massive amounts of hormones raging around."

Check. My Medusa joke from a couple weeks ago suddenly didn't seem funny anymore.

"Extreme exhaustion, necessitating naps." She tilted her head all the way to the side. "I've never napped in my life except for the three times I was pregnant."

Check. Brynne was sleeping right now at my sister's house. I wanted a smoke, and then another, and to just keep on going until the whole pack was gone.

"Breasts get very tender to the touch, a little painful. Again, it's the hormones starting the process for milk to feed the baby."

I just gaped at her, and I'm sure my mouth was hanging open like the village idiot's as she talked about hormones and breasts and milk production. *This cannot be happening. It can't. Not now.*

But my sister rambled on, scaring the absolute shit out of me with every subsequent sentence that came out of her mouth.

"This last part is something that happens and trust me, I would rather not say, but I suppose I should tell you anyway since you asked." She held up her hand to stop me from speaking. "I don't want to hear if it's true or not. I *really* don't need to know."

"What?!" I yelled at her. "Stop fucking around and tell me!"

Hannah glared at me and then slowly changed it into a smirk. "Pregnant women get very randy and want sex all the time. Their men are usually too stupid to realize why they're getting lucky with the extra shagging all of a sudden." She got a kick out of telling me that one, I am sure. "It's definitely the hormones." Hannah folded her arms and waited.

"We need to go back," I said in a strange voice. Even to my ears I didn't sound normal. All I could see was Brynne begging me to fuck her in the shower before I came here. *Oh my God.* Petrified shock didn't even begin to cover the enormity of this bomb drop.

As I stood there beside my sister, gazing out over the Somerset coast, on a warm summery day in July, with my niece chasing the dog over the grass, I knew two things were an absolute certainty.

The first was that Brynne wouldn't take the news well at all.

The second part came to me quickly and with extreme clarity. The reaffirmation that I was a very, very, lucky man for reasons I could only admit to myself. I wouldn't even tell Brynne the reason. It was all for me to know and to keep private. Very simple logic, really. And the more I thought about it, the easier it was to accept the possibility.

If Brynne is truly carrying my child . . . then she can never leave me.

7

♠

"What could cause her pills not to work right? Brynne told me she's been on them for several years. Explain this to me," I demanded.

Freddy looked at me sympathetically. "Relax, mate. It's not the end of the world. She won't be forced into anything. We live in 2012. There are options."

"Oh, fuck!" The idea that she could be pregnant was enough to process at the moment, but even thinking about what Fred might be suggesting was even worse. "A termination, you mean?"

"Yes. She's within her rights, and it is one option. Adoption is another," he said softly.

I flopped down into a chair, set my elbows on my knees and leaned my forehead on my hands. I just sat there and breathed. As much as I was in shock, I knew that terminating the pregnancy was out of the question. Out of the fucking realm of possibility. No way would I allow my child to be killed or have it hushed away. I just hoped that Brynne felt the same way I did. *What if she doesn't?*

"Well, you two need to have a talk and then she should have a test to confirm. If you want me to do one and speak to her I will, but you're going to have to go there first, E, and discuss it together."

I nodded into my hands and hauled arse up from the chair. Fred clapped a hand on my back in support. "But how? If she's taking her pills, why would this happen?" I persisted. Maybe in some far reaches of my pathetic attempt at denial I hoped a bell would ring proclaiming it was time to wake up.

Freddy smiled and shook his head at me. "Things change, other medications can diminish the effects of contraception, condoms blow out, people get drunk and have a go, they get illnesses that alter their body's ability to metabolize the drugs, and most important, *nothing* is one hundred percent effective. The only thing is celibacy." He gave me a look. "Condoms?"

I shook my head and looked down at the floor.

"Ahh, well then, if you've made deposits in the bank, my man, it can happen very easily."

I winced. "How do I go upstairs to her and tell her I think I've knocked her up and she needs to have a test? How?!"

Freddy went to the wet bar, poured me a vodka double and handed it over.

I gulped it down and he slapped me on the back a second time.

"I don't think you're going to have to go upstairs to do it," Fred said.

I snapped my head up to ask him what he meant, and felt my knees go weak again.

Zara and Brynne walked into the room, hand in hand and smiling wide. She looked so happy . . . and beautiful . . . and . . . pregnant.

"Oh, hi." I smiled at Ethan and wondered why he looked at me like I'd grown a second head. "What are you guys gossiping about in here? Man talk?"

Ethan chuckled nervously and looked a little pale. He looked terrified, actually. *Now that's very weird.*

"Is everything okay? Did you get a call from Neil?" I asked, starting to feel uneasy myself. "Did he find out who sent that text last night?" I put my free hand up to my neck and tried to still the panic suddenly rising up.

The thing with Ethan is he grounds us. He's the sure one, exuding confidence at every turn. He makes me feel safe, so seeing him look like he did right then . . . worried . . . well, it scared the shit out of me.

He came right over and pulled me close up against his chest. "No. Nothing like that." He kissed me on the forehead and held my face, looking much more like the Ethan I know and love. "He's still working on your phone." He shook his head. "Don't even think about that damn text, okay? Are you thirsty? Would you like some water? How about you sit down and get off your feet." He led us over to the couch and practically shoved me down onto it.

"Um . . . okay." I shook my head and narrowed my eyes at him, mouthing, *"What the hell?"*

"Nothing, baby. You just look tired. How was your nap?" His voice sounded strange.

I frowned back at him. "My nap was great, but I didn't sleep a terribly long time." Zara crawled onto my lap and I began smoothing over her long curls. "While you were off having ice cream I got a tour of Hallborough and some pictures of Mallerton's portrait of Sir Jeremy and his Georgina for Gaby . . . and sent them off."

"That's nice," Ethan said, dragging a hand through his hair.

"Yeah . . . it was *nice*." I looked over at Freddy and got a strange vibe from him too. We'd had a great conversation earlier while the rest of them were gone, and he'd given me a tour of the house. Now he looked like he just wanted to get the hell out of the room. "What is going on? Why are you both acting so weird?"

Ethan shrugged and held his hands up in helplessness. "Baby . . ."

Freddy came over to where I was and held out his hands for Zara. "Come with Daddy, little one. Uncle Ethan wants to talk to Brynne."

"Oh, okay," I said, reluctantly handing her over. "I wanted to hear all about your trip to get ice cream with Uncle Ethan." I made a sad face at Zara.

"The ice cream was nice," she said from up in her father's arms. "Mummy told Uncle Ethan she would bet the house that you is very preggers and going to be parents whether you likes it or not." She smiled sweetly. "I shared with Rags so Uncle Ethan and Mum could yell about your preggers."

Several things happened all at once. I was on my feet instead of the couch, but had no idea how I got there. I could see myself standing up, right in the middle of Hallborough's beautiful Georgian drawing room with its elegant furniture and paintings and rugs. I could see Ethan's handsome face and the afternoon sun filtering in through the tall windows. And all those particles swirling in the air—the kind that are usually invisible, but when the sunlight hits just right, you can see them lazily floating, suspended as if by magic. Come to think of it, I was floating too. The ceiling held me back from drifting away into the sky and probably farther into outer space. I would have kept floating away. I know I would have if it weren't for the ceiling.

Ethan cursed and stumbled toward me. I kept hearing my name. Over and over I heard my name called. I could see everything. I was standing there. Ethan was flying toward me. Freddy was running out of the room so fast with Zara it looked like a blur of movie footage that was sped up. The room suddenly felt warm; no, it felt hot. Like an oven. I looked down from the ceiling at Ethan rushing toward the "me" standing in the drawing room. He reached out his arms, but then everything slowed down. Real slow. Ethan kept moving but his speed reduced even further. I didn't think he'd ever reach me. I blinked and tried to make sense of what Zara had said. Freddy had already taken her out of the room, though, so I couldn't ask her about it. I even heard her little voice ask Freddy, "Daddy, what's preggers?"

"I love you." I woke up to those words coming from Ethan's lips. I was back on the couch, but this time I was lying down. Ethan was on his knees on the floor stroking over my head and hair with a whole lot of concern in his eyes. "You're back . . ." Ethan closed his eyes then opened them again. He looked pretty shaken up, probably a lot like I felt. *Get in line, buddy. That was an out-of-body experience I just had.* I could check that one off my life list now.

I remembered.

And the weight of the knowledge compressed my chest until I gasped in a huge breath and struggled to sit up. Ethan kept me down and shushed me. The urge to flee was great. It was as if my subconscious knew that panicking wouldn't help a bit, but like with an addiction you do it anyway even though you know it'll only make things worse.

I shook my head at him. "I'm not, Ethan. I'm *not* pregnant. I take my pills and I've never missed a day . . ."

He just kept stroking my hair with one hand, resting his other on my shoulder.

He was afraid I was going to run. I know Ethan and I can see how he thinks sometimes. He was holding me down on that couch so I couldn't leave him, or run away, or take off, or bolt. *You are a very wise man, Ethan Blackstone.*

Because that is exactly what I wanted to do.

"Remember what I just said to you, Brynne." His voice was hard but also vulnerable. I could hear the worry in it.

"That you love me?"

He nodded slowly, never taking his hands off me.

"But I am not pregnant," I insisted. "Let me up."

"Brynne, you need to have a test and then we'll know

for certain. Hannah and Fred think you could be . . ." he trailed off, his voice so unsure. "Hannah helped me get some pregnancy kits from the chemist's for you to . . ."

I pushed at him hard. "Let me go!"

"Brynne . . . baby, please just listen—"

"Let. Me. Go. Now!"

He backed off. I sat up and folded my arms beneath my breasts. I felt so hot and thirsty and just plain old wrong at the moment I couldn't be a very good judge of much of anything.

"Don't freak, okay? We need to discuss this like adults." His jaw ticked from the grinding of teeth.

"Yeah," I sneered at him. "Discuss. That would've been a good idea before you talked to your sister and Freddy about me. Ethan!? Why would you do that? Why?"

"I didn't. I had no idea. Hannah brought it up to me and then Fred got involved. They think you could be pregnant. Sick last night, napping all the time, and . . . other stuff."

"What other stuff?"

Ethan looked like he would rather swallow a mouthful of glass than have this discussion with me right now.

He grimaced. "Would you just take the test?"

"No! I won't just take a test because you and your family think I should! What other stuff?!" The irrationality I knew I shouldn't be allowing in was getting the old security guard wave-through. *Welcome to HorrorLand, please park in lot You're-Royally-Fucked and make your way to the main gate, where you'll be greeted by your worst nightmare.*

He brought both hands up to my chest, cupped a

breast in each and squeezed. I winced from the pain and the panic pumped up another notch. I remembered this kind of pain from before. I'd felt it before. *Noooooo!*

I pushed his hands away sharply. "You talked about that with them?! Oh my God!"

"It wasn't like that, Brynne. I didn't talk about you. Hannah just assumed some things and when I asked for an explanation she told me about . . . symptoms." He lowered his voice. "You have all those symptoms. You're getting sick and taking naps and they hurt . . ." He gestured at my chest and trailed off, the wariness in his voice making me feel like a bitch again. I knew I could dish out bitchiness in spades when the occasion called for it. This could be considered one of those times.

I leaned forward and buried my hands in my hair and just sat there, staring down at the floor and tried to process. Ethan let me be, which was a damn good thing because I wanted to lash out and bite like a trapped animal would do. *Symptoms . . .* My periods are never much and I've missed them completely before. My doctor assured me it was normal with the particular kind of birth control pill I take so I'd never worried about it. Truthfully, though, I'd not needed to worry because *when you aren't having sex with anyone, you don't have to worry you'll get pregnant!* Before Ethan, sex was sporadic and always protected. I wasn't fool enough to let a guy go without a condom when we didn't know each other very well. *So why did I with Ethan, dumbass?* Hell, Ethan had only used a condom *one* time. Once. *Lots and lots of opportunities for the little swimmers to find a way in. Again, I'm a huge enormous dumbass.*

Being sick the night before had felt very odd, because as soon as I puked it was like nothing was wrong with me at all. The same thing happened at breakfast this morning. I was really hungry, and then when the food came I just wanted toast. Come to think of it, my stomach felt weak right now. That late lunch of a roast beef sandwich was not settling in well. My breasts did hurt. I'd taken naps the last two days.

Everything illuminated and came together in a flash of understanding and terrible anxiety. Why was Ethan so calm? He must be appalled too if this was true.

"It can't be true. It just can't," I said to no one in particular.

"Remember what I said, Brynne," he said with an edge.

I reached out with my hand and he grabbed it, too overwhelmed to really answer him. What could I say to him anyway? Sorry, my birth control pills malfunctioned? I'm a fucked-up mess and always have been, I might as well get knocked up so I can screw up my life some more? Or, I know this is complicating your stressful life, Ethan, I'm really, really sorry about that, but we're pregnant.

I swallowed convulsively. Watery saliva began pooling in my throat. More came, and then more, and I knew I would be horribly sick again. I struggled to manage the effects of the nausea that overtook me so suddenly.

I lost.

Lurching up, I ran for the closest bathroom, my mind desperately trying to remember the floor plan of this huge labyrinth of a house. My hand over my mouth, I stumbled into the powder room just off the solarium and flung myself over the toilet. I puked my guts out until there was nothing left to come up.

I wanted to run away.

I'd been here for the second time in less than twenty-four hours with my girl and it sucked. Especially for her. Talking seemed like a pointless exercise, so I didn't. I just held her hair and let her go to work on expelling the contents of her stomach. I wet a cloth with cold water from the sink and handed it to her. She took it from me, pressed it over her whole face and groaned. I felt completely helpless. *You did this to her and she hates you for it.*

Fred tapped on the open door. "House call," he said kindly.

"Can you give her something, Fred?"

Brynne took the cloth away from her face, looking pale and about ready to cry. Fred smiled at her. "I can give you an anti-nausea but it'll just be symptomatic."

"Please," she answered, nodding her head.

"What does that mean, just symptomatic?" I asked.

Fred spoke to Brynne. "My dear, I don't feel comfortable doing a treatment on you if we don't have a confirmation. Are you ready to try a test?" He spoke gently. "Then we'll know for sure and you and E can decide what's best for the two of you. We really need that test first, though." He gave a quick nod.

"Okay." That was all she said and she spoke to Fred without even looking at me. She seemed rather cold and sort of detached, like we were strangers now. That hurt.

I desperately wanted her to look me in the eyes, but she wouldn't. She just held the wet cloth to her face and kept her eyes locked on the wall.

Fred set the two test kits down on the sink counter. Hannah had helped me choose them in the village earlier, because I sure as hell didn't know what I was doing. After that conversation with my sister, she'd convinced me I needed to buy some pregnancy tests. This was surreal. It really was. Here we three were standing around in a bathroom trying to pretend this was standard operating procedure when, in fact, it was totally fucked up. My Brynne at metaphorical gunpoint practically being forced into a surprise pregnancy test, and with me knowing about her past and the other time she was impregnated.

FUCK! I wanted to punch the wall again but didn't dare in this place. These walls were worth too damn much.

Lots of crazy thoughts flooded my brain. *What if she hates me for knocking her up? What if this breaks us? What if she wants a termination? What if she isn't even pregnant after all and this scares her off?* I was terrified but I still wanted to know. Now. I needed some answers.

"Right," Fred said, "we'll talk in a bit and work on getting you to feeling better, my dear." He eased out of the small room to leave but turned back to say something else. And there was Brynne standing stiffly with downcast eyes like a cornered animal. It broke my heart to witness. It really fuckin' did. "Brynne, we're here to help and support in any way that we can. I mean that and I know that Hannah does too."

"Thank you," she answered in a small voice.

With Fred gone it was just the two of us. Brynne didn't move, she just stood there. It was awkward. I wanted to touch her but was afraid to.

"Brynne?"

She lifted her eyes and swallowed, looking miserable and pale. The second I moved toward her she backed up a step and held up her hand to keep me away. "I—I need to be alone . . ." Her bottom lip trembled as she choked out the words. So different from when it turned up in a sexy smile. Brynne usually smiled a lot more than I did. Her whole face lit up when she did it. Whenever she smiled, it made me want to smile in return. She made me want a lot of things I'd never cared about before too. But she wasn't smiling now. She was scared to death.

It killed me to see her like this. "Baby, remember what I said." I stepped out of the bathroom but I didn't want to. I wanted to be right beside her when she found out. I didn't want to leave her alone. I wanted her in my arms telling me she loved me and that we could do this. I needed that from her right now, and I knew I wouldn't be getting it.

She met my gaze as she started to shut the door slowly. "Don't forget," I said just before it closed and I was facing an elegant carved door instead of my girl, who was struggling on the other side of it.

Time passed slowly as I waited for her to come out. My dread grew exponentially as the minutes ticked away. I checked my mobile for messages and responded to some of them when I got to a text from Neil: **Have news on Fielding. MP rpt.**

I dialed and waited for the connection, staring at the

bathroom door and wondering what was happening in-side. My mind went on full alert as I transferred into pro-tection mode.

"Boss."

"A missing person? Fielding is missing? Please tell me that's not true."

Neil sighed. "Yeah, report was filed just a few days ago by his parents, who live somewhere in the Northeast; Pennsylvania, I think. Last confirmed contact was the thirtieth of May. According to the report, he didn't show for work. His apartment checks out. Passport left behind and no evidence of a hasty flight. The consulate of course has no record of travel outside of the U.S."

"Fuck, that's not nice news, mate."

"I know. The possibilities are endless. His father sus-pects foul play, and has said so in interviews to the papers."

"I bet Oakley's camp loves the press." I said sarcasti-cally.

"No accusation, though. Senator Oakley is not men-tioned, so the connection hasn't been made between Montrose and Fielding to Lance Oakley."

"So let's extrapolate this. Congressman Woodson's plane goes down the beginning of April. Oakley's name starts popping up as a replacement almost immediately. Montrose gets in a bar fight and takes multiple stab wounds to the neck and chest on April twenty-fourth. The motherfucker dies two days later in hospital. Suspect unknown. Tom Bennett contacts me and I take over here on the third of May with Brynne at the Andersen Gallery. Fielding's last sighting was the end of May. Everything's quiet for a month. Text from ArmyOps17 to Brynne's mobile last night, the twenty-ninth of June."

"Yeah."

"What's your gut telling you about Fielding? You've seen the reports."

"I think he's dead in a shallow grave somewhere or maybe in the Pacific feeding the fish."

"Connected to Oakley, you think?"

"Hard to know. Justin Fielding had a drug problem. Cocaine, apparently."

One of the reasons Neil and I worked so well together was our thought processes were so in tune. Neil wasn't a babbler. He said what was needed and didn't pad the conversation with useless crap. Just the facts. And his instincts were dead-on, so when he said he didn't know, that meant things were still falling into place.

"Okay then. We have two of our video perps out of the picture, one dead and one confirmed missing. The third is on active duty in Iraq and a very improbable suspect. The text came from inside the UK and from someone who saw the video at some point in time because they knew the song that was on the original."

"That's about right."

"How do you feel about a little trip out to California?"

"I could do that. Can work on my tan and kill two birds with one stone."

"All right then. Have Frances set you up for early next week. I can't have you gone until I'm back in town."

"How is Brynne feeling? Better, I hope." Neil asked in a soft voice.

I groaned into the phone and grasped at what to answer. *I'm saying fucking nothing!*

"Um . . . she's still feeling ill. Fred's helping her though." I rushed out a quick good-bye and ended our call fast. I could talk about work all day long, but personal stuff was not something I had any experience with, nor did I have a desire to start discussing.

I checked my watch and headed for the door. Twenty minutes had passed since she'd closed the door on me. Seemed like ages ago now. I rapped my knuckles a couple of times. "Brynne? May I come in?"

Nothing.

I rattled the handle and called her name again, louder this time.

Silence.

I pressed my ear to the door and listened. I couldn't hear a thing going on inside the bathroom and started imagining the room's layout. It is, after all, part of my training to understand the structure of buildings and the fastest way to exit them. Sometimes when things come to you in sudden clarity it is truly frightening. This was one of those times. The solarium abutted the bathroom on the other side of the house.

I knew then. I knew it before the text came through a moment later on my mobile from her: **I hav to . . . so sry. WATERLOO**

8

♥

Please give me the strength to do this, I prayed. All I could see was the way Ethan's face looked before I shut the door. What was he thinking right now? He probably wished he'd never heard of me. I felt so ashamed and foolish. It didn't change how I felt about him, though. I loved him the same as before. I just didn't know how we would get through something like this and survive as a couple. How could we?

I turned on the faucet and drank about a gallon of water right from the tap, rinsed my mouth and washed my face. I looked like Frankenstein's bride from the old black-and-white film. My eyes looked frightening, as wide as Elsa Lanchester's were in that movie. I wanted to pretend this wasn't happening, but I knew I couldn't. Those are the thoughts of a child, and I'm not a child! I'm turning twenty-five in two months. How could a person make so many mistakes in twenty-five years?

I reached for a test package and opened it. My hands

were shaking as I held the test stick with the key on the side in plain English. Minus sign for not pregnant and a plus sign for *"You're so pregnant, you irresponsible slut."* I felt that sensation again where my body seemed to want to float away. I closed my eyes and breathed, bringing myself to a place where I could go forward, and then I heard Ethan's methodical voice softly through the door. He was on a call, talking through some of his work business, most likely. I stupidly wanted to laugh at the absurdity of the situation. I was in here taking a pregnancy test and he was on the other side calmly going about his life. How in the hell could he even manage it?

I looked around my prison at the beautiful walls, and that's when I saw it. A door. I don't think they ever used it, but that didn't mean it couldn't be used. I didn't think, I just did what I'd wanted to do when Zara had first made her comments to me.

I ran.

It felt like hardly any time had passed, but I found myself approaching the rocky shore we'd run along this morning and knew I'd been at it for a good while. The farther I ran, the guiltier I felt for leaving without a word. Ethan would be so hurt. Hurt? He's going to be fucking angry! There would be hell to pay. I wondered if he even knew I'd taken off yet. I closed my eyes at the thought of him finding me gone and knew I needed to make contact. I remembered something he'd said to me a long time ago. It was when he asked me to pick my safe word. Ethan had told me it was for when I needed some space and that he would respect it. He had kept his promise the other time I used it on him.

Ethan was honest with me. I believed that he would keep his word so I sent him the text, silenced my phone, and kept on running. I don't know what I hoped to accomplish, but the physical exertion helped me. Adrenaline needed to get burned off somehow, and this was something I could at least control.

I ended up at the end of the pier and right at the Sea Bird Café, where we'd eaten just hours before. *How fast things can change in a day.*

Ethan had told me, "Remember what I said to you, Brynne." He'd repeated it several times. He wanted me to know he loved me. That was Ethan, always reassuring me when I got irrational. But this . . . It was just too much to consider, and I didn't want to face it. I didn't want to face the truth . . . but I knew I had to. Running around like a fool in a seaside village wasn't going to help anything.

Pull yourself together, Bennett.

Well, that got me the strength to push inside the café doors. I walked up to the first employee I found and told her I'd eaten breakfast there that morning and thought I might have left my sunglasses in the loo. She waved me through and in I went.

I slipped the test stick out of my pocket and did my thing, very angry at myself for being in a public restroom instead of in the house with Ethan there waiting for me. Supporting me. His final words to me a very firm "Don't forget." Assuring in his way that he was there for me. *I am so stupid.*

I tried to hold in the sobbing I wanted to let out so badly, and didn't even look at the indicator. I capped it and just shoved it back in my jeans pocket, washed my hands and bailed. I'd never felt so utterly weak and pathetic and lost. *Well, yes you have. Seven years ago was much worse.*

The warmth of the sun was starting to wane in the late afternoon and the wind had picked up, but I wasn't cold. Nope. I was sweating as I followed the return path back the way Ethan had led me this morning. I knew where I wanted to go. I could sit there and think for a while . . . and then . . . What then? What would I do then?

The forest path was not as bright as it had been that morning and had definitely lost some of its fairy-tale quality, but I pushed on to my destination and hardly noticed. The metal gate latch opened just as it had before and clanged loudly behind me once I stepped through. I ran up the long gravel drive, kicking up small stones behind me as I plowed on. I hurried, somehow needing to see it again. I breathed a sigh of relief when the mermaid angel statue came into view. Yes. It was still there. I chastised myself for thinking it would be otherwise. It was real and not a figment of my mind. *You are so losing it.*

I sat right down at the foot of the statue and felt my heart pounding. It beat so hard I'm sure it moved the skin above it. I wasn't dressed for running, but at least I had on shoes that worked.

I sat there for a long, long time.

The sea looked darker and more blue than it had that morning. The wind was sharper and a hint of rain could be found on the breeze. The smell was a good smell to me; earth and water and air all blended. The smell of life.

Life.

Did I have a little life starting inside me? Everyone seemed to think so. The idea of the three of them discussing me like some kind of lab rat still made me see red. Secrets again. Ethan knew I did not do secrets. I just cannot handle them and I doubt I would ever be able to. When I am the last to know things, even if they are small, it takes me right back to that moment when I first saw the video of me on that pool table being . . . fucked like I was nothing but trash. Worthless. Ugly. So very ugly.

It's my hang-up. My cross to bear. I hope there comes a day when I can close the lid on that Pandora's box and keep it closed, but it's not happened yet. Since meeting Ethan the lid has been knocked off several times.

It's not his fault, though. I do know that much. It's mine. I made choices like everyone does. I have to live with them. The old cliché "reap what you sow" makes a lot of sense, actually.

I wasn't ready to look at the test yet. I just wasn't. I guess it made me weak, but I don't claim to be all together in the head. That's Dr. Roswell's job, and I've given the poor woman plenty to work with over the last years. She would have a field day with this news. I'd need a third job just to pay for the extra therapy.

So back to what could be. Pregnant. A baby. A child. Ethan's baby. The two of us parents . . . I'm quite sure that when Ethan suggested we should get married, he didn't have becoming a father in mind. *He'd make a wonderful father, though.* I'd seen him with Zara and the boys. He was so good with them. Playful but with some common sense. He would be the kind of father I had. The best. If that was something he even wanted. And I was terrified, because I just did not know the answer to that question.

Picturing Ethan in the role of daddy is what broke me. The tears came then, and I couldn't hold them back for even one more second.

I cried there on the grass lawn of a beautiful stone manor perched along the Somerset coast, at the foot of a mermaid angel that looked out to sea. I cried until there were no more tears in me and it was time to move on to the next stage of this process. I'd already done denial and anger. What was next? Bargaining? Ethan would have something to say there. I felt guilty again for leaving him at the house. He was going to hate me . . .

Strangely, the crying jag helped, because I did feel marginally better. I was terribly thirsty, though.

I needed water and figured dehydration was the culprit. All that puking and running will do it to you. I looked around for a faucet and spotted one. I walked over and turned the handle to let it flow for a bit before cupping my hand and bringing the water to my mouth. It tasted so nice, I drank handful after handful until I was satisfied. I did my best with my face too, trying to wash away all the tears and snot and absolute disgusting mess I was by now.

I came back over to my place beneath the mermaid angel and again watched the sea for a time. My wet face felt cool in the breeze until it dried in the wind.

It's time to look now.

Time to look and see what the cards had in store for me. I was as ready as I would ever be, I decided. As I reached into my pocket for the stick, I felt another wave of nausea take hold of me and wondered how I could possibly vomit up anything else.

Apparently even water wasn't welcome in my stomach, because I was reduced to kneeling over the rocks and heaving again as all that lovely, refreshing water came right back up.

I stayed back the whole time. I gave her the space she asked me for and respected her wishes.

Until she got sick again.

I couldn't let her suffer through that alone. Not my girl. Not when she needed some help and compassion from someone who loved her. Seeing her sitting beneath the mermaid statue and then weeping her heart out had been hard to watch. I didn't have any other choice, though. I wasn't letting her go it alone outside in public where she was at risk. It just wasn't going to happen like that. I'd made sure the GPS was activated on her mobile after that morning she went out for coffee and met up with Langley on the street. *The cocksucker.* And since she had her mobile with her and turned on, I had been able to track her movements for nearly the whole way. The stop into the Sea Bird Café surprised me, though. I wondered why she'd done that. The statue made much more sense to me. It was very peaceful here. I could immediately see why she'd come back to this place to be alone.

"I've got you," I said as I touched her back and gathered up her hair—again—for more times than I cared to count.

"Oh, Ethan . . ." she choked out in between the heaving, "I'm sorry . . . I'm sorry—"

"Shhhh, it's okay. Don't fight it, baby." I rubbed over her back with one hand and held her hair with the other. "It's just the water you had coming up now."

When she was finally done she drooped like a wilted flower, hunched over the ground looking so very ill. I knew I needed to get her back to the house as soon as possible. She was in desperate need of Fred's doctoring and some rest.

I pulled her up to me on unsteady legs, her tragic state shredding me from the inside out. I couldn't help but feel horribly guilty for doing it to her too.

"Th-thank you for coming to f-f-find me," she chattered, her lips looking more blue than anything. She was chilled and shivering, so I took off my shirt and put it on over hers, hoping the extra layer would warm her a little.

She was compliant, allowing me to take charge, and that was a massive relief. Taking care of her was something I could do. I didn't need much, just the assurance she wanted my help. Wanted me.

"I'll always find you." I picked her up and started walking down the long drive of Stonewell Court to where I'd parked outside of the gate. She closed her eyes and put her palm on my chest.

Right over my heart.

It always amazed me at how easy it was to carry her. I knew why. It was because *she* carried my heart with her wherever she went. My heart was in her hands, and carrying her was some form of self-preservation, maybe. Holding her, holding me up.

I couldn't explain it, but I understood it. Made perfect sense to me.

I said it again. "I'll always find you, Brynne."

As soon as I got her back to Hallborough, Fred told me to take her upstairs to our room and put her into bed. She was asleep when I laid her down. She didn't even wake up when I took off her shoes and tucked the blanket around her.

My baby looked awful. I'd never say that out loud, but she did. It didn't mean she wasn't still the most beautiful woman in the world, though. To me she was. My beautiful American girl.

Fred came around to the other side of the bed and pinched the skin on her arm a few times. He took her pulse from her neck and then her temperature at her ear. "She's severely dehydrated with an elevated pulse. I'd like to stick her with an IV. She needs the fluids right away or she could be in trouble. Her body mass is low and she can't afford to—"

"Can you do that here so she doesn't have to go into hospital?"

"I can but I have to run 'round to the clinic to get what I need, and someone will have to monitor her the entire time."

"I'll do it." I looked back at her sleeping, hoping she was having a good dream at least. She deserved that. "I'm not leaving her."

"And what's the verdict? Am I going to be an uncle or not?"

"I don't know, Fred. She never said. We still don't know . . ." I wanted to know so very badly, though.

As soon as Fred took off, I pulled back the covers to get her out of her jeans. I wanted her comfortable in this bed since she was going to be in it for a good while. *Hell yes she would!* She'd get some rest if I had to tie her down to the fucking bed.

I'd found some soft leggings to exchange for the jeans, and a pair of fuzzy purple socks she liked to wear around at night. Brynne had beautiful feet and loved to have them rubbed. I'd seen her slather her feet with lotion in the evenings and then put on socks like this. She said it was why they were so soft.

I unbuttoned her jeans and pulled them off her long, sexy legs in one smooth swoop. Her blue knickers came with. I could see her body as I had seen it many, many times, so perfectly made and utterly captivating, but I didn't think about sex right now. I stared at her belly, so flat and hollowed, and thought about what might be growing inside there instead.

Are we having a baby?

Brynne might be scared to death about the possibility, but if it was true, there wasn't a doubt in my mind she would be a wonderful mother. My girl was brilliant at everything she did.

She moved her head restlessly on the pillow but didn't wake. The soft words I spoke at her ear were whispered, and I hoped she could hear me somehow. Slipping on the leggings, I quickly followed with the socks, grateful just to have my hands on her skin in some kind of useful service.

Having her back safe was the most important thing; even so, a "Waterloo" directed at me for the second time in our relationship hadn't been nice. But in the end I was glad she'd used it when she needed to. She'd even given me a little "I'm sorry" before typing the word in her text. I sighed. I knew Brynne was doing the best she could, and at least she was honest about telling me when she needed some space and a little time. I felt like I was being the only way I knew how to be. I didn't know what I could do any differently.

Putting her into a loose T-shirt was a little more challenging. I settled for her Hendrix shirt because it was so soft and I wanted her to be as comfortable as possible. Grateful the closure of her bra was situated in the front, I popped it open to reveal her beautiful tits and thought they looked no different to me than before. *Just perfection, is all.* But looks can be deceiving, and I'd seen how she reacted when I touched them earlier. *How in the motherfuck did I get her pregnant when she is so careful about her pills?*

Despite everything, my dickhead cock reacted at the sight of her naked flesh. I wanted to twist the damn thing off for getting us into this mess, but knew that was pointless. The only way to keep that fucker away from her would be from inside my grave.

Which might be soon, from the speed at which we were traveling. By God, I could hardly keep up, and felt like I'd aged a year in the past twenty-four hours.

In a rush to finish dressing her, I lifted her off the bed gently to push the T-shirt over her head and down her back. I smoothed it over until her beautiful bare skin was covered up again.

I couldn't resist kissing her on the forehead before

tugging her arms through the sleeves. She never woke throughout the whole process, which did not soothe me one bit. I didn't want her feeling sick, but needed to have her *back*. So very badly. I tried to keep my emotions in check but it wasn't easy, especially when my Sleeping Beauty wasn't going to awaken from her slumber just because I'd kissed her. So where did that leave me in this clusterfuck of a weekend? Fairy tales really are full of shit when you get right down to it.

As I pulled the blankets in to tuck around her, something fell off the foot of the bed with a muffled thud. Her phone? Most likely Brynne's mobile, in the pocket of her jeans. I reached down to retrieve it off the floor and saw something else had slipped out of her pocket. It was just lying there in the bunched-up blue fabric. A white plastic stick with a purple cap on the end that foretold a portion of our future.

I knew what that white plastic stick was, but I still didn't know its secret. The test indicator window was facing the floor.

9

♥

I opened my eyes to find Ethan dozing in the comfortable chair next to the bed. He had his arms folded in tight and his long legs stretched out on the matching ottoman. He was so beautiful to me it almost hurt to look at him for very long. I was still amazed that he'd come to find me. How could he want this? How was it possible? Why wasn't he running for the hills?

My left arm felt funny and I figured out why when I saw the tube taped to it, which led straight up to the IV bag hanging on one of those poles on wheels.

I sat up in the bed, looking for the clock to check the time. How long had I been asleep? The clock read just after ten-thirty. The afternoon's events came crashing back in a blasting wave and I braced myself for more pain and suffering, but it never came. I guess all the running and crying and puking had sucked all of the reacting out of me. Instead, I was warm in a soft bed with Ethan watching over me with an IV in my arm. Okay, that was a little scary. I must have been in terrible shape when Ethan brought me here if I needed intravenous liquids.

I settled back down into the covers and indulged in watching him sleeping in the chair. It couldn't be very comfortable for him. Poor guy. He had to be exhausted from everything that had happened, and everything we had done in the last day and a half.

I wasn't ready to face it all yet, but I did feel much better than I had in hours, and . . . safe. Very safe in Ethan's care, the way he'd made me feel since the night I'd met him and he took me home in his car. I let myself drift back to sleep again, content with the knowledge that, at least for now, I wasn't alone.

When I woke the next time, Ethan's chair was empty. The bedside clock read a little after one-fifteen in the morning, so I surmised he must have gone to bed. Another bed. Somewhere else. I took a deep breath and tried to suck it up. Turning into a puddle of jelly wouldn't help me a bit. But it sure felt good to fall apart sometimes, especially when you had someone to catch you. *Like Ethan . . .*

I realized I needed the bathroom, so I flicked the covers back and gingerly crawled out of bed. Feet were a little shaky and muscles very sore, especially my legs and abdominals, but I had to smile at the socks on my feet. Ethan must have put them on me. *He really has to love me.* I truly believed that he did, but I guess I was afraid that a pregnancy would kill that love, in all its newness and fragility. We were moving way too fast for this to possibly work. *Right?*

The IV pole had to be rolled along with me, or I would risk ripping out the needle imbedded in my wrist. I shuddered at the look of the ugly thing, glad I didn't remember getting stuck with it in the first place. The pole was a little awkward, but I managed to get in and take care of business.

The first thing I did afterward was brush my teeth. I actually moaned at the divine taste of toothpaste and the feel of a clean minty mouth after far too many revolting spells of barfing. *It's the little things . . .*

Next I tackled my hair, which I have to say looked pretty damn horrific. I didn't even want to think about what might be dried in there. I really wanted a shower, but I knew there was no way to navigate it out by myself when I was still hooked up to an IV. Brushing and braiding my hair into one long rope on the side improved things somewhat, but I still looked like hell. I eyeballed the bathtub.

"What are you doing out of bed?" Ethan barked from the doorway, a heavy scowl on his beautiful face.

"I had to go to the bathroom."

"And are you finished?"

I nodded and looked longingly at the magnificent marble bath.

His eyes followed mine to the bathtub. "Don't even think about it. You're getting back into bed." He pointed, still glaring.

I raised both brows. "Are you telling me where to go by pointing?"

"Yup. And it's thataway." He jerked his thumb for emphasis and stalked over, lifting me off my feet with no trouble. "Grab onto the pole, baby, it's coming too."

I squeaked and grabbed the pole. His clothes felt cold as he pressed me against him.

Ethan wasted no time in getting me back into bed and my IV organized. "Why do I need this, anyway?" I asked.

He leaned in, bringing his lips very close to mine. "Because according to Fred you were so severely dehydrated you would've been admitted to hospital in your condition when I found you." His eyes were hard but his voice was soft as he told me the brutal truth.

"Oh . . ." I didn't know how else to respond and was beginning to feel emotions rising up that threatened to overtake my fragile grip on keeping it together. I brought my unfettered hand up to the side of his face and touched him, the stubble of his beard a mixture of soft and rough, well familiar to me by now. Ethan closed his eyes as if he was savoring my touch, and that made me sad. He needed some comfort too.

"You were outside smoking, weren't you?"

He nodded and I saw something flicker in his eyes like regret and maybe even shame. I felt even worse. He certainly didn't need my judgment right now. I'd put this poor man through the ringer in the last day and night, and he was still here by my side. He'd come to get me, and told me he loved me, and took care of me when I was sick. He'd done all of that and what had I done? I'd run off in self-pity and gotten myself so ill I would be in a hospital right now if not for Freddy being a licensed physician.

"I'm so sorry . . ." I whispered. "I hurt you again . . . and I'm so, so sorry for doing it."

"Hush." He brought his lips to mine and kissed me sweetly, smelling of mint and spice, and letting me know he was still right with me. My rock of strength.

"I'm glad you're here—I woke up before and saw you sleeping in the chair . . . and then the next time you were gone . . ."

"Where else would I want to be, baby?" He brushed his thumb over my lips.

"Away from me?"

He shook his head slowly. "Never."

"But I still don't know what the test says, because I never looked." I started to crumble.

"Neither do I," he said right back, smoothing my hair.

"How can you not know?"

"I don't," he answered softly. "When I pulled your jeans off you it fell out onto the floor."

"And you didn't look at it?" I asked incredulously.

He shook his head and smiled. "Nope. I wanted to wait for you and do it together."

I flung my arms around his neck and lost it. I tried to be quiet about it at least. Ethan just held me and stroked my back. He really was too good for me, and I did honestly wonder what I'd ever done to deserve someone like him.

"Get in bed with me," I said against his shoulder.

"Are you sure that's what you want?"

"Yes, I'm sure that's what I want!" I answered, blubbering through more sappy tears.

Ethan must have liked my answer, because he wasted no time getting ready to join me.

I worked on drying my eyes as Ethan slipped out of his jeans. He kept his boxers on, though. Not that they ever were much of a deterrent when we wanted to be naked, but I don't think either of us were capable of much more than sleep right now. We were both treading on ground that seemed entirely made of eggshells.

Ethan slipped under the blankets and put his arm beneath me as he did often. I settled on my side and tucked in all along his body so I could rest partially on his chest. My left hand was the one with the IV, which forced me to keep it on top, but I still rubbed circles over his chest through his shirt. I burrowed into him and breathed in his delicious scent.

"You smell so good. I must smell like pig slop."

"Well, I really couldn't say, my beauty, because I've never been close enough to pig slop to know how it smells." I could tell he was smirking. "When were you?"

I grinned and mumbled. "It's metaphorical pig slop I'm talking about, and that works just as well. Even better, probably."

"I agree with you on that one. I'll take the metaphorical pig slop over the real stuff any day." He massaged the back of my neck and teased me. "If you do smell like pig slop then it's pretty nice, actually. In fact, I would go so far as to say that I fucking love the smell of pig slop."

It worked. He got me to laugh a little at least and that helped me find the courage to tell him I was ready to face up to what fate had in store for me.

"Ethan?"

"Yeah, baby?"

"How did you know I would go back there—to the mermaid angel?"

"I set up GPS on your mobile a while ago." His muscles flexed around me a little tighter. "Even though I didn't like seeing *Waterloo* in that text," he said, pausing to take a breath, "I'm glad you did what you needed to do." He kissed my forehead. "And that you had your mobile on you and powered up. I'm going to have to insist you always keep it on you when we are apart. We need to talk about the security again too."

"Why? What happened?"

He dismissed my questions with more kisses, then murmured a very firm "Later" against my lips.

I could tell he meant business by his tone and let it go. He was right anyway. We had other stuff to deal with first.

"I—I want to look at the test now."

"Before you do, I need to say something." Now Ethan was the one who sounded anxious. I could feel him tensing his body and I didn't like the change one little bit. It scared me what he might say. And if he did say what I feared, then I knew it would be the end of us. There was one thing that I simply couldn't do. I knew I wouldn't be able to. I'd had been down that road before and I couldn't go there again and survive.

"All right. Tell me." I felt my stomach clench in a bundle of nerves but was determined to listen. I had to know. I closed my eyes.

"Look at me." He traced his finger all along the side of my face and ended at my lips. "I need you to look me in the eyes for this."

I opened them to find his full attention focused on me. The intensity of the way he conveyed his needs to me was almost blinding.

"Brynne, I want you to know—no, I need you to *be-*

lieve—that whatever the test reads, it won't change my feelings. It may not be the plan I had in mind with you, but if it is the path . . . then I'm not veering off it. I know where I want to go and who I want with me." He put his hand on my belly and held it there. "You. And anyone else we might have made together are coming with *me*." His expression showed so much determination, but I could see some vulnerability in his eyes too, almost fear.

His words were so certain, even a little hard. I thought I understood what he was telling me, but wanted to make sure. A flicker of hope started burning inside my heart and I dug deep, deeper than I ever had before, to find the courage to ask him the next part.

"So . . . so you wouldn't ask me to have an abor—"

"Fuck no!" He cut me off. "I can't do a termination, Brynne. It would feel wrong to me . . . and I really hope you feel the same."

I shuddered out a long deep sigh. "Oh, thank God!" I felt the tears welling up in my eyes. "Because I know I couldn't go through with an abortion, even if you demanded one. My mom tried that on me before and it just—it just sent me over the edge. I know I wouldn't be able to . . ."

He kissed the rest of my response away and then rested his forehead on mine. "Thank you," he whispered, with soft lips caressing my face.

I just breathed for a bit and let him hold me close up against his body. I needed to take it all in and understand his feelings, and I was so very relieved. "So you would be . . . glad?"

He didn't even hesitate. "I don't know if *glad* is a word

I would use to describe how I feel about the possibility of us becoming parents, but I do know what my conscience tells me, and if we are pregnant . . . then I guess it was fate for it to happen like this, and we just have to do it."

Ethan's eyes looked so blue right then I was sure I could drown in them. "Do you believe in fate?"

He just nodded. No words; instead he offered a gesture that felt more intimate than if he'd spoken it.

"Okay, where is it?"

"Where's what?"

"My test. It was in my front pocket of my jeans."

He got a blank look for an instant and then started to laugh. It was pretty uncharacteristic even for Ethan, considering the circumstances.

"What's so funny?" I demanded.

"I just realized I don't have it anymore. Freddy knows. He's the only one who knows the truth."

"How does he know and not you?"

"Well, he had to go to his clinic to get all the supplies needed for your IV and while he was gone, that's when I found it had fallen on the floor." He kissed the side of my temple. "I was just staring at it on the floor when Fred walked in. He asked me if I would look at it. I told him to read it, but not to tell me. And that's what he did. He looked at the test and then put it in his shirt pocket, I think. He was really focused on getting some fluids into you, and quite frankly so was I. You were completely out of it. You never woke up even when I undressed you. You scared me to death." He squeezed me a little. "Don't ever do that again, please."

"Trust me, I don't want to feel that sick again, thank you very much. It's awful . . ." I trailed off, realizing we still were without an answer to a question that really needed one.

"Wait, the second test—" I reminded him.

"Yeah, I was just thinking that myself. I wonder if it's still downstairs in the powder room." Ethan sat up in bed and reached for his jeans. "I really hope so for Fred's sake, because I doubt he'll appreciate being woken up at two in the morning to give us the first one."

"Are you going down to see if you can find it?"

"Mmm-hmm," he said, "I've been waiting for hours to know the truth and I don't want to wait any longer." He gave me another intense look as he pulled on his pants. "Okay with you?"

I nodded and took another deep breath. "I want to know too."

He stood up and checked my IV bag before dropping down to kiss me quickly on the lips. "Don't go anywhere, baby."

"Oh, I won't," I said sarcastically, "I want this out of me." I indicated to my wrist.

"In the morning, he said. He'll remove it then." He smoothed my hair in that gentle and soothing way he had. "The drip is going in very slowly now." He gave me a really nice smile. I loved seeing it. I loved when Ethan smiled, period. Because it changed his whole face to where he really looked . . . happy.

"I'll be right here waiting, then." I nodded.

He lost the smile and got serious again but turned back at the door, in his jeans and bare feet, his hair in disarray from dragging his fingers through it, his beard looking scruffy.

He took my breath away.

Heading down the grand staircase, I was able to take my first relaxed breath in hours. Well, maybe relaxed is not accurate, but the dread that had been crushing me like an anvil on my chest had lifted enough that I could breathe without physical pain.

She was back in the land of the living, for one thing. We were on the same page with unplanned pregnancies for another. The rest of it would have to be dealt with one step at a time.

First step was to find the unused test kit.

It wasn't in the powder room where I'd last seen it, and that made sense as this house was a working hotel most of the time. Hannah wouldn't leave something like that out in a room where guests might find it. I hadn't expected it to still be there anyway.

I hit the kitchen next. I had an idea where she might have put it and went to switch on the lights. The pantry was huge, with one whole wall devoted to nonfood items and supplies for the business. I scanned each shelf, and then bingo, there it was. The box I'd purchased in the Kilve chemist's shop earlier in the day sitting on the shelf with the soaps. I read the package again. "Over 99% accurate" and "As accurate as a doctor's test" had to mean something, right?

As I went back through to leave the kitchen I passed the shelf with the photograph on it of my mum with Hannah and me. I stopped and picked it up. As I studied the picture, I realized this was the way I always imagined her. Her beauty captured in this photo for the final time before she went away and became something else. I looked at the image of me at four, at how I leaned into her and how she was touching me, my hand on her leg, and wondered if I'd ever told her I loved her. I had in my dreams and prayers of course, but wondered if I'd ever said the words to her so she heard them coming from me. There was nobody I could ask, though. Even if there was, I don't think I could ask them the question. It would be cruel to make my dad or Hannah try to remember something like that.

I thought about where I was headed and what Brynne and I would be doing a few minutes from now, and wished so badly that my mother could have known about us. That I could ring her up and say, "I have some news, Mum, and I hope you'll be pleased to hear it."

I brushed my finger over the image of her lovely face and set it back on the shelf, somehow feeling the connection was there and that it was possible for her to know about me. I held that hope close to my heart as I turned out the light and went back upstairs to my girl.

Brynne was sitting up in bed looking beautiful and anxious, and the protective urge that flowed from me was so incredibly intense, it made me pause. And I realized something important. I knew in that moment that anyone who dared to try to hurt her or our potential child would have to kill me first to get to them. Wow. I shrugged it off because it didn't matter about me, anyway. If anything ever happened to her, I'd be finished.

This was my truth.

"You found it?" she asked in her sweet voice.

I waved the package in front of me as I came forward. "One missing test."

"Okay, I'm ready." She spoke quietly and held her hand out.

I placed the package in her lap and picked up her right hand. Instead of kissing the top, I turned it and pressed my lips to her wrist. I could feel her pulse beating. Her eyes filled up and got watery, so I smiled and told her the truth. "Everything will work out the way it's meant to, baby. I have no doubts like that."

"How can you not?"

I shrugged. "I just know that we are going to be together, and if this is part of our future then we'd better go forward with it." I pulled back the blankets and helped her out of the bed.

"I can walk," she told me. "And I promise that I will come out the same door I went in this time." She looked down at the floor, ashamed.

I could afford to be cocky at the moment, so I grabbed the chance even though it made me a bastard. "Yeah, I'm pretty confident of that, my beauty. You'd have a tough time getting down the staircase with that pole and me not noticing."

She lost the look of shame immediately and glared beautiful flashing eyes at me. "I can think of a good use for the pole."

"That's my girl." I led her to the bathroom, rolling the pole for her, unable to curb my smart-ass mouth. "This really is a very fine pole, you know. It probably has a good many practical uses—"

She shut the bathroom door in my face and left me standing there on the other side for the second time, waiting for some information that I now hoped would be true. It's weird, but from the start, I embraced the idea almost as soon as it was suggested. The idea of a baby was a daunting prospect, sure, but we were intelligent people and had to have more going for us than many people do when they start a family. Our child would just cement us more solidly together, and that was a beautiful thing in my eyes. I knew what I knew, even if I couldn't admit it to a single other person on this earth. *If I've gotten my girl pregnant, if we've made a baby together and it's growing inside her right now, then I'll never lose her, she'll never leave me, nothing can ever take her away.*

I didn't see how anything or anyone could dispute my logic. Yet again, it made perfect sense to me.

10

♥

When I opened the bathroom door to come out, test in hand, Ethan was still there where I'd left him when I'd shut it on his smirking face. God love him for trying to tease me and make a stressful situation a little easier. If I had to read him, I would say he was handling the possibility of being a father *very* well.

Actually, he almost seemed to be hopeful I was pregnant. I wondered why, and could certainly tell that he and I weren't in the same place in the head about this at all. Far from it. Ethan was a lot older. Eight years older. Years that made a significant difference when faced with the imminent possibilities of marriage and a family. Life was happening much too quickly and it terrified me. The only thing keeping me from going bat-shit crazy was his attitude about the whole situation that we could do this.

I still didn't really see how it was possible for me to even be pregnant at all. I had some major questions for my doctor, I knew that much. Like how in the hell do birth control pills just not work when they are never missed and taken religiously for years?

He put his arm around me and started walking me and my pole back to the bed. "You waited for me right here?" I peeked up at him.

"Of course I did," Ethan said, taking my chin and holding it up to meet his lips in a slow, deliberate and very wet kiss. I needed it. He always seemed to know when I needed affection and reassurance, and was very generous in doling it out.

I pressed the test into his hand and watched his eyes widen. "I want you to look at it first. You look and then tell me. It takes a few minutes to give a result." My voice sounded about as fluttery as I felt.

He smiled down at me. "Okay. I can do that. But first, it's back to bed for my girl."

Ethan kissed me on the forehead first and then set the test on the bedside table and left it there. He put me in the bed, ditched his jeans again and crawled in next to me. He drew me close and arranged us just as we'd been before. I rested my head back on his chest and laid a palm over the hard muscles. I had a lot to say, but hardly knew where to start. Best to start with the most important piece of my speech.

"Ethan?"

"Yeah?"

"I love you so much."

The instant I whispered the words, his whole body relaxed. I felt the hardness in him soften and I knew he had been waiting for that declaration from me, probably for a while, throughout the many hours of this day-slash-nightmare. I knew I couldn't say the words as often and as easily as Ethan could, and did, and even though I tried to show him, I realized that I did hold out on him a little, and it wasn't right for me to do that. I could try to make an effort for his sake.

"I love you t—"

I shushed him with my fingers over his lips and lifted my head up. "I know you do. You tell me all the time. You're better than me at expressing your feelings, and I want you to know that I see it. I see it in how you take care of me and how you touch me and how you show me by being so solid and just . . . *there* for me." I took in a deep breath.

"Brynne . . . it's the only way I—"

"Please let me finish." I pressed my fingers back over his lips. "I need to say this before we look at the test and I lose it completely, because I'm sure I will either way it reads."

His blue eyes said so much, even though his mouth stayed closed. He kissed my fingers, which were still covering his lips, and waited for me to continue.

I took another big breath. "I ran away from you for the last time. I won't hit you with a 'Waterloo' again. It was terrible to just take off like that and I'm very ashamed I was so weak and selfish. I acted like a child and I cannot even imagine what your family thinks of me right now. They must be praying I'm not pregnant, just sick with some horrible flu, because I'm sure they see me as a crazy American freak who is trying to trap you—"

"No. No, no, no, no, they don't think that," he interrupted, his lips finding mine and silencing my speech for good. He rolled me under him, very careful of my left wrist, stretching my arm up and out of reach of getting bumped. So very Ethan-ish of him. Taking charge of me in the only way he knew, and in the way that I needed him to. *How did he always know?*

He kissed me thoroughly, pinning me beneath him and finding his way deep inside with his tongue, sweeping in a wide circle over and over around mine. I felt that glorious sensation of being invaded that came whenever we were together. His need to be inside me coupled with my need to have him there.

He lifted his head and held me under him, one hand propping his body up and the other holding my cheek. He had his serious face on now. "I know the truth, Brynne. I was there from day one with you, remember? I know how hard I had to work to get you." He dipped his head and dragged his stubble up my neck to lick below my ear. "I wanted you then, just like I want you now, like I'll always want you," he whispered through nibbles and lip bites up my neck and across my throat, working his way back to my mouth so he could swallow me again.

I blossomed under his intimate caresses, finding my way to where I needed to be.

He pulled back, his beautiful, hard features over me, reflected in the shadows of the one lamp in the room. And right there in the early hours of the night, buried in the middle of an experience that had the power to change our lives forever, my Ethan spoke the most perfect words.

"I wish I could make love to you right now. Now. Before we know what it says . . . because it will change nothing that I feel in here . . . for you." He picked up my right hand and laid it flat over his heart.

"Yes, please," I managed before falling into a place somewhere so far into love with him it laid me bare. This thing with him and me was truly irreversible.

He rose up from me and sat back on his knees. His eyes were piercing blue, asking for permission because he was like that with me. Ethan knew what he wanted and would take it from me, but he needed to know I was willing.

I was. No words were exchanged because they weren't necessary. Not really.

I slowly raised my other arm to match my left one and arched my back, offering myself to him in a way I know he loved. Submitting myself to his care and knowing he would take us to a place where we could be like that together in the way we understood so well.

He pulled off his T-shirt and tossed it. My eyes soaked in the cut abdominals and solid curves of his deltoids and biceps. I could stare at him for hours, but usually didn't get nearly my fill of looking.

He pushed my shirt up and over my head, leaving it bunched around my left arm. It would have to stay there, because I was still connected to the IV. He drew his hands down, hovering just above my skin, not touching as he swept his eyes over me. It reminded me of a pianist poised just before beginning to play a piece. It was beautiful to watch him.

He bowed over me, starting at the hollow of my throat,

and drew downward with his tongue as far as he could go. He dragged it achingly slow over my sternum, down my stomach and to my navel, where he gave some special attention to the indentation. He never got near my breasts and the obvious evasion got me undulating for him, my body already on fire, craving his touch.

He looked up from my navel just before reaching for the waistband of my leggings. He drew down with his tongue as his hands drew down the leggings, right over the center of me, to lick at my sex. His tongue pushed between the folds and found my clit swollen and aching for him. I bowed off the bed and moaned as he devoured me to the brink of orgasm with his lips and tongue.

"Not yet, my beauty," he rasped against my pussy, slowing down the flick of his tongue to keep me on the edge of climax without crashing over. He pressed a palm over my stomach and with the other hand managed to pull the leggings straight down and off my legs completely with a little lifting help from my raised hips.

He opened one of my legs wide and high and growled a sound of pure carnal lust, staring down at me spread for him, his other palm still planted on my belly. Ethan had me totally exposed and bared, pinned by his hands when he descended again and inserted his tongue, penetrating me as far as he could go. He worked magic with that tongue of his, and I felt myself falling as everything within my body was pulled toward a release. I might die if he didn't give it to me.

"Say it to me now," he commanded with a harsh breath at my center.

Again, I understood him. I knew precisely what he wanted to hear.

"I love you, Ethan! I love you. I love you so much . . ." I sobbed my declaration, barely able to form audible words.

He heard me, though.

Ethan wrapped his perfect tongue around my pearl and sucked it hard. I went off like a nuclear explosion, slow at first, and then a rolling pause just before the incendiary blast that broke me apart into countless fragments. Pieces of me that could only be collected and reassembled by one man. Only Ethan could do that. This truth I understood implicitly. The one who had the power to take me apart was also the only one with the power to put me back together again.

Ethan's blue eyes were hovering over me when I opened mine. He'd moved back up my body, his hand where his mouth had just been, long fingers sliding slowly up inside me, his thumb just pressing on the bundle of nerves in a decadent sensation of pleasure.

I floated there, still breathing hard, looking up at him, accepting his kiss and his intimate touches. The taste of me on his lips always made me feel cherished for some reason. Like he wanted to share his experience with me. He brought his fingers up from where they'd been buried deep and pressed them, curved, into my mouth, sliding them in and out along my tongue. It was intimacy on top of more intimacy. Ethan whispered erotic things to me about how I felt and looked and tasted and smelled, and what he was going to do to me next.

I was impatient for more, though, especially feeling

his cock hard and huge against my leg, realizing he had pulled off his boxers at some point. I tried to get closer by circling my hips against his stiff length. He chuckled and whispered something about giving it to me in his own sweet time.

I returned to the thought that I might be dead by then.

"My Ethan . . ." I tried to touch him with my hand, but he just dragged my arm back up over my head and gave me a look that needed no translation. I rolled my head from side to side, needing more and feeling desperate.

"Tell me what you want," he crooned against my neck.

I arched again, trying to meld us together, but Ethan controlled the speed. "I want—I want to feel you inside me," I begged him.

"Mmmm . . . you will, baby," he chanted huskily. "Now you will. I'm going to give you my cock—very . . . very . . . slowly. So slow and so far up in you you'll feel every molecule of me . . . inside you."

I *would* die.

I felt him shift into position between my legs, widening me, his hard length tipped already and slowly rocking against my soaked flesh, but he didn't enter me yet. I knew what he was doing. He was savoring, drawing out the anticipation, treating me to every small sensation of touch and pleasure, so slowly, as if we had forever. I had a gentle and very patient Ethan loving me tonight.

He propped up on his hands and rocked his hips a little more each time, still slow and controlled as he moved in infinitesimal strokes with just the tip of his penis kissing the hot flesh of my pussy over and over and over again.

His body pulsed above me, our eyes locked and burning at each other, when he dipped his head down to touch his forehead to mine. Only once that connection was made did he thrust into me all the way, finally giving in to the completion of the act, burying himself to his balls as the most erotic wheeze came out of his throat.

I cried out from the glory of it.

Ethan found my lips again and thrust his tongue into me in tandem with the elegant sliding thrusts of his cock, taking his time to bring me along. I knew he would hold off until either I came again or was about to.

His pace increased steadily and I squeezed my inner walls as hard as I could around him, trying to get every bit of him there was to have. I knew it was working when he swelled even tighter and began to make those harsh breaths with every thrust. The sounds he made were beautiful to me, building in my head along with the gripping pulses at my core, barreling me toward another climax.

When he covered one nipple with his mouth and tugged on the other one in a gentle pinch I was suddenly there, crashing uncontrollably along like a tidal wave does, bringing everything with it. Ethan stared me down as he blew apart with a shuddering roar and filled me up with hot bursts, the last few strokes furiously fast before slowing to gentle rotations that drew the last bit of pleasure out between us until falling into a hovering stillness.

I was full of him now and I didn't want the feeling to go. I wanted to stay like this with him forever. In this moment, it felt like forever was a glorious possibility.

But he rolled onto his back and took me along with

him until I was on top, my left wrist completely unbothered by all that we'd just accomplished. Now he allowed me to use my hands to touch him. I brought them to his chest and splayed them there, feeling the pounding of his heart against my palms.

He cupped my face and kissed me for a while, whispering more words about how much he loved me and that I was his no matter what happened in our lives, that he would never stop loving me. He drew a hand along the length of my back, following my spine slowly up and down.

After some more intimate moments passed in his arms, he murmured with a soft brush of lips to mine, "Don't fall asleep yet."

"I won't."

"Are you ready?"

I nodded and whispered, "Yes."

"And nothing changes us."

"*Nothing* changes that we love each other," I clarified.

"I knew you weren't all beauty and no brains from the first time I ever heard you speak," he told me with a wink.

He reached for the test stick on the bedside table and brought it up to the light.

My heartbeat picked up the pace, and it wasn't from the beautiful orgasms. "It shows a minus sign for negative and a plus sign for positive," I blurted.

Ethan gave me a very pointed raise of one brow. "Thanks for the tip; I think I might have figured that part out, baby."

He squinted at the stick.

I laid my cheek down on his chest and tried to breathe.

He just looked at the thing, and then his hand started moving slowly up and down the curve of my spine like before.

It felt like ages of time passed but he remained quiet, just rubbing my back absently with his hand, still connected, his cock still buried inside my body even in its half-hard state, until I couldn't bear another second of waiting.

"What does it say?" I whispered.

"You have to look at me."

The self-doubt I'd known for years, the one I had a close, personal relationship with, crept right back in to wreak havoc on all the good feelings we'd just enjoyed together. That fear nearly paralyzed me, but Ethan wouldn't allow it. He kept up the rubbing, and even nudged me a little to release me from the fear that gripped me.

"Forget about everything else and look at me, Brynne."

I took a mouthful of courage and lifted my eyes.

From the first moment I knew Ethan, his feelings were always evident—from the expressions on his face to the tone of his voice to his body language. It was easy to know if he was pleased, annoyed, relaxed, aroused or even happy. The happy-Ethan expression was not frequent, but I'd seen it enough times to recognize it.

When I looked at the face he was showing me now, I was certain about one thing.

My Ethan was happy—truly happy about the fact that he was going to be a father.

11

♠

"From the records sent by Dr. Greymont, I'd concur with his findings that you're about seven weeks along, Miss Bennett."

The doctor had age going for him, and the fact I'd been taught to respect my elders, because I sure did not like where his hands were right now. Dr. Thaddeus Burnsley had a condom-sheathed ultrasound probe up her snatch as he determinedly searched for the beating heart of our baby.

Good thing he was focused on the monitor and not her quim. It was rather awkward, but hell, it was part of the process, so I'd better get used to it. I have no idea how anyone did that job, though. Pregnant females all day long with their parts out on display? Good lord, the man had to have the constitution of an ox. Fred had referred us to him, so here we were for the first appointment. Ethan Blackstone and Brynne Bennett, prospective parents of Baby Blackstone, arriving sometime early next year.

"So that would be the middle of May?" Brynne looked over from where I sat at her shoulder. I winked and blew her an air kiss. I knew what she was thinking. She was figuring that I impregnated her almost immediately. She would be right too. The caveman in me was pretty proud of myself, as I did the metaphorical Tarzan beat-on-the-ole-chest routine. Good thing I was smart enough to keep my trap shut about it.

"It would seem so, my dear. Ahhh, there we are. Hiding as they like to do when they're so small. Right there." Dr. Burnsley zeroed in on a small white blob, in the middle of a larger black blob onscreen that had a heartbeat clipping along at a fast pace, floating in its watery world, making its presence known.

Brynne made a little gasp and I squeezed her hand. We both stared transfixed at the enormity of what we were looking at. What a test tells you becomes very different when you can actually see it with your eyes and even hear it with your ears. *I'm looking at another person. That we made together. I'm going to be a dad. Brynne will be a mum.*

"So tiny," she said in a soft voice.

I couldn't imagine how Brynne was absorbing all of this, because I was feeling more than a little overwhelmed. I don't know why, but it suddenly hit me that this was real and we were going to be parents whether we liked it or not. *Hannah's words exactly.*

"About the size of a blueberry and very strong from all indications. Has a robust heartbeat and the measurements match up." He pressed a button that printed a sheet of images and removed the probe. "You're looking at a delivery date in the first part of February, from all indications. You can get dressed and then meet me in my office. We'll talk some more."

The good doctor handed the photos to Brynne and left us.

"How are you doing, my darling?"

"Trying to take it all in," she said. "It's different actually seeing him . . . or her . . .". She sat up on the table and looked down at the photos, studying them. "I still can't believe it. Ethan, why are you so calm?"

"I'm not, really," I answered truthfully. "I'm fucking shaking in my shoes. I want a smoke and a drink and I'm sure you'll be brilliant at everything and I will be a complete useless idiot."

"Wow. That's a big change from last weekend." She smiled at me. We'd been through this already with Fred. I knew she wasn't mad. We'd talked it through and both had had our freak-outs at different times and moved on. This was just the first official doctor's visit and there would be plenty more. We'd both accepted that the sun kept rising and the earth kept turning, so best to just get on with it.

I came over and peered at the pictures. "So the size of a blueberry, huh? Amazing that the little bugger can make you so sick."

She poked me in the arm. "Did you just call our baby a *little bugger*? Please tell me I did not just hear you say that!" she scoffed.

"See? I'm already doing it. Totally useless idiot insulting our blueberry-sized baby." I pushed my thumb at my chest.

She laughed and leaned into me. I wrapped my arms around her and lifted up her chin, very glad to see a light in her eyes. If I could make her laugh, I knew she was doing okay. Brynne wouldn't be able to fake her feelings with me. If she was sad or really struggling with this, I'd definitely know. Hell, we were both fucking terrified, but I knew without a doubt that she would be very, very good at motherhood. There wasn't a sliver of hesitation in my mind that it wouldn't be the case. She'd be a perfect mum.

"I love you, mother of our blueberry-sized baby." I kissed her, brushing my thumb up her cheek, thinking she looked very bright and glowing right now.

"Thank you for being the way you are with me. If you were any different . . . I just don't think I could love you like I do. You know?" she whispered the last.

I whispered back and nodded, "I do know."

She hopped down and pulled on her lacy knickers and then her tan trousers and shoes. "I'll see what I can do to get you on better terms with the blueberry," she gestured toward her belly, "I have connections."

Now she made me laugh. "All right, you sassy thing, let's go have our chat with Dr. Banana Probe so we can get out of here."

"Funny. Did I ever mention how sexy you Brits sound when you say *banana*?"

"You just did." I grabbed her bum and kissed her again. "I'll give you my banana if you want."

Her mouth opened in surprise but she trumped me good. My girl reached her hand right up and cupped my cock and balls. She gave me a good tug and pushed her lovely tits into my chest. "Your *banana* needs a little work if you're going to be doing anything nice with it."

"Holy shit, my sister was right. The hormones make you pregnant females wild for cock. I might die from so much sex."

She shrugged and turned to leave the exam room. "Yeah, but it'd be a fun way to go, wouldn't it?"

I took her hand and followed her out, thanking the gods for pregnant hormones, and wearing what I am fairly sure was an idiotic grin on my face.

"Everything looks very good. I want you to start pre-natal vitamins, and I approved of the anti-nausea Dr. Greymont prescribed, so continue with that as needed. You've stopped all of your other medications?" Dr. Burns-ley questioned in his efficient manner.

"Yes," Brynne answered. "Dr. Greymont said that my antidepressant probably interacted with my birth control pills and that's how . . ."

"They can be interactive, yes. That is why the instruc-tions recommend double precautions. I'm surprised the dispensary didn't offer counseling for a new medication."

"I don't remember if they did, but it's not safe for me to take them if I'm pregnant, right?"

"That's correct. No alcohol, no smoking and no medi-cations apart from the vitamins and the anti-nausea to get you through the next month. After that time you'll find your appetite increasing and less trouble with the nausea, so you won't need it. I really want you to get some calories in, though. You're very slim. Try for a small gain if you can."

"All right. What about exercise? I like to run a few miles in the morning."

Good point. Already impressed with her intelligent and thoughtful questions as she went through everything with the doctor, I just sat there listening and tried not to look too stupid. I didn't miss the part about the smoking either. I heard that message loud and clear. I had to quit. It was fucking imperative that I quit. I couldn't smoke around Brynne or the baby for the sake of their health. *So what does that say about what I'm doing?* I knew what needed to happen, I just didn't know how I would manage it.

"Right now you can continue with all of your normal activities, including intercourse."

A long pause from the doctor at this point had me thinking nice thoughts about my hormone-ravaged sweetheart and all the ways I could help her out. She, on the other hand, was blushing beautifully, making me hard, and ensuring the rest of my workday at the office would pass achingly slowly as I tortured myself with plenty of erotic thoughts about what might be in store for me when I got home. *Such a lucky bastard I am.*

"And exercise in moderation is always healthy."

Oh, I'll give her plenty of exercise, doctor.

Dr. Burnsley glanced back in her chart again. "But I see here that you work at a gallery conserving paintings. Do you have exposure to solvents and chemicals, substances of that nature?"

"Yes." Brynne nodded and then looked at me. "Constantly."

"Ahh, well, that's an issue. It's harmful for fetus development if you to ingest fumes that contain lead, and since you work with very old pieces, that is precisely what you'd be in contact with. Modern household paints are no problem, it's the older chemical compounds that are worrisome. You'll have to stop that immediately. Can you request some other form of work during your pregnancy?"

"I don't know." She looked troubled now. "It's my job. How do I just tell them I can't touch solvents for the next eight months?"

Dr. Burnsley lifted his chin and offered a pleasant expression that didn't fool us for a moment. "Do you want a healthy baby, Miss Bennett?"

"Of course I do. I just didn't expect—" She gripped the arms of the chair and took a deep breath. "I'll figure it out somehow. I mean, I can't be the first conservationist to get pregnant." She waved her hand and then pulled it through her hair. "I'll talk to my advisor at the university and see what they can do."

Brynne gave him a fake smile that told me she wasn't happy with this little development, but she wasn't going to argue with his medical advice. My girl was sensible about the stuff that mattered.

I knew how important her job was to her. She loved her work. She was brilliant at it. But if there were dangers with the chemicals, then the job would have to go for the time being. Money was never an issue with her and me. We'd never really talked about it at all. For all intents and purposes she was already moved into my flat, and there was no question of where we were headed down the road.

She would be my wife, and what was mine would be hers. We were having a child. Our path was clear, but the nuts and bolts of organizing everything had yet to be sorted. I knew what I wanted, but the timing was so hellish right now there were literally no spare minutes to delve into plans. Not until the Olympics were behind me, at least.

After the weekend pregnancy bomb dropped on our heads, we'd raced back to London and back into work. We hadn't even told our parents yet, and had my sister and Fred on secret squirrel, under threat of death if they spilled the news before we did.

We were trying to acclimate to everything on top of the immense buildup of obligations for my business, the Games being only twenty-one days off. There was hardly time for this meeting right now. I wished for a smoke. Or three.

Once we were out of the doctor's office, I put my arm around her and kissed her on the top of the head. "That was fun, baby. Dr. Burnsley is a charming fellow, don't you agree?"

"Yeah, he's awesome," she said sarcastically with arms folded beneath her breasts.

"Aww, come on, he wasn't that bad," I cajoled, "he used the banana probe on you."

"Oh my God, you are a jackass!" She shoved at my shoulder and laughed silently. "Only you could make a joke about that hideous situation and make it funny!"

"But it worked, and that is the point of it," I told her as we walked.

"I'm kind of worried about my job. I never thought of the possibility I'd have to stop." She sounded down about it.

"Maybe a leave of absence would be a good thing, though. It would give you time to plan for what we've got coming." I looked down at her stomach but tried to be optimistic and light about it. Best to not delve too deeply and remind her she was going to have to give up something she loved for the next months. "I know I would adore having you home more and you'll need to have plenty of rest. Maybe this way you can start a project or something that you've wanted to work on but didn't have time for before."

"Yeah," she answered noncommittally. I thought I could see the cogs in her pretty head turning with ideas. Hard to say what, because if Brynne wasn't in a sharing mood, then I certainly wouldn't know. "I'll figure it out."

"Of course you will." I squeezed, bringing her a little closer, hating that I had to leave her and go back to my office. I wanted hours in bed just wrapped up in each other. It was really all I wanted.

I stopped us on the sidewalk and turned her to me. "But please don't worry about it too much. I'm taking care of both of you." I put my hands on her belly. "You and the little bugg—er . . . um, I mean . . . blueberry, are my top priority now."

She smiled and then her bottom lip started trembling, and her lovely eyes that were very greenish-brown under the summer sky got very wet. She put her hand over both of mine. I watched as one lone tear dripped down my girl's beautiful face.

I widened my mouth into a smile I could feel. I loved having her like this. Needing me to take care of her and knowing she was going to let me. I really didn't need a lot.

Just her love and the acceptance of mine along with my care.

She rolled her eyes in embarrassment. "Look at me. I am such an emotional freak mess right now!"

"I *am* looking, and you forgot something, baby. You're a *gorgeous* emotional freak mess." I brushed away the tear with my thumb and licked it off. "I mean, if you're going to go all out and be a freak mess, you might as well look gorgeous doing it."

I got her to laugh a little. "Now, do you fancy a sandwich for lunch?" I looked at my watch. "I wish I had longer for something a little nicer than takeaway."

"No, that's fine. I have to get back too." She sighed and then smiled at me. "I have an announcement to make at work, it seems." She took my hand and curled hers around it as we walked.

We happened to be right across the street from the saltwater aquarium shop when we came out of the delicatessen with our sandwiches and settled on a bench to eat. I pointed it out to her and asked if we could stop in quickly as soon as we finished because I wanted to arrange service for the six-month checkup for my tank.

Brynne took a second look at the shop and grinned. "Fountaine's Aquarium." Her grin got wider as she took a bite of her turkey sandwich.

"What? What's making you grin like the Cheshire Cat?"

She didn't answer my question, but instead asked one of her own. "Ethan, when did you get Simba?"

"Six months ago, I just said."

"No, what day did you get him?"

I thought about that for a moment. "Well, now that you ask, I believe it was Christmas Eve, actually." I looked at her and tilted my head questioningly.

"That was you! It was!" Her whole face lit up. "I was shopping for a present for my aunt Marie and it was so freezing cold. I had a bit of a walk ahead of me, so I dipped in there just to get out of the cold for a few minutes and it was nice inside. Dark and warm. I looked at all the fish. I saw Simba." She laughed to herself and shook her head in disbelief. "I even talked to him. The clerk told me that he'd been sold and that the owner was coming to pick him up."

Realization dawned on me in a sudden blast. "It was snowing." I said in amazement.

She nodded at me slowly. "I went to the door to leave and brave the cold again, and you walked in. You smelled so nice, but I never got a look at you because I couldn't take my eyes off the sight of the snow. It had started while I was inside the shop getting warm—"

"And you were shocked as you looked out the door and saw it. I remember . . ." I interrupted her story. "You were bundled in purple. You had on a purple hat."

She just nodded, looking beautiful and maybe a tad bit smug.

I swear Brynne could have pushed me over onto the cobblestones with her pinky finger if she'd wanted—I was that floored by what she'd just told me. Talk about the divine hand of fate. "I saw you step out into the snow and check yourself in the window of my Rover before you walked off."

"I did." She brought a hand to her mouth. "I can't believe that was you . . . and Simba, and we actually spoke to one another, two strangers on Christmas Eve."

"I can hardly believe we're having this conversation," I repeated, the amazement still evident in my voice.

"And it was so, so beautiful when I came out." She glowed at me as she remembered. "I'll never forget what it looked like."

"So I smelled good, huh?"

"Very." She gave her head a little shake. "I remember thinking whoever got to smell you all the time was a lucky girl."

"Man, I missed out on months and months of you smelling me. I don't know if I'm happy about knowing this news or not," I joked, but really was quite serious. Would've been nice to have met before all this mess. Maybe we'd already be married . . .

"Aww, baby, that's so sweet," she told me, shaking her head at me like I was crazy but she loved me anyway.

"I love it when you call me *baby*."

"I know you do, and that's why I say it," she said softly in that gentle way she had. The one that made me insane to possess her and have her splayed out naked underneath me where I could take my time crawling my way up inside her, making her come and come some more, calling out my name—

"What are you thinking about, *baby*?" she asked, interrupting my inner erotic ravings, just as she should have done.

I told her the honest truth, in a whisper, of course, so nobody else could hear me. "I'm thinking about how many times I can make you come when I get home from work tonight and have you naked, and I'm all over you."

Brynne didn't respond to my little speech with words. Instead, her breath hitched as she swallowed hard, making the hollow of her neck and throat move slowly in tandem with the flush that started creeping up to her face. Mouthwatering . . .

The slight breeze made strands of her lovely brown hair dance across her face occasionally, necessitating that she brush it away every so often. Brynne had that certain special something— a *joie de vivre* that others recognized. When I had her in my view like this, it was hard to ever look away. I knew it was hard for others too. I didn't like other people noticing her and looking. It was terrifying for me, and I knew why. Their attention made her vulnerable as a target, and that was something utterly unacceptable to me.

My eyes tracked the courtyard out of habit, scanning the patrons of the delicatessen as they came and went. It was a nice day for July, and crowded. The Games were going to turn this place into a mob of ungodly proportions. That worried me too. There were thousands of people coming into London for travel now. More athletes and teams were arriving each day. Thank the bloody gods I didn't have that load on me. My VIP clients were going to be enough of a crush and a headache.

I was still cautious all the time with Brynne, and I had very good reason to be. Until I knew who'd sent the text to her phone I wasn't taking any chances. Especially with Neil in the States. He'd be returning on Saturday with what I hoped were some leads on who this motherfucker was. If it led back to Senator Oakley's camp, then that shit scrape was going down. I knew a few in government, and I would reel in favors if it came down to that. Calling my bluff on a serious threat to Brynne was like poking the rattlesnake with a stick. I was prepared for whatever I had to do in order to protect her.

"Are you finished?" I asked, noticing she'd stopped taking bites of her sandwich.

"I am. It's baby steps right now." She laid her palm on her stomach. "Literally."

"I know, but you have to eat. Dr. Banana Probe said so. I heard him clearly and he is the absolute authority on these things." I gave her an arch of the brows.

"Well I'm pretty confident that the good doctor would avoid food too if he spent as much time as I do hung over a toilet, puking his guts out after eating some."

"You poor thing—and you have a very good point, my beauty." I leaned in to kiss her lips. "What have I done to you?"

She scoffed and kissed me back. "I think that's fairly obvious, considering where we just spent the last hour."

"But the medicine helps, right?" I brushed her cheek, keeping our faces close. I really fucking hated seeing my girl suffer.

She nodded. "Yes. It works miracles." She stood up to go throw away her sandwich wrapper in the bin. Even that small feat garnered attention from those in the immediate vicinity. I spotted at least three men who eyed her and one woman. No wonder photographers wanted her for their pictures. *Damn the cocksuckers.*

Brynne was oblivious to every bit of it, which just made her more of a rarity.

We stepped into Fountaine's Aquarium and grinned at each other when we crossed the threshold, both remembering the day we'd spoken as strangers and fate had a say about a few things. The shop was busy and we had to wait in the queue until another attendant came up front to help.

Beside us stood a woman wearing her child in a backpack sort of sling contraption. I remember Hannah using a similar device for Zara when she was a baby. Except this child was not happy about it. Not even a little. I felt quite sure that if the little bloke could've spoken, the air in the shop would've been tinged blue with *fuck you*s and *bugger off*s. He screamed and kicked, trying to worm his way out. The mother of this creature just ignored it as if there was nothing untoward about a wailing and writhing mini-human on her back screeching loud enough to shatter the window glass.

I took a glance at Brynne and got wide eyes from her. Was she thinking what I was thinking? Will our baby do this? *Oh, please, God, no.*

We moved up in the queue, with only one more in front to wait through when the red-faced minion with the full-sized lungs really started working it. I thought my head was going to explode. The woman backed up, effectively shoving the little demon right up in my face. The shop was so close I got cornered up against the counter with nowhere to go. I reared my head back as far as I could, thinking maybe calling the shop to schedule would have been the best idea.

Brynne was trying very hard not to laugh at me when

the situation deteriorated even further, which I didn't imagine to be possible. Oh, it was very possible. The creature let loose with a bum blower less than a foot from me. Not only did it possess the power to peel paint off walls, but it sounded very wet, which affirmed it couldn't have been merely an arse cruncher for him. That tyke was squirming in a load of shit to which I was far too close right now. The mother turned 'round and gave me a glare as if *I'd* done it. *Fucking hell, get me out!*

Brynne was shaking beside me with her hand over her mouth, when the clerk asked what he could do for me. I tried not to leap over the counter and beg him for an oxygen mask. I don't know quite how I transacted my business with the screaming and the revolting odor, and then Brynne rushing for the door saying she'd wait outside. *Yeah, get out, baby, before you asphyxiate. Run, and don't look back!* Smart girl I've got, no secrets there.

When I managed to escape the shop, Brynne was on the sidewalk watching the foot traffic. She saw me and burst into giggles. I dragged a hand through my hair and sucked in a huge breath of air. Clean fresh, pure, London air. Well, maybe not pure, but at least my eyes weren't watering anymore. Or maybe they were—my vision was blurry and I craved a smoke.

"Are you okay?" I asked her, wondering if that offensive back in the shop had made her puke.

"Are you?" she laughed up at me.

"Fuck me into next week. By all that's holy, that was frightening! Tell me that was an incarnation of Satan back there!" I nodded. "Am I right?"

Still laughing, she put her arm through mine and started walking us to the car.

"Poor Ethan got a load of smelly baby," she giggled.

"Okay, *that* was not a smelly baby!" *More like really fucking effective birth control.* "Good God, I don't think there are adequate words to describe what that was."

"Aww, you're scared." She made a face of fake concern.

"Fuck yes, I'm scared. Why aren't you?"

Brynne laughed harder.

"Please tell me our little blueberry will never behave like that."

Shaking with laughter now, she reached up to kiss me, and told me how much she loved me again. "I think I need a picture of this, baby. Smile for me."

She took out her mobile and snapped a photo, still laughing in her beautiful way that reminded me what a gift I'd been given when she decided to love me back.

12

♥

Dr. Roswell's beautiful turquoise fountain pen made the nicest sound in her notebook as she made her notes.

"So the university cannot really alter the program for me. I'll still have to do the conserving practicum at some point. But they were happy to give me a leave of absence from the Rothvale and have approved my substituting in some research work."

"And how do you feel about that?" I knew she was going to ask me that.

"Um . . . I'm disappointed, of course, but don't have a choice about it." I shrugged. "It's weird, but even though I am scared to death about having a baby, I'm more afraid of doing something that might hurt my baby."

Dr. Roswell smiled at me. "You're going to be a wonderful mother, Brynne."

Well, that remains to be seen. "I have no idea how to be a mom or how I got into this situation." I held my hands up. "I don't even recognize my life compared with what it was two months ago. I don't know if I'll be able to ever get the kind of job I've trained for all these years. There's a lot I don't know."

"That's very true, but I can assure you that it's true for everyone, everywhere."

I pondered her very wise and eloquent statement. The woman could say so much with such few words. How could any of us predict the future or know what we could or would be doing? It's impossible to know. "Yeah, I suppose," I said finally.

"And Ethan? You haven't said much about what he wants."

I thought about him and what he might be doing right now. Working hard to keep all those celebrities safe at the Olympics, barking orders in meetings, on conference calls barking more orders, and stressing. I worried about him even though he wouldn't hear word one from me about it. He just spread himself a little thinner and never complained. *But his nightmares keep coming, don't they?*

"Ahh, Ethan is very matter-of-fact about this. He never showed me anything but support from the first moment. He didn't seemed scared or trapped or . . . anything like that. I'll be honest, I expected him to feel that way. We haven't known each other that long, and most men would want to run hard and fast in the other direction when faced with an unplanned pregnancy, but not him." I shook my head at her. "He was adamant we not terminate. He said he couldn't do it. That me and our baby are his priority now."

She smiled again. "He sounds like he's thrilled, and that must give you some feelings of security."

"It does. He wants to get married as soon as we can organize it after the Olympics are finished. He really wants an announcement to go out about an engagement." I looked down at my lap. "I've been holding off on that part, and he's not happy with me about it."

She wrote something down and asked her next question without looking up. "Why do you think you are resistant to an engagement announcement?"

"Oh, God . . . I don't know. The only way I can describe it is a feeling of helplessness, a lack of control in my life. It's like I'm being swept along in a current. I'm not struggling to keep afloat or in danger of drowning, but I cannot get out of it. The current pulls me along and takes me places I never thought I would go." I started to feel a little emotional and wished I hadn't said anything to her, but it was too late. The confessions were starting to pour out of me now. "I can't go back to the beginning. I can only go forward, whether I want to or not."

"Do you want to get out?" Dr. Roswell offered up options, just like I knew she would. "Because you don't have to have a baby, or get engaged, or married, or any of it. You know that, Brynne."

I shook my head, looking down at my belly. I thought about what we had created and felt guilty for even voicing my worries. "I don't want to get out. I love Ethan. He tells me he loves me all the time. And I need him . . . now."

"Brynne, do you realize what you just said?"

I looked up into her smiling eyes and knew I was going to spill the rest.

"I need Ethan. I need him for *everything*. I need him

in order to be happy, and to be the father of this baby we made, and to love me and care for me . . ." My voice trailed off to a whimper that sounded so pathetic I loathed myself in that moment.

Dr. Roswell spoke so softly: "That's very scary, isn't it?"

The tears started coming and I reached for a tissue. "Yeah," I sobbed, taking a moment to get the next part out, "I need him so badly . . . and it makes me utterly vulnerable . . . and what will I do if some day he decides he doesn't want me anymore?"

"It's called trust, Brynne, and it is by far the hardest gift to give away."

She was right about that.

Dinner alone pretty much sucked. I wouldn't complain to Ethan, though. I understood how busy he was at work and there had been lots of evening events for him lately. I cleaned up from my vegetable soup and French bread dinner, which so far was staying put in my stomach. Thank God for the anti-nausea medication, or I was sure I'd be dead by then. The vomiting seemed to be behind me for the most part, if I kept to very simple food and took the meds regularly. Both Freddy and Dr. Burnsley said I had something called hyperemesis gravidarum, or in plain English, severe morning sickness. In my case it started as evening sickness and serious dehydration, and could eventually cause malnutrition if left untreated. Lovely. So suffice it to say, I was trying my best to eat.

I'd gotten a text from Ethan about an hour earlier telling me he would be home late and eating dinner at his office. I understood, but that didn't mean I had to like it. The Olympics were huge and it was exciting as the buildup to the opening ceremonies grew. I really did understand the demands Ethan was under at work, and it made me feel better to know that he hated it as much as I did, if not more. He told me all the time how much he wished he could just stay in for one of my home-cooked dinners and cuddle in front of the television together and have sex for dessert.

Yeah, me too.

I was a wreck emotionally and I knew it. I was lonely, and hormonal, and far too needy at the moment. I hated feeling needy.

I looked longingly over at the Miele coffeemaker, which had to be worth more than my boot collection, and sulked as I wiped down the granite worktop. No good coffee for the next seven months was gonna suck about as much as the lonely dinner did tonight. I didn't do decaf and figured torturing myself with only one cup a day wasn't worth the hassle.

I was finding my inner Zen and gaining a close personal relationship with herbal teas instead. Raspberry and Tangerine Zinger had been pleasant surprises, I must admit. I made a cup of the Raspberry Zinger and called Benny.

"Hello, my lovely darling."

"I miss you. What are you up to tonight?" I asked, hoping I didn't sound too pathetic.

"Ricardo's here and we're just done with dinner."

"Ahhh, well, why did you even answer the phone?

You're busy. Sorry for interrupting, I just wanted to give you a drive-by love blast."

"No, no, no, my sweet. Not so fast. What is going on with you?" Ben was without a doubt the most emotionally intuitive man on the planet. He could sniff out the smallest innuendo and go wild with possible scenarios. I'd seen him in action enough to know.

"Nothing is going on with me," I lied. "You're busy and have company. Call me tomorrow, okay?"

"No. Ricardo's sorting out some work business on a call of his own. Start talking."

I sighed into the phone. *Why did I call Ben again?*

"I'm waiting, darling. What is going on with you?"

"Ben, I'm fine. Everything is good. I've moved in with Ethan and he's very swamped with work and the Games coming. I'm just doing my thing."

"So you're alone tonight?" Ben was going to ask me for details, one after the other. I am so dumb sometimes.

"Yes. He's so busy right now with organization meetings."

"Why on earth didn't you call me? I'd have taken you out for a spin."

"No, you have plans with the fantastically handsome Ricardo, remember? I've not felt like going out for a spin the last days anyway."

"You're not feeling well?"

Fuck. "No, Ben, really I'm good. I was just home alone and missing my friend and wanted to hear your voice is all. We haven't talked since the boot photos you took."

"Oh, God, they're gorgeous. I'll send you some of the proofs on email."

"I can't wait to see them." I couldn't wait, but Ethan sure could. He was still voicing his displeasure at my modeling, but I wasn't budging on the issue. Especially now. If I couldn't work at the Rothvale on the paintings, then I sure as hell was going to have plenty of time for my other job of modeling. At least now, before my body got big. I hoped to even do some pregnancy-themed shots. It was something that crossed my mind, even if I couldn't share my news with anyone. Ben didn't know anything yet, and neither did Gaby.

They were both going to kill me for not telling.

"So you've moved in with Blackstone, huh?"

"Yes, Ben. I did. Ethan demanded it, really. After what happened at the National Gallery the night of the Mallerton Gala, he sort of put his foot down. I'm keeping the lease on my flat to help ease Gaby's way through the end of the year, but yeah, we are now cohabitating."

"When's the wedding?" Ben asked dreamily.

I laughed at him. "Would you stop!"

"I'm serious, girl. You're so headed there, and if I know anything at all it's that Blackstone loves you well and good, my darling."

"You really see that in him?"

Ben scoffed into the phone. "A person would have to be dead not to. I'm happy for you. You deserve it, and so much more."

Oh, we've got the more *coming all right.* "I'll be crying if you utter another word, Ben, I mean it." I wasn't lying this time.

He seemed to get my vibe and lighted the tone. "You

have to let me help you choose your dress. Promise me," he pleaded. "Vintage, fitted, handmade lace . . ." The dreamy voice was back. "You will look a goddess, you know, if you let me have at you."

I smiled into the phone and thought about how surprised Ben would be to find out he and Ethan were on the same team on this one. "I'm not saying a word, buster. I gotta go but I loved hearing your voice. I've been without it too long."

"Me too, lovely girl. Text me your free days and let me take you to lunch next week?"

"Will do, Ben. Love you."

Wow, that was a close one, I thought as I hit End. Better not call Gaby either. Second that on Dad, Mom, and Aunt Marie as well. Gaby would have my pregnancy planned out and the hospital scheduled after just one look at me. I knew I couldn't hold out much longer. Ethan was pushing for the announcement of our engagement, and if I knew one thing about Ethan, it was that he usually got exactly what he wanted.

Being a sucker for punishment, I logged into my Facebook next.

A message from my high school friend Jessica was sitting in my inbox. We'd kept in touch through Facebook since I'd moved to London. I didn't have a ton of friends on my profile and kept it pretty private. Ethan had checked it out thoroughly and given the okay. He said that the threat was from people who already knew me, where I lived and worked, so having a Facebook page wasn't going to matter either way.

Jessica Vettner: Hey honey. How are you? I'm just doing the same old with work and life and you'll never guess who I ran into today. Karl Westman from Bayside. Remember him? He's still mega hawt too!!! LOL He asked for my number. :D Karl's been working in Seattle and just got transferred back here to Marin. I bumped into him at the gym of all places. I still go to First Fitness over on Hemlock. I see your dad there sometimes and we share the same personal trainer! Your dad is a sweetheart and really proud of you. ☺ He talks about you all the time and said you're doing more modeling and loving it. I'm happy for you, Bry. I would love to just see you again! When are you ever coming back to SF for a visit?? ♥ Jess

Wow. That was an unexpected blast from the past. Not Jessica, but Karl. I don't think she remembered, but I sure did. Karl was the boy I dated for a while once Lance left for college. Karl, who made Lance insanely jealous when he found out I wasn't just waiting around for him to come home from university and fuck me, or so that was the story I knew. The reason Lance and his buddies abused me on that pool table and thought it would be a fun idea to make a video of it.

I never saw or talked to Lance again or even Karl. I know Karl tried to get in touch with me a few times before I was shipped away to New Mexico, but I wouldn't see him or any of my old friends, apart from Jessica. I just couldn't go back to that place in time; that was the same reason I hadn't been back to my hometown in four years. I had no intentions of ever going back.

It was weird thinking about all that again. There were no hard feelings about Karl, no feelings period. Karl had actually treated me pretty decently considering what my reputation had been in high school, but I'd shut down after the incident and was unable to look anyone in the eye who had seen the images of me on that video. I wonder what Karl thought when he saw it. Was he trying to comfort me because he felt sorry for what had happened, or was he hoping to get some more action out of me? Who knew? I'm sure I never knew at the time, nor did I much care. I was too busy trying to find my way out of this life.

I wrote a happy-happy-nice-nice message back to Jess wishing her luck with him, and logged out of Facebook.

I had a new life now. In London . . . with Ethan . . . and the baby I was having.

Neil sat across from me and looked more affected than I'd ever seen him in my life.

I didn't blame him, really. Telling him that we no longer need worry that Brynne might have got tainted food or drink at the gala had been just the start of his shock.

"Blow me down!"

"I've waited a week to tell you. We've not even shared with our parents yet and she's been struggling with severe pregnancy sickness."

He turned his head and winced. "Is that you, E? You should hear yourself speaking."

"What?" I couldn't wait until Neil was in my shoes. Hell, he was getting married in a few months and it wouldn't be far long after that, I'd wager, before he came into my office looking like he'd been brained with a large stick.

"You going on like it's nothing. You'll be a dad, mate."

"Well, what would you like for me to say? It's not like we planned for her pills to fail, and really, it changes nothing in the end," I said, sneering. "Thanks for the tip. I am aware."

Neil cracked a grin. "You're pleased." He laughed and shook his head. "You're quite chuffed about it, aren't you?"

I was, and I had no reason to lie to him. "Yeah, I am. I'm marrying her too. And it will happen well before you and Elaina do it," I challenged, daring him to raise an eyebrow about that. "The sooner the announcement goes out wide the better, I say. Let the senator and his goons read about it in the celebrity gossip. BLACKSTONE TO MARRY AMERICAN MODEL, FIRST CHILD ON THE WAY. The more publicity the better, I say. How about: PREGNANT AMERICAN MODEL BEAUTY WEDS FORMER SF CAPTAIN, SECURITY DETAIL FOR THE ROYAL FAMILY? That sounds a bit better, I think. The guest list will be impressive, I can promise you that much. Every celebrity I know will be getting an invitation. The higher her profile, the more layers they'll have to break through to get to her. Can you imagine if any U.S. official got caught laying a hand on her now? They'd likely have a war on their hands. The more elevated her celebrity, the harder it becomes for her to ever be a target. It's calling their bluff, and I'm fully prepared to fuck them quite rudely." I faked a grin.

Neil nodded. "I'm happy for you, E. Brynne is your cure, anyone with eyes can see that." He paused before asking, "How does she feel about being a mum?"

I couldn't help the surge of pride that swelled in me when Neil asked that last bit. "You know how Brynne is. Very sensible about the important things, and this is one of them, but I know she's frightened like anyone would be. Fuck me, it's terrifying!" I reached for a Djarum Black and lit it.

"Yeah, but you two will manage to make a go, I'm sure," Neil said before changing the subject. "How did Len do while I was gone away?"

"Fine. Solid, dependable, Len. In fact, he's at the flat right now and I imagine as we get closer to opening ceremonies it'll be Len on her most of the time. I'm going to need you to run things here when I'm off."

Len was Neil's replacement for Brynne duties. He drove her wherever she needed to go, and basically guarded the entrance to the flat at any point I wasn't in there with her. I couldn't and wouldn't take the risk that she be exposed to vulnerability. The closer we dug into the Senator Oakley camp the more clues pointed back to the senator's possible involvement in what I now believed to be cleverly camouflaged hits on Montrose and Fielding. There were clues that Fielding was dead, but no telling when his corpse might make an appearance, if ever. Neil had pegged what was surely Secret Service lurking around Fielding's abandoned apartment in Los Angeles. That fucker had been taken down, I'd bet my Victoria Cross on it.

"Time to go from here, boss. It's too late for you to be lurking, and your woman is home alone," Neil said.

"Agreed on that." I sighed at the thought of the late nights still to come in the next weeks, took a long drag on my cig and extinguished it. I really was making improvements on tapering down. Sometimes I just let them burn without smoking them.

Neil clapped me on the back as we went out. "So, Dad, we need to get you good and drunk in celebration at first opportunity. You've knocked up your girl and you're getting shackled to boot." He shook his head again like he was still in shock. "You don't do anything lightly, do you?"

"'Fraid not," I grumbled.

The flat was dark and silent when I let myself in. All I wanted was to get my hands on her. I always had a moment of panic if I came in and the place felt empty. But that was stupid because it was so damn ridiculously late to be coming home from work and I'd just relieved Len of his duties at the door. Of course she was in the flat! She would be asleep and the place dark.

I ditched my jacket and started working on my tie as I headed for the bedroom. I'm grateful I never made it in there, because I would have had a heart attack when I found our bed empty.

I stopped dead in my tracks when I spotted her stretched out on the sofa, her e-reader set on her stomach, iPod wired up with music, and just took her in. Her long legs tangled in a throw blanket, an arm stretched over her head, hair spread out beneath her.

Only the light from the city shining in through the bay windows lit the room, but it was plenty for me to see her with. She had on a pair of my black silk boxers and a little green top that showed enough of her soft curves to make me hard. It didn't take much to bring me to life, regardless. The more we were forced to spend time apart, the worse I got with irrational need. I wanted her. All the time. Want. Need. Desire. I was losing my mind and I'm pretty sure Brynne knew it. She worried about me and that knowledge just made me love her all the more. I finally had someone who cared for me because of *me,* not how I looked or how much brass I happened to have.

Her eyes opened and she found me.

I stayed planted at least seven feet from where she was and kicked off my shoes. She sat up on the couch and stretched, arching her back and chest toward me in invitation.

We still hadn't spoken a word to each other, but so much had already been communicated. We were going to go at it like beasts and it would be excruciatingly good. Like always. So . . . having a mutual strip show, huh?

Sounds goddamn perfect to me.

Me first. I had more clothes to get rid of than she did. I think I was smiling. If it wasn't showing on the outside, I had a fucking clown grin going on the inside.

I worked the buttons on my shirt slowly, watching her watch me as her eyes grew smoky. I shrugged it off my shoulders and let it drop to the floor. I kicked it away with my foot and blinked at her.

Your turn, my beauty.

She did a move that I dearly love, and one she does so well it ought to be illegal. She raised her arms and crossed palms behind her neck and dragged them upward through her hair, flexing her neck in a stretch before bringing her hands back down to the bottom of her skimpy green undershirt. She peeked up at me and paused.

I growled low in my throat. Purely instinctual and utterly impossible to hold in. I needed to devour her right now.

Slowly she pulled the green scrap upward, revealing the satin skin of her stomach, a slight delay over the mound of her breasts, and then a little bounce as they fell free, and the top went on a little fling through the air. She straightened her arms and set them palms down on the couch.

I took a step closer as I whipped my belt out of the loops and dropped it to the floor with a clank. My tongue rolled over my lips as I imagined how her perfect tits would taste once I got to them. *So fucking sweet.*

I unbuttoned and unzipped and let my trousers fall off my hips. They got the same kick across the hardwood as my shirt had received.

Brynne stuck two fingers in her mouth and pulled them out slowly, circling one of her nipples, now budded up tight and dark pink.

Sweet Christ, I will surely die tonight.

I pegged her hard, willing her to understand me.

I need that mouth of yours on me, baby.

She looked up at me with hooded eyes and intercepted my message. She slipped her hands under the elastic at the waist of my shorts she liked wearing so much, and shifted her hips up, taking them off and along her legs. She dropped the black silk from her fingertips and leaned back like a goddess on a dais, her legs slightly curved, one arm stretched out, one bent at the elbow. It was a pose. Not unlike one she might do for a portrait. But this pose was just for me.

She looked so beautiful I almost didn't want to move. I needed to drink her in first. I needed to get drunk on her. I could never get enough of looking at my Brynne.

I took a step and got rid of a sock. Another step and I lost the second one. It was just me and my shorts now.

Brynne licked her lips as I moved right to the edge and waited for her to touch me.

My body was wound tight as I could go, my balls ached and it was all I could do not to mount up and get buried inside her.

She sat forward and touched my cock through the silk. I thrust it into her hand and rolled my head back. I felt the shorts going down my thighs and stepped out of them quickly. My shaft was gripped in one hand, my sac in the other. And then I felt her soft tongue on me.

"Fuuuuuuuck, baby . . ." I breathed as she took my cock and worked it in and out of her mouth in deep pulls. She raised her beautiful eyes and met mine as she sucked me to the back of her throat over and over. Hot. Deep. Expertly. I wanted to hold my orgasm off but knew I wouldn't be able to with the way she was working out my cock. It was too fucking good and I needed it too much. I was lost in her and it felt so goddamn wonderful, I never wanted to be found again. Lost for forever in this moment with her. I could die a happy death right now, and I would definitely be smiling.

"Ahhh, fuuuck, I'm going!"

She pulled off my cock and went for my balls with a lick and a squeeze. I wrapped my fist around the base of my cock and jerked it hard. Once. Twice. Third time and I started to go off right into her open mouth. Sexiest fucking thing ever. My girl taking me down like that, her mouth open with her tongue out, waiting to catch my spunk.

Holy hell, I'll be doing this again.

A shuddering roar came out of me as I erupted and was blown into next year.

When I became coherent again, I was on my knees with Brynne stroking my hair and my cheek resting on her lap. I was going to need a minute or two to come back down to Earth. "You know how to welcome your man home from a shit day," I mumbled, starting to roam my hand up her smooth leg.

"I missed you tonight." She spoke softly and kept rubbing my head. Her touch always felt divine.

"I missed you more," I said on a groan, "I hate being away from you at night."

She relaxed a little. I felt the change in her as she loosened under me. I inhaled deeply, breathing in her scent, the floral mixed with her skin that sent me into a sexual haze so very deep I'm sure I buried some of my humanity. My beast appeared at the scent of her arousal. Made me want to do very kinky things to her.

My head came up and my hands went to her knees. I spread her legs before me and stared at her bare pussy. She was beautiful on display for me. *Only me?* I put that painful thought aside and focused on my treasure for the moment.

"Christ, you're soaking, my beauty. You need some attention, don't you?"

"Yes . . ." she whispered, her mouth falling open as she started to breathe heavily.

"I've been remiss." I jerked her hips to the cushion edge sharply and held her open. "You must forgive me." I blew on her cleft and loved the response I got, undulating hips and a soft, sexy moan. The sounds she could make . . .

My cock was ready for more just from hearing that throaty purr. I dived in and drew a deep lick through her pussy, parting the lips so I could get to work on the nub that made things feel really nice. She bowed her hips up again and made more sexy sounds for me.

I feasted. No other way to describe it. I sucked and licked, nibbled and nipped, and I could have stayed there for a long, long time doing it. The taste of her always made me crazed.

When I felt her tighten around my tongue and the two fingers that had found their way inside her heavenly cunt at some point, I prepared for what was certainly coming. Her all over me.

"Are you ready, baby?" I managed to ask, lips against lips.

"Yeeeees . . ."

Her cry came out soft and drawn low on a vibrating breath. So purely beautiful to me, I almost hated to take her forward and lose the sound of it. "Come for me." I focused on her clit and clipped my teeth onto it. "Right. Now!"

It was an order, and like other times, she performed to perfection for me. Her whole body arching upward, rolling out a low, shuddered cry from deep within her throat as I pushed my fingers inside and curled them into her.

I watched with my eyes, tasted with my tongue, heard with my ears and felt with my fingers as my beautiful girl reached her climax. The only sense I didn't use as she came apart was that of speech. There were no words to describe her, nor were there ones I could coherently form in the moment; she was a work of art, and I was speech-less.

13

♥

Ethan scooped me off the couch and into his arms. I lifted my eyes and got that wave of emotion again as his blues found me. I loved him so much I knew the fear. I'd heard others speak about it. I'd read about it in books. Now I understood. The fear that you have when you finally give your heart away to another person. It makes you very vulnerable to loss. If you never love anyone, then you'll never be hurt when they don't love you back or when they leave you.

I finally had the practical experience of understanding. It sucked.

Ethan sensed my newfound knowledge, I think. He studied me with intuitive eyes that looked very dark blue at the moment, and ducked his head down to meet my lips. He kissed me there in front of the window while holding me naked in his arms. I melted into him and gave in to my goddamn emotions.

He carried me down the hall to the bedroom and broke the kiss to lower me down to the bed. He saw.

"Oh, oh, baby . . . don't cry," he whispered, cupping my face and settling against me.

I couldn't help it. There was far too much inside me to leave it there. "I just love you so much, Ethan," I blubbered and then closed my eyes in an attempt to find some small sliver of sanctuary from my emotions.

He took over, stretching out against me so that our bodies aligned from head to toe when he started kissing me. Everywhere. "I love you more," he whispered as his lips trailed over my tears and brushed them away. He moved on to my jaw and then my neck and throat, the warm draw of his tongue over my skin settling me into some control over my urge to weep.

"I know what you need, and I'll always be here to give it to you." His hand reached up to weave fingers into my hair as his mouth closed over a nipple and sucked. And just like that he took me away into another world. A place where I was cherished, and where I could forget about a time when I never dared to dream about being loved like this.

Ethan alternatively flicked his tongue between my nipples, pinching with his lips, pulling them up and hardening the tips to sharp aching points as he held my hair in a firm grip. The tugging of my hair arched my chest up to meet his mouth. I needed what he did to me. So very badly.

When he lifted his head from my breasts, I protested the loss of his mouth on me and the pleasure it gave. He wanted to look at his handiwork. Ethan loved to look at our bodies during sex. There was no part of me he hadn't had a good look at or touched in some way. It gave me confidence when he looked and I knew he liked what he saw.

"Does that feel good when I suck on your beautiful tits and make them hard?" He tugged on my hair.

"Yes! I love when you suck them." I was starting to feel desperate.

"Do you love it when I bite them?" He clamped his teeth over one, not hard enough to hurt badly, but enough to give me a jolt of ecstasy along with a twinge of pain that brought out a moan.

"I think I take that as a yes," he muttered. "You're so fucking gorgeous when you make sounds . . ." He bit the other nipple, making me gasp and craving much more. Ethan had shown me, beyond a shadow of a doubt, that I was indeed a sexual creature. When he got me into this state even I would class myself well into the category of nymphomaniac.

His hand left my hair as he reached down to open my legs wide so he could stare at my pussy. "But this is what I want now," he rasped, stroking over my cleft, spreading the slick wetness from my earlier orgasm backward to lubricate my other opening. We'd been working on this for a while, and Ethan was taking his time in getting us there. I'd never done anal sex with anyone else; he would be the first. It felt nice to be a virgin in this way and give something to him that wasn't going to go to anyone else.

He pushed two fingers in and lifted his eyes as he did. "I want this, baby. I want into every part of you because you're mine, and you always will be."

The sting of pressure filling me up made me flex

against the invasion. "I know," I panted against his lips brushing mine. His words only helped me to feel more of what I needed to know from him, I focused on that and let myself go to a good place in my head. *You're mine, and you always will be.*

"Relax for me. Let me in here, and I'll make it feel so good." He started stroking with his fingers slowly, working in deeper with each penetration. "Baby . . . so fucking tight. I want to claim this tonight."

"Do it," I breathed, rolling my head to the side, "I want you to . . . finally do it . . ."

Ethan took hold of my chin, turning me back to face him as he pressed his fingers farther inside me and took possession of my mouth with his, thrusting his tongue in deep with forceful swirls. "I love you," he said harshly. "So much I don't know what to do with myself most of the time, but I do know what I want to do here." He withdrew his fingers, then slid them back into my virgin asshole.

I cried out from the intensity of the slide as it burned a path straight to my center.

"I have to know every bit of you, Brynne. I'm greedy and I have to have it all, baby." He started a slow rub of my clit with his thumb in tandem with his finger penetrations. "I have to be inside your beautiful, perfect ass because it's you and I have to know what it feels like to be there."

I shuddered beneath him and his touch, incapable of much more than a simple yes. The second I uttered my agreement, he pulled off me and turned me over. He took his time arranging me as he wanted. My hips were tugged back so I rested on my knees. My arms were stretched forward and made to grip the headboard. My knees were spread farther apart, and then . . . nothing. I could hear him breathing, and knew he was studying me again. My Ethan had a touch of voyeur kink in him and it only served to make me hotter knowing I was fulfilling his fantasies.

I hung there in anticipation when he covered me, his chest pressing onto my back, his mouth at my ear. "Are you sure?" he asked with a warm brush of his lips and then a lick just below my earlobe.

"Yeeees," I shuddered out my answer on a long breath.

His lips met the back of my neck and swept down my spine in a worshipful caress. The closer he moved toward his destination, the more my body lit up in sensations building low in my belly. I started to shake.

"Easy, my beauty, I got you." He pressed a hand to my lower back and then smoothed over one cheek. "You are exquisite like this," he murmured as his hand rolled up the other cheek to grip my hip. "Utterly exquisite and perfect." I felt him shift his weight around behind me and heard the side-table drawer slide open. Slick drops of lube met my skin as he worked it around. "Breathe for me, okay? I'm going to take care of you so good."

I nodded to let him know I'd heard but I couldn't speak. All I could do was suck in air and anticipate what would happen once I felt him there.

The tip of his cock bumped through my folds and slid deliciously along my clit, sending out sparks that made me thrust back for more contact.

"Yes, baby. You'll get it." The blunt head of him pressed

forward on me. The pressure was intense, and I couldn't help the contraction of my muscles. "Relax and breathe." He gave another push and the tip of him was in, my opening stretching to accommodate his size. "One more, baby. Almost there. I'm going in slow but steady, okay?" His hands held my ass as his cock moved deeper, propelled by a desire on both our parts to complete this union. There was some pain, but it was a very erotic sort of sensation that released something inside me. I wanted to feel it. I really did. I needed to understand what it was to give myself to Ethan completely.

The immense pressure building was already forcing a response within me and taking me forward for an orgasm. I pushed backward on his cock to let him know it was okay to keep going. "Ahhhhh . . . oh, God," I said, shuddering as he pressed forward again, the stretched feeling increasing to the point of pain until it seemed impossible, my body burning up. Then suddenly a give as he filled me up completely on a stinging thrust that took him all the way home. I closed my eyes on his shout and froze at the sensation.

"Fuuuck, you feel so good!" He held himself still and caressed both sides of my ass with his hands. "Baby . . . oh, fuck me . . . okay?" He was having trouble with words and I certainly understood that. I was having trouble holding still, and could feel the shakes returning. The convulsions weren't pain-induced, but involuntary reactions to the incredible assault on my erogenous zone. There was minimal pain because Ethan had prepared me slowly for this experience, taking me with care, as was his way with most everything. "Look at you, shaking." He stroked my hips reverently. "I'll stop if you tell me to. I never want to hurt you, baby," he said clearly but I could hear the strain in his words. "You feel so crazy good, I'm—I am—fuck, it's so good!" I could tell he was as affected as I was, hanging there suspended, waiting for the other to share. Ethan and I had always connected very honestly when it came to sex. I don't know why everything was so easy, but it was and it always had been so.

"I'm—I-I'm okay," I stuttered, "I want you to keep going."

"Fuck, I love you!" he groaned harshly.

Ethan withdrew slowly, the drag sending more of those sensory sparks down my center, and then thrust back in deep again. Each penetration slow and controlled. Each joining a little deeper than the one before it. I was shocked at the intensity of the pleasure building inside me as he picked up the pace steadily. His hands held me secure and his cock owned me in the last and final way possible.

As everything built low in my core, racing toward something explosive, I could tell Ethan was in the same desperate condition as I was. He began to start in with the dirty talk and the heaving breathing as he slipped a hand down over my clitoris and rubbed in a circle.

His touch to that little bundle of nerves sent me over the edge. "I'm going to come!" I sobbed. As I bowed my head down into the sheets to brace for the onslaught, I felt him swell to inhuman hardness inside me as his cock continued on in a relentless rhythm.

"Oh, FUUUUCK!—so am I!" he bellowed through the tight thrusts that connected us over and over again.

I convulsed beneath him and blew apart, utterly bone-less, and only able to hold on as he kept on with his pur-pose. A moment later I felt him leave me and flip me over, my body still reeling with the most explosive pleasure I'd ever experienced.

"Eyes!" he barked.

I opened mine and latched on to his fiery blue orbs. The sight of him was magnificent to behold. He looked like a pagan god, slick with sweat and all straining mus-cles as he kneeled between my legs, gripping his cock, and ejaculated all over my breasts and throat.

He was so very beautiful in that moment.

Sometime later I heard the bath running and opened my eyes, my body heavy with sleepy satisfaction. Ethan was right there watching me, all intense and serious in his expression, his fingers trailing through my hair.

"There she is." The hard lines softened as he leaned in to nuzzle over my lips. "You get sleepy after I make you come."

"I think I needed a little nap after all that."

The frown returned. "Too much? I'm sorr—"

I shut him up with my hand over his mouth. "No." I shook my head. "If it'd been too much I would have said."

"Did it feel good?" he asked carefully, a worried brow creasing his beautiful features.

"Oh . . . yes."

"Did I hurt you?" The sound of concern in his voice melted me even further.

"Only in the nicest way," I told him honestly.

The furrow disappeared and a look of relief replaced

it. "Oh, thank holy fuck!" He lifted his eyes upward like he was saying a prayer and then trained them back on me, which was absurd, really—thanking heaven for anal sex with an f-bomb declaration of gratitude when I'd given my blessing?

"Because I *really* want to do it again sometime." He looked so very relieved, and possibly even a little smug about me. I was glad to have made him happy and comforted to be shown, yet again, how much I could trust Ethan with my heart, and my body. He excelled in taking care of me. I hadn't really seen just how much he wanted to, and just how good he really was at doing it. Sexually and emotionally.

Ethan was brutally honest about stuff, sometimes so much so I blushed outwardly for his frankness. Inwardly though, I knew it was part of the reason he worked so well for me. I had to laugh a little at him too. Only Ethan could get away with sounding sweet about his hope for more backdoor sex for us and not have it come out crude and harsh.

How in the hell does he do that?

My kinky, foul-mouthed, romantic gentleman lover.

The perfect combination, in my opinion.

"Okay . . ." I told him, and leaned forward for a kiss.

He kissed me for a while in his gentle and precious way, as was typical. I looked forward to the after-sex kissing session. Ethan always wanted to kiss me after, and it always felt like he was making love to me again, only just with his lips and mouth. He pressed into me from above and held me underneath his hard body, his hips settled in between mine, his lips all over me, my lips, my throat, my breasts. He didn't stop until he was good and satisfied either.

Ethan knew how to demand from me. And I am quite sure his instincts are just that basic—hardwired primal directives that he cannot help but to answer. I'm sure about him, because it works the same way for me as well. I want to accept him, and submitting during sex is a way to give Ethan those things he asks me for so candidly. It gets me hot too. I love the things he says and asks from me when we're in the heat of fucking.

He lifted his lips away and looked over me with glassy blue eyes. "I love you so much it scares me sometimes. No . . . it scares me most of the time." He shook his head idly. "I hate leaving you alone here so much. It's not right." He sighed heavily. "I hate it so badly. I get—I just turn into a sort of raving madman, and I hope it's all not . . . too much. That I'm not too much." He touched his forehead to mine. "I see you and I just have to be with you like this." He trailed a hand over my breast and cupped it over the now dried effects of his orgasm, which looked to have been mostly wiped off me at some point. Maybe he'd done it while I dozed. I'd been so out of it from that cataclysmic climax he'd given me, I had no idea.

"Well, I'm not complaining." I held his face. "I like your version of a madman, if that's what you call it, and just so you know, I was lonely tonight, missing you and feeling worried about everything, but then you came home look-ing like you would die if you didn't have me, and . . . well, it was just what I needed to make me feel better. When I'm alone with my thoughts, I tend to start worrying about things that I shouldn't. Doubt creeps in. You are the first person to really help me with all the doubt. You just erase it all when you touch me and show me how much you want me."

He just stared, his eyes wide. "Are you real?" he whispered, brushing up my face with the back of his fingers in a cherishing caress. "Because I'll want you forever."

Ethan had asked me that question before and I loved it. "When you say things like that my heart beats faster."

He put his hand over my left breast and held it there. "I can feel your heart. It's my heart too."

I nodded. "It is your heart, and I am very real, Ethan. I've wanted everything we've ever done together, and you own my heart now." I touched his face in the same way, just inches apart, drowning in his eyes.

Ethan sighed heavily, but it sounded like one of relief and not of worry. "Come on, my beauty, have a bath with me. I need to wash you and hold you for a while." He picked me up and carried me into his travertine masterpiece of a bathroom, and helped me into the tub. After he settled in behind me, I stretched back and rested against his firm chest. His arms came around to swirl water up over my breasts and shoulders.

"I called Benny tonight," I offered after a moment.

Ethan soaped up a bath sponge and drew it up my arm. "How is Clarkson? Does he want to take more pictures of you?"

"We didn't talk about that."

"But he will." Ethan's response was nothing new. He

didn't like me modeling, and he really didn't understand how much I needed it either. I wasn't in the habit of throwing it in his face because I didn't want him getting all upset and unreasonable again. Every time I went for a photo shoot he got irrational, so it was easier to just avoid reminding him.

"I think Ben's getting suspicious, and I'm sure Gaby would be too if she'd seen me in the flesh, but we've only spoken on the phone."

Ethan drew the sponge over my neck. "It's time to tell them, baby. I want it announced and it has to be something big. I know that much."

"Big how?"

"London press? Celebrity guests? Posh planning?" I stiffened in his arms. He tightened his hold around me and whispered, "Now, don't panic, okay? Our wedding has to be an . . . event that will be newsworthy enough so that *everyone* knows about us."

"Like the senator?"

"Yes." He paused. "We think that Fielding is dead too. He's been missing since the end of May."

"Oh, God! Ethan, why didn't you tell me?" I jerked forward and turned halfway around to look at him accusingly.

He tightened his hold around me and pressed his lips to the back of my neck. He was attempting to soothe me, I suppose, and lucky for him his tactics usually worked. Ethan was able to settle me down with just a gentle touch.

"I just got confirmation, and when I first suspected it we were at Hallborough, and you were so desperately sick . . . Don't be angry. I had to tell Neil about us too. He knows we're pregnant. And before you get mad about that, you should know he's very happy for us. You know everything there is to know, Brynne." He kissed my shoulder. "No secrets."

My brain started putting it all together and the very idea gave me goose bumps. "You're worried they will try to get to me too, but if our relationship and wedding are made into celebrity news then they won't dare to?" I could hear the fear in my voice and hated it. I couldn't imagine that Senator Oakley would want me dead. What had I ever done wrong except date his son? It was Lance Oakley who'd done the damage, not me! Why did I have to live in fear over something I didn't cause? I was the victim here, and as much as I loathed the idea, it was the truth.

"I cannot take the risk with you and I won't, not ever." Ethan kissed my neck and swirled the sponge down my belly. "I always say you are brilliant because you are. You understand, then."

"Yeah, I get it. I understand that a powerful political party may want to snuff me out, but that doesn't mean I have to like a façade wedding." I could feel Ethan tense behind me and figured he wasn't happy with what I was saying.

"I told you I would do whatever it takes to secure your safety, Brynne, and I will. I promise you, the venue and the guest list don't change a goddamn thing about the purpose. Not for me, they don't," he ground out. "And I want the fact that we are expecting a baby to be part of the announcement as well. It just makes you more of a precious commodity." He shook me lightly. "Which you are."

Yeah, my man was not happy at all. He sounded a little wounded too, and I felt guilty yet again for being so unappreciative. I guess it was just one more thing to discuss with my therapist. While I was grateful Ethan wanted to marry me and was willing to make a commitment to our child, I hated that threats from fuck-knows-who were the driving force behind his proposal.

"I'm sorry. I know I am not making this easy on you, Ethan. I wish I could be different about this." *In so many ways, I wish it.* "But you should know it's not really every girl's dream to have a celebrity wedding because someone might be trying to kill her."

"There's a lot more motivating me than that," he growled, "and you know it." Ethan thrust up the drain plug and heaved himself out of the tub. He offered his hand to assist me, his expression a little angry, a little hurt, and a lot beautiful in all his magnificent wet nakedness.

Yeah, a baby we started together by accident is driving it too.

I accepted his hand and let him draw me out of the tub. He snapped down a towel and started drying me from head to toe. When he got to my stomach he bent down and planted a gentle kiss right over where our baby would be growing.

I gasped and felt tears starting again, fully unable to bring my emotions to heel, and wondering how I'd ever make it through everything intact. Why did I have to be so weak?

He lifted his eyes up. "But I love you, Brynne, and I have to be with you. Isn't that enough?"

I lost it. Completely and totally, and for the goddamn zillionth time. Tears, sobs, hiccups—the whole nine yards. Ethan got the deluxe emotional package from me tonight. Poor guy.

My outburst didn't seem to faze him, though, as he took charge, putting me back into bed, sliding in alongside me and drawing me close. He drew his fingers through my hair and just held me for a long time with no more demands, no questions or inquiries. He let me be, offering his comfort and strength generously without the prospect of anything in return.

He was thinking. I could hear the cogs grinding around inside his head as he pondered me. Ethan did that quite a bit, actually, the thinking without saying anything.

I was too, though. I remembered something Dr. Roswell had said to me more than once. Whenever I expressed my fears about the future, she said: "You'll get through one step at a time, one day at a time, Brynne."

Another cliché, yes, but one that was spot-on true, as Ethan liked to say sometimes. Spot-on true.

I'll get through this one step at a time, and Ethan will be here to help me.

"It is enough, Ethan," I whispered. His fingers stilled in my hair. "It is enough for me. You are enough."

Ethan kissed me, gentle and soft, his tongue slipping inside to tangle around lazily like there wasn't a care in the world for us right now. I felt his palm sweep down to rest low on my belly and he held it there, warm and protecting.

"We're gonna be okay, baby. I know we are. All three of us."

I buried my face in his chest and nuzzled. "When you say it, I believe you."

"It will. I know this." He lifted my face up and tapped his head with his finger. "I have visions, just like you have those super powers of deduction that you told me about once." He gave me a wink.

"Really." I added some sarcasm, just so he'd know I was over my snit about the wedding and could go back to acceptance.

"Yup. You, me and our little blueberry will have our happily ever after."

I had to shake my head at him. "We don't have a blueberry anymore."

He feigned shock. "What happened to blueberry? Don't tell me you ate it."

"You idiot." I nudged him in the ribs. "Blueberry is now raspberry."

"Where are you getting this information?" he asked, one eyebrow quirking up.

"Website called Bump dot com. You should check it out. It'll tell you everything you need to know about fruits and vegetables."

He laughed. "I love when you play with me," he said, taking my chin. "Especially when I can see the light in your eyes and you look happy. It's all I really want. You to be happy with me, about us, our life together."

"You do make me happy, Ethan. I'm sorry about how I am lately. A hormonal wreck crying over everything, moping, being difficult, ugh . . . I hate the sound of myself even apologizing to you right now."

He shook his head. "Nope. We'll have none of that. You don't need to apologize, baby. All you need to do is agree to the announcement of our engagement. I wrote it out today. It's ready to go."

He looked so earnest in his request, and I realized in that moment the time for avoiding my fears about marriage, a baby, the stalker, everything that scared me, really, was definitely over. Going forward was the only option now.

"Okay. I'm ready."

"You are?" Ethan looked more than a little surprised. "Just like that, you're now ready?"

"Yeah. I am. I know you love me and I know you will take care of us. I finally admitted to myself with Dr. Roswell that I need you. I love you and I need you." I cupped one side of his face with my hand. "Let's do it."

I got one of those spectacular and rare Ethan smiles that made it all worth it. I did indeed love making this man happy. It filled something in me, made me feel warm inside.

"We need to tell our parents and families. How do you want to break the news?" he asked softly.

"Hmmm . . . good point." I looked at the bedside clock reading one o'clock in the morning. "How about now?" I said.

"Now?" He looked unsure for a moment before he figured it out. "You want to tell your dad first." I could tell he was doing mental calculations. "It's five o'clock on a Friday, do you think you can get ahold of him?"

"I'm pretty sure I can. Get dressed."

"Huh?"

I slipped out of bed and started pulling on yoga pants and a T-shirt. "I want to Skype him and tell him that way."

I smirked, feeling pleased with my idea. "I doubt he'd appreciate hearing he's going to be a grandfather with you naked on Skype looking like you do right now," I said with a long, measured look over his bare, muscled skin, "so get dressed, please. I can guarantee he'll want to talk to you once I tell him what you've done to me."

"Princess, you look so pretty. I love seeing your face on here. To what do I owe this honor, and what in the hell are you doing up at one a.m.?"

I grinned at my dad and actually got butterflies in my stomach at the prospect of telling him our news. Somehow I knew he would be happy for me. He'd never judged me in the past, and he wouldn't now. "God, I miss you. I would give anything to have you right in front of me for this, Daddy." My handsome dad had a pool towel around his neck and wet hair.

"I just did forty laps, and it felt great. My weekend is off to a good start. The weather's been so nice for the pool. Wish you were here to enjoy it with me."

"Me too. Are you taking your blood-pressure pills like you're supposed to?"

"Of course I am. I'm in great shape for an old codger."

"Oh, please, you're about the furthest you can get from being a codger, Dad. When I imagine an old guy, you're definitely not it. I even got a message from Jess on Facebook telling me how she sees you at the gym and how adorable you are. You must have to scrape the ladies off you when you work out."

He laughed and brushed my comment away. I always wondered about that part of his life. He never talked about dates or women, so I really didn't know much. He had to get lonely sometimes. Humans weren't meant to be alone. I wished he could find someone who made him happy.

"Jess is a sweet girl. We talk mostly about you, Brynnie. You didn't answer my question either. Why are you up so late?"

"Well, Ethan and I have something important to say and I didn't want another moment go by before talking to you."

"Okay . . . you're smiling, so I think this must be happy news?" He lifted his chin and looked a little too smug. My confidence faltered just a little, until I felt Ethan come up behind me and sit down. He put his hands on my shoulders and leaned forward so my dad could see him in the monitor. "Hey, Ethan, so you're going to make an honest woman of my daughter? Is that what this big announcement is all about?"

"Ahhh . . . well—um . . . we wanted to tell you a few things, actually, Tom."

"Well, I'm dying to hear it," Dad said, obviously loving that he had Ethan squirming on Skype, a monstrous grin on his handsome face. God, I hoped he was happy once he heard the words.

I went for it. A big ole fat belly flop into the deep end of the metaphorical swimming pool that was my life.

"Daddy, you're going to be a grandpa."

I felt Ethan's fingers grip my shoulders a little harder, and watched the big grin on my dad's face morph into a look of complete shock.

14

♠

I pulled up to the redbrick house where I'd grown up in Hampstead and parked on the street.

"This is my dad's house."

"It's lovely, Ethan. An elegant English home, just like I imagined it. The yard is beautiful."

"Dad likes to keep his hands dirty with it."

"I've always admired people with a green thumb. I'd like to have a garden someday but I don't know much about plants. I'd have so much to learn," she said wistfully from inside the car. "Do you feel good when you come here? Does it still feel like home to you?" She sounded a little homesick to me.

"Well, yeah, it does. It's the only one I ever had until I bought mine. And I know my dad would be happy to teach you anything. My mother's garden is in the back of the house. I really want you to see that." I swept my eyes over Brynne, looking beautiful as usual in a flowery dress and some purple boots. God, I loved when she wore her boots. The clothes could go but the boots could stay . . . any time. "Are you nervous?"

She nodded. "I am . . . very."

"There's no need, baby. Everyone loves you and thinks you are the best thing to ever happen to me." I gave her a slow kiss on the lips, tasting her sweetness before we had to go out in public, and my constant need to have my hands on her would have to be curbed for the next hours. *It sucks to be me, then.* "Which you are," I added.

"Oh, come on; I remember how my dad interrogated you . . . and how your voice cracked." She giggled. "The look on his face was priceless, wasn't it?"

"Ahh, I guess so. I don't really remember his face. All I could think about was how grateful I was to have thousands of miles between us, you know, to save my cock from being twisted off."

"You poor thing." She laughed, holding her hand over her stomach.

"Are you feeling well? How's our raspberry behaving this evening?"

Brynne reached up to hold my cheek. "Little raspberry is cooperating so far, but I never know what will set me off. Nighttime is my nemesis for some reason. Just gonna take it slow."

"You look so beautiful tonight. Dad is going to be thrilled." I picked up her hand and kissed it on the palm, then pressed it back over her stomach.

"You're going to make me cry if you keep that up." She covered my hand with hers.

"Nope. No tears tonight. This is a happy time. Think

about how happy your dad was last night when we told him. Well, at least after he realized he was too far away to castrate me, he was." I flashed a quick wink.

"I love you, Blackstone. You make me laugh, and that's something. Let's do this thing."

"Yes, boss." I came around and got my girl out of the car and up the steps to the door. I rang the bell and waited. The soft slide of a warm body slinked against my leg. The cat had grown some since the last time I'd come over here.

"Soot, my man. How the hell have you been?" I picked him up and introduced him to Brynne. "This is Soot, the self-proclaimed owner of my dad. He's sort of adopted him."

"Aww . . . what a handsome kitty. Such green eyes." Brynne reached out to pet him as Soot lowered his head into her hand for a rub. "He's really friendly, huh?"

"Oh, yes he is—"

The door opening interrupted us. Brynne's aunt Marie, with a welcoming smile on her face, stood just inside my dad's front porch. "Surprise," Marie said. "I bet you two weren't expecting to see me here, were you?"

I laughed awkwardly, in reality a bit caught off guard, but I recovered well in spite of my shock. "Marie, if this isn't a most lovely surprise, I don't know what is. Are you helping Dad with dinner?"

"I am," she said. "Please come in, you two." She greeted us both with kisses and hugs. Brynne and I exchanged a quick glance. I'd bet brass Brynne was as surprised as me to see Marie here.

As soon as I got a look at Dad, I knew something was

up. He wiped his hands on a kitchen cloth and greeted us. A warm embrace and a kiss to the hand for my girl, and a rather cool frosty nod to me. Soot leapt out of my arms and headed off somewhere.

"Marie and I had already arranged for dinner here tonight when you called and asked to come over," Dad said.

Really? Another quick flash connect with Brynne and the struggle on both our parts to play it cool here was immediately obvious. So Dad and Marie were . . . ? Nice. I still thought Marie was hot for a mature woman. The idea dawned on me that maybe my dad was annoyed I was breaking into his romantic evening. Well, shit. "Why didn't you say so, then?" I asked. "We didn't need to do it tonight."

My dad shook his head at me and kept up the reserve. If I didn't know any better I'd say he was giving me the cold shoulder. Just me though, not Brynne. He bestowed a warm smile on her and said, "Oh, I think you did need to do it tonight, son."

What in the hell? Did he know something already? I was going to crack some heads around if my sister or Fred had spilled the beans. I narrowed my eyes at him. He stone-faced me right back.

Marie broke the tension. Thank holy fuck. "Brynne, my darling, come help me with the dessert. Raspberry trifle, and it's going to be divine."

I got the urge to smile when she said *raspberry*, my eyes flashing to meet Brynne's. She gave me a smiley wink and followed Marie into the kitchen.

"What's with the brush off, Dad? Are we interrupting

your evening or something? You could have said tonight wasn't good, you know."

Dad set his jaw and raised both brows, letting me know who was leading this little exchange. Amazing how a parent has that power. Taking me right back in time to my teenage years and squirming in the hot seat for some cock-up mess I'd gotten myself into.

"Actually, you are interrupting my evening, but that is neither here nor there. I'm always happy to see my son. No, I'm more incredulous that I've had to wait for the call from you, Ethan." He speared me with searching eyes.

"Can we stop speaking in code here? You're obviously bent about something."

"Oh, yes, something," he said curtly.

"What do you mean by that?" My voice cracked. Fuck! I was in trouble now. Dad knew? How?

"I think you know, son. In fact, I know you know."

"You do?" Yeah, voice still cracking like an opera singer onstage. "How is that possible?"

He actually softened his expression a small bit. "It seems that a great deal of things are possible, son. Imagine my surprise to call up to Hannah's and have my granddaughter tell me gleefully that Uncle Ethan and Auntie Brynne are preggers."

Oh boy! I immediately went for my beard and dragged a hand over it. "So the little monster told you, huh?"

"Indeed." Dad still kept up the harsh expression. "Zara had quite a bit to say about it."

I held my hands up in surrender. "What do you want me to say, Dad? We got caught, all right? It wasn't intentional, and I can attest we were as surprised about it as everyone else was!"

He folded his arms over his chest, seemingly unaffected by catching me off guard. "When is the wedding?"

I looked down at the floor, suddenly feeling ashamed I had no answer for him. "I'm working on it," I mumbled.

"Please tell me you're getting married right away." Dad's voice was getting louder. "You cannot wait until after the baby is born like some of these celebrities do!"

"Would you lower your voice?" I demanded. "Brynne is . . . well, she's wary of commitment. It's scary for her . . . because of her past."

Dad flashed me a glare that told me pretty much what he thought of my explanation. "Too late for that, son. He snorted. "You're already as committed as it gets. Having your child born without benefit of a legal marriage will be even scarier, I can assure you it will be. For you and for Brynne." He shook his head at me. "Forget about the past, you need to think about the future." He zeroed in on me like a dog after a steak. "Have you even proposed to her? I don't see any ring on her finger."

"I *said* I was working on it," I snapped. *And I really fucking am, Dad!*

"Time won't stand still, Ethan."

"Really, Dad? Thanks for that bit of advice." My sarcasm would have earned me a cuff along the jaw in my younger years. Now I just got narrowed eyes and another blast of frigid. An idea came to me that he might have shared our news already. "Does Marie know too?" I asked haughtily.

"She does not." Dad gave me another hostile look with

eye-roll added in before heading back to Brynne and Marie in the kitchen.

I stared at his retreating back in irritation, deciding some distance for now would be best. No sense in having a family row and upsetting *everyone*. Better just for me to suffer. I planted my arse on the sofa instead and wished for a cigarette. Or a whole pack.

Funny how the parents all reacted so differently to our news. Tom Bennett was happy for us, after he got over his initial shock, I think. He never demanded a wedding date, but simply wanted to see that we were happy and that I loved his daughter and was committed to taking care of her and our child. He'd even suggested plans to come over for a visit toward the end of fall, which thrilled Brynne.

Brynne's mum didn't ask about a wedding date either. Mrs. Exley was a different story, true, but then she didn't like me, and I am sure she didn't like the fact she was going to be a granny either. Too fucking bad for her then. A whole lot of cold silence had met us on the other end of the line when we rang her to share. Brynne hadn't wanted to tell her mum on Skype as we had done with her dad, and I now understood why. Mum must've given off some evil looks when she heard our news and my sweet girl certainly didn't need to see them. It had been bad enough trying to comfort her after putting down the phone. Yeah, the lines had been drawn in the sand and my opinion set. Brynne's mum was a judgmental cow who clearly cared about her social position more than she cared about her daughter. Hopefully our dealings would be minimal.

So, yeah, my dad's insta-hostility over our lack of a wedding date rather took me by surprise. Especially when two ounces of patience would put an end to his rabid concerns.

Within moments, Soot found my lap and made himself comfortable. He stared up at me with clear green eyes as I stroked his sleek, shiny coat, wondering how the nice evening had evolved into getting my King Dickhead crown handed to me on a velvet cushion.

"I have a plan," I said to the cat. "I do. I just haven't shared with anyone yet."

Soot blinked his clear green eyes at me in total understanding, and purred.

Ethan pulled my chair out from the dinner table and helped me up. "I want to show Brynne the garden," he announced.

"But shouldn't we help clear away dinner?" I asked.

"No, please, my dear, let Ethan show you his mother's lovely garden. I want you to see it." Jonathan's tone was final on this matter. I didn't even contemplate arguing.

I looked up at Ethan and took his offered hand in mine. "Well, okay, if you don't mind. The salmon and béarnaise was really nice. I'm impressed with your cooking skills, Jonathan." I winked at Marie. "I knew about my aunt being a kitchen witch, but you surprise me."

Jonathan shrugged. "I had to learn." I instantly felt bad for reminding everyone of the loss of Ethan's mom. A young boy had lost his mother, but Jonathan had lost his wife and soul mate. It was such a sad thing, but Jonathan had been prepared with years of practice in dealing with awkward moments like these, and he glided through this one like it was nothing. "Marie and I were quite a duo tonight, though. I did the fish and rice, she did the salad and dessert." Jonathan flashed my smiling aunt a dashing wink. I wondered if they were . . . dating; a weird thought to think of them together romantically, but one that made me happy if it were true. Maybe they were just friends, but they sure did look cute together. I wondered what Ethan thought about seeing his dad with a woman.

Ethan pressed his hand to my back and led me outside. Soot bounced along ahead of us before jumping onto the brick base of an enormous garden urn flanking a secluded bench surrounded by deep purple larkspur and light blue lavender.

"This is so pretty, just like an English garden on a postcard." I shrugged up at Ethan, who was looking really intense for a simple garden tour. He had his jaw set tight and a determined expression on his face. "Is it hard for you to see your dad with Marie?" I asked carefully.

He shook his head. "Not at all. Marie's hot." He grinned. "Go Dad, I say."

"Well, that's a relief. I was a little worried there for a moment. You seemed . . . tense during dinner."

He pulled me down onto the garden bench and wrapped me in his arms, burying his head at my neck. "Do I seem tense now?" he muttered against my hair.

"Not as much," I answered with a rub of my fingers at the base of his neck, "but your muscles here are very tight. When are we going to tell them? I thought we would have done it already."

"We'll make the announcement when we go back inside. I need a moment alone with you first."

"I'll take a moment alone with you." I smiled into his handsome face looking so intently at me, the illumination from the garden lights reflecting in his blue eyes like tiny sparks. He leaned down to kiss me and swallowed me up with his expert technique. My stomach did a little flip at the sight of him looming, still just as affected by him now as I had been from the first moment we locked eyes that night in the Andersen Gallery back at the beginning of May.

Ethan kissed me in his father's garden for far more than a moment, but I could have done it all night. His lips and tongue were magic from the beginning and still were. Ethan made me feel precious when he kissed me. No other man had ever made me feel so loved.

He pulled back finally and held my face in his hands. His thumb brushed over my lips in a caress that dragged over my bottom lip just enough to send the message. A "you're mine" gesture that did strange things to my insides. The simplest touch from Ethan could do that, though, and I was familiar with the feeling by now. It just made me love him more, if that was even possible.

"I bought you something when we were at Hallborough. I found it in an antiques shop when I went into the village and knew it was for you. I've been waiting for the right moment to give it to you." He pulled a small rectangular package out of his jacket pocket and placed it in my lap.

"Oh . . . I have a present?" I lifted the package and unwrapped the soft blue tissue. It was a book. A very old and very special book. My heart started thumping hard as I realized precisely what Ethan had given me. "*Lamia, Isabella, The Eve of St. Agnes, and Other Poems* by John Keats?" I choked out in complete shock.

"Do you like it?" Ethan's expression was hesitant and I realized he might have struggled over this gift, unsure about whether or not I'd enjoy it. An early edition Keats had to cost a fortune, and this one was an early edition. Bound in green leather and still bearing faint gold embossed lettering on the spine, it was a work of art to me.

"Oh my God! Yes, you could say that, baby. This is a beautiful, magnificent gift. I'll cherish it always." I carefully opened the cover and held it up to one of the garden lamps to see. "There's an inscription. 'For my Marianne. Always, your Darius. June 1837.'" I brought a hand up to my neck and looked over at Ethan. "It was a lover's gift. Darius loved Marianne, and gave her the book."

"As I love you," he said softly.

"Oh, Ethan. You're going to make me cry again if you keep doing things like this."

"Well, I don't mind your tears, really. I never have. And especially when they're not sad ones. You can cry happy anytime you want, baby." He leaned down to touch his forehead to mine. "I adore the taste of your tears," he said before pulling back.

I touched his cheek and whispered, "I love you too. And you give me far too expensive gifts."

"Never, baby. I'd give you the world if I could. You never ask for anything. You're so generous with yourself and you humble me with your spirit. I'm in awe of you most of the time. It's true." He nodded to emphasize his words. "I'm not lying."

"Now it's my turn to ask you if you're real."

His eyes roamed over me as he nodded again. "I think I became real when I met you."

My heart dropped down to the cobblestones beneath my feet when Ethan got up from the bench and knelt in front of me. He took my hands in his.

"I know I'm a bit rough around the edges and I know I've trampled my way into your life, but I do love you with all my heart. Never doubt that. You're my girl, and I want you and I need you with me forever. I would have wanted a future with you regardless. The baby coming is just more of a sign that this is right. We're right, my beauty. We're so right together."

I couldn't speak, but I agreed with him. We were so right together.

All I could do was look into his beautiful eyes and fall more in love with everything that was Ethan Blackstone. My amazing man.

The paths we take in life are never clear, and nobody can predict the future, but the night I laid eyes on Ethan, I knew there was something special about him. When I went to his flat that first time to be with him, I knew. I knew the decision would be life-changing too. For me it had been. He was everything I could have ever dreamed of in a partner, and even more about him that I never could have possibly imagined. Timing is always off. You deal with what comes, when it comes into your life.

Ethan was simply . . . the one for me. I squeezed his hands with mine. It was the only response I could give, considering my heart was beating so fast I felt sure I would float away if he wasn't holding on to me.

"Brynne Elizabeth Bennett, will you make me the happiest man alive and marry me? Be my wife and the mother of our children." He tilted his head and whispered the rest. "Make me real. Only you can do that, baby. Only you . . ."

"Yes." I nodded fast.

I don't know how I managed to even respond with that one little word. I heard myself speak it aloud, but all I could really do was look at him. Look down at him kneeling before me and feel the love he was pouring out back to me. There was so much more I could have said, but I didn't. I wanted to just be in the moment and remember how I felt when Ethan asked me to make him real.

I understood what he meant when he said that to me. I understood it because I shared the same feelings about him. He'd brought me out from the dark and into the light. Ethan had given me back my life.

Something cold and heavy slipped onto my finger. When I looked down to see what it was, the most gorgeous ring was perched on the fourth finger of my left hand. Antique, ornate, and huge—a hexagonal deep-purple amethyst, set in platinum with diamonds, glittered up at me. I held it in the glow of the garden light so I could really get a good look. It was magnificent, beautiful and far too extravagant for me, but I loved it mostly because Ethan had chosen it. My hand shook and the tears started. I couldn't have stopped them for anything. It was a good thing he'd just said he didn't mind my tears because they would be dripping all over him in another moment.

These were definitely of the joyful variety, though.

"I-I want to m-marry you. I d-do. I love you so much, Ethan." My words came out on a sob. I just was so overcome by him I could hardly absorb everything, and I'm sure my state of hyper-hormonal didn't help either.

Ethan picked up my hand and kissed it, the familiar brush of his goatee paired with his warm lips comforted me in a way that I couldn't describe with words. He just made me feel cherished, and he always had. I belonged to him now, and I was embracing the realization with open arms. It had taken me a bit of time to make it, but I'd gotten there. I had accepted Ethan's love and offered to him my whole self in return. Finally.

I never knew it was possible to be so happy in life.

Whiskers teased my flesh. A hot tongue flicked over my nipple, swirling it into a tight, tingly bud. I arched into his mouth and moaned a luxurious sound of pleasure, which only seemed to spur him on. Somebody was wide awake and intent upon making me come before breakfast. The very best way to start my day.

My eyes fluttered open and locked onto his, my waking like a signal light giving the go-ahead to drive on through. I loved waking up to Ethan like this. His weight pressing me down, his hips settled in tight between my legs, his hands pinning mine to the bed. He flared his eyes as his cock filled me up with a determined slide. I voiced my pleasure and arched up to meet as much of him as possible. He just took my mouth with his tongue and found another part of my body to claim.

It was good to be claimed by Ethan. So good.

He moved slow and steady, building the rhythm up with deep thrusts that ended with a little grind each time he swiveled his hips. I squeezed my inner muscles hard around him, knowing it would help him along and get me to my release that much faster. I was greedy for it these days.

"Not yet, baby. You gotta wait this time," he rasped down at me, "I'm coming with you, and I'll tell you when."

I felt him roll us quickly, settling me on top, but he wasn't content for me to ride him like that. Ethan hefted himself up to sitting position and clutched me hard at the hips so he could maneuver me over his cock, bringing me down very deep with each plunge, our faces within inches of each other's as our bodies connected. He could see everything written in my eyes; how much I loved him, how much I needed him, how much I wanted him.

"Ooooh, God . . ." I shuddered, trying desperately to control the crash about to consume me, knowing it was impossible because Ethan was a master at giving it to me. He was a master at directing the sex too. His dominant nature came out in full force, controlling when I could orgasm. He would make me wait sometimes. Today was one of those times. I had no worries about the eventuality of where he would take me, though. The waiting just made what was coming at the end so much better.

"You feel like heaven down on my cock," he said, his lips

finding mine again, silencing any more words for the moment. "So wet for me . . . and your tight cunt squeezing me. I love your cunt, baby." I waited for this part of the ritual— the dirty talk from him. Nothing could get me hotter than the stuff that came out of his mouth. Well, maybe what he actually did with his mouth. And his cock. Ethan could get away with saying "cunt" and not make it sound nasty. The word didn't hold the same meaning among Brits anyway. It wasn't the horrific slur here that it was back home. Ethan's erotic ramblings made me insane with lust.

I took him in and let him have me, the merging of our tongues only gaining in intensity as he drilled into me with his cock from below, my movements controlled by him, lifting and dropping me over and over again down onto his swelling shaft. I felt him get harder and prayed for the end to swallow me.

"Please . . ." I begged on a whimper that he swallowed up with his mouth and tongue.

"Does my beauty want to come?"

"Yes, I want to so badly!"

I felt his hands leave my ass where he'd been guiding me and move up to pinch my nipples. "Say my name when you do."

The sharp sting bit into me, breaking the huge wave of sensation I'd been holding back, allowing the crash to happen. "Ethan, Ethan, Ethan . . ." I chanted, collapsing forward onto him, no longer able to rein in my body. Everything became involuntary for me after that, but I was aware of him climaxing. I heard his harsh groans and I felt the heat of the spurts of cum shooting deep inside me, reminding me that this was how we'd started our baby. Just like this. Our bodies connecting in a wicked frenzy until nirvana occurred and nothing else mattered.

He held me up, his hips grinding slowly to work the very last ounce of pleasure out of this encounter. I purred against his chest and never wanted to move. Ever.

"Well, good morning to you, Mrs. Blackstone," he said on a soft laugh.

"Mmmmm . . . it was, wasn't it?" I moved over his hips, and flexed around his cock, still semi-hard inside me. "I'm not Mrs. Blackstone yet."

He gasped in a breath, "Easy there, my beauty, don't kill me off before I can make an honest woman of you."

I laughed. "I think I'm more in danger of that than you are. God, you do crazy things to me." I nuzzled his lips and nose, loving our time together and the knowledge that Ethan was all mine for the next little while until he had to leave for work.

He was so stretched with the Olympics and working so hard, I was determined to help him in any way I could. Giving him some mind-blowing sex to start off his day was one way, and I got to share in the benefits of that too.

"I love doing crazy things to you. I love you." He kissed me sweet and slow. "And you'll be Mrs. Blackstone soon enough, so you might as well get used to me saying it."

"Okay. I think I can do that for you." I splayed out my left hand and looked at my ring again, the dark purple stone looking almost black in the dull morning light. "And I love you too." It still shocked me a little, seeing it there on my hand. I was engaged to Ethan, and we really were getting married. And I really was having his baby. When did the bottom drop out from beneath me? I had to keep telling myself this was not a dream.

"Do you really like the ring?" he asked softly. "I know you like antiques and that was so unusual I hoped you might like it instead of something modern." He held my face to his and rubbed over my jaw with his thumb. "But if you want a different one, just say. I know it's not a conventional engagement ring and I want you happy in all things."

I clutched my left hand with my right one protectively. "I love my ring and you're never getting it back," I teased. "You know, in certain light it almost looks black sometimes. A black stone." I smiled wide at him.

He smiled back at me as realization dawned. "Good?"

"Very good, Mr. Blackstone. You have remarkable taste with your gifts, which are far too extravagant but that I love all the same. You spoil me rotten."

He rotated his hips down below, reminding me our bodies were still connected. "My prerogative, and I've hardly gotten started, baby. Just you wait." He winked.

"I haven't given you any gifts," I said, plucking at the sheets bunched under my knees.

"Look at me." His voice was all seriousness, the teasing gone.

I lifted my eyes to meet his blazing blue ones.

"Don't say that. It's not true. You've given me this." He took my hand and placed it over his heart. "And this." He put his hand over my heart. "And this." He put both our hands over my belly and left them there. "There *are* no greater gifts, Brynne."

15

♥

The shopping expedition proved my theory that this would be an exercise in lunacy.

"What do you mean you're not wearing these shoes?" Benny held up what had to be at least a six-inch Louboutin stiletto encrusted with crystals. "They're hot. You can pull it off, luv. Will make your legs miles long."

I rolled my eyes at him. "And the point of that is?"

"To look sexy?"

I shook my head at Ben. "No, darling. The point of the day is to get married, not to look like I work for an escort service." I pointed to my belly. "Pregnant, remember?"

"Yeah," Gaby said sarcastically at my left. "I still can't believe you kept it a secret from me for nearly two weeks!"

"Sorry, it wasn't intentional, and have I mentioned that it was a total shock to my system? In more ways than one." I returned the sarcasm right back with good measure. "I'm barely starting to feel human." I frowned. "Emphasis on the *barely*."

Gaby shook her head. "I bet," she said, looking over a

rack of dresses in hopes of finding something that could pass for a maid of honor's. "Seven weeks, Bree. We have seven weeks to get this wedding together. It's insane."

"I know. I wish we could have a little more time to plan this, but Ethan wants it done as soon as possible. We get a whole two weeks' leeway after the Olympics finish up." I lowered my voice to a whisper. "He thinks being married in a big public event and announcing we are expecting will deter whoever is watching me from taking any action. I can only hope he's right." My stomach did a little flip, but I pushed the fear away. I really didn't have time to worry about who might be after me anymore. I was having a baby—another person to protect now. It surprised me how easy it'd been to fall into that role too. Biology was hardwired into us, I realized. Protecting my unborn baby was just a natural instinct that I had to follow. I took a deep breath and reminded myself that Ethan had me well guarded, and that I didn't take risks. Not anymore. No, that freaky message on my old cell had spooked me thoroughly, along with the idea that two of my attackers on the video were most certainly dead. I looked over to where Len was literally standing guard, the bridal shop not deterring him even the slightest little bit. He was my shadow these days, with Ethan and Neil so busy with the Olympics. I smiled at him and saw the softening of his expression for just an instant before he went back to guard duty, scanning the room and keeping the crazies away. Thank God.

Gaby must have sensed my worry, because she put her arm around me. "You've been through so much. How in the heck are you not stark raving mad by now, girl?" She barely paused to take a breath. "Color? You want us in a shade of purple or lavender?"

"That is a very good question. One I've got no answer for." I shrugged. "I was referring to the stark raving mad inquiry," I told her with a sigh, "and I would love you in purple if you find something that strikes your fancy. I want you and Elaina to feel good in whatever you choose, Gab. And your dresses don't have to be the same at all, or even the exact same shade or material. I want you guys to wear what you love. You'll be beautiful in anything—"

"Okay, enough useless prattle, ladies. We have to find a wedding dress, and time is slipping by," Ben announced imperiously with a theatrical look down at his watch. "Can you tell me what your requirements are in a gown, darling? If I know what you're looking for, I can do this." He snapped his fingers on both hands with a flourish.

Gaby rolled her eyes at Ben's announcement. "That's a little bold, Ben. You are a guy. What makes you think you can locate Bree's wedding dress out of the million shops in London?"

Ben looked at Gaby and clucked at her. "I'm gay. 'Nuff said, woman. When have I *ever* steered you wrong?" Ben gave Gaby a thorough long look up and down. It was no secret he picked out her clothes all the time, and that she always took his suggestions to heart. Ben was good with fashion and design. God, I loved them both so much.

"I like your earlier suggestion, Benny. Something vintage-inspired, simple—lace is pretty, and I want sleeves. They can be short, but no sleeveless gown for me." I gestured with my hands over my stomach. "Maybe a higher waistline would be best, in case I start to explode. A little splash of purple, maybe?"

Ben rolled his eyes. "You don't look up the duff at all, darling." He cocked his head curiously. "Will you have a bump by August the twenty-fourth?"

"I don't know and don't start, please. All the guests know I'm pregnant so it's not like we're trying to hide the fact. Trust me, I've heard all about it from my mother already. Like she thinks pretending we aren't having a baby will be more respectable somehow. Ugh, I loathe the drama she creates. Why can't she just be happy for me? She's going to have a grandchild, for Christ's sake!"

Gaby placed a hand on my shoulder. "Bump or no bump, you'll be beautiful, and your mom will just have to get over it. We'll wow her with such a gorgeous wedding and you such a lovely bride, she won't have a choice but to love the whole thing."

They were sweet for telling me so, but I didn't have high hopes about turning my mom around. She didn't want to hear about Ethan and our relationship. She had actually had the gall to tell me I was throwing my life away on Ethan and our baby. She asked what the last four years had been for if all I was going to do was get pregnant again. That hurt. She really thought so little of me. The first time was not my fault, and this time . . . well, I didn't intend to get pregnant. I know Ethan and I acted irresponsibly, but I wouldn't regret this outcome. I couldn't regret it. I touched my belly and rubbed over the area back and forth. Conceiving our baby had been done in love no matter what my mom said, or what I thought of myself. That much I knew was true. I loved Ethan and he loved me. There was no other choice I could make, whether my mom understood the concept or not; there was no other choice in this world for me.

"Thanks, you guys. Really . . . I don't know how I'd pull this together without you two in such a short time," I said with a sigh. "Even Elaina and Hannah are hard at work. I hope we can actually pull this off."

"As if we couldn't," Ben scoffed. "You'd have to hold me at gunpoint to keep me away from helping you with this posh, A-list celebrity, country-manor wedding *that Her Majesty has been invited to!*"

"Yeah, well, let's pray she doesn't come. Thank God for Elaina turning me on to that little wedding planner—Victoria something. I've been assured she will take care of anything having to do with queens and princes. I wouldn't know the first thing about the protocol involved with having royalty at one's wedding." I looked at Ben and Gaby and threw my hands up in the air and swallowed hard as the realization hit me. "I think I'm gonna be sick."

"Nope. No more sick, my darling girl," Ben said determinedly, hanging his long arm over my shoulders. "We're going to sit down for a nice lunch and get fortified first, then it's back to work finding the perfect dress for your posh country celebrity wedding. Which is happening in seven short weeks." Ben looked upward and crossed himself. "We can do this."

I couldn't resist texting Ethan over lunch. He seemed to enjoy our banter and usually replied if he wasn't in a meeting, and sometimes even when he was. Naughty texts too. I grinned as I typed: **I might hav to go naked 2 marry u. No dress luck yet. Havin lunch now ? ♥ U**

I didn't have long to wait before my phone vibrated. **No baby. U have it wrong. OK 2 B Naked for honeymoon ONLY! Dress essential 4 wedding. xx**

I laughed out loud and gained the unwanted attention of my friends. I tried to cover my mistake by delving into my salad. Didn't have a chance of working, though.

"Sexting again?" Ben asked with a smirk.

"Sorry. It happens spontaneously." I tilted my head and shrugged. "Blame the hormones?" It was worth a shot to use the hormones at least once in my defense.

"Gotcha, darling," Ben said with a grin, his nosy radar on full alert. I swear he could charm a nun out of her panties if he wanted to. Some scary shit, the way he figured things out.

"They just have to look at each other and the people in the room could spontaneously combust by merely watching them." Gaby's voice was laced with sarcasm again as she took a big swig of her wine.

I pouted that I couldn't join her in a glass, deciding it was okay to be insanely jealous of her right now. "Don't be a bitch, Gab, you're already pushing it by teasing me with wine. I can't help it if Ethan gets me to spontaneously combust."

Gaby laughed and refilled her glass of Chardonnay. "It's no surprise Ethan got you pregnant. I imagine it was hard for the two of you to take in enough food and drink to keep yourselves going in the early days. All you did was have at it like rabbits."

I gave her my best stone face. It lasted all of ten seconds before I started giggling. "It really, really was."

We were goofing around, being idiots when my phone went off. Mom? At this hour? She never called me at her mornings.

"Shit! It's my mom calling. Do you think she could sense me talking smack about her?" I decided to let it go to voice mail.

"The theme music from *Psycho* is the ringtone for your mother?" Gaby asked, her French fry stopped in midair.

I shrugged. "Ethan put it on there for me." Uncomfortable silence. "He's always playing around with apps and gadgets." The silence grew steadily louder. "I mean, if the shoe fits . . ." I valiantly tried to latch on to something light and amusing.

Benny saved me when he started laughing and it became contagious. Hell, if I had to put up with this sucky animosity from my mother, I might as well try to find the little humor there was to be had. Ben had met her and lived to talk about it. My mom tolerated him, but she loved Gabrielle, so I'm sure Gaby thought I was being a tad harsh. I wasn't. Ben could attest to the fact.

A minute later, my phone signaled a new voice mail, which was no surprise. My mom left voice mails all the time. She knew I screened her calls, and it just pissed her off more than she already was with me. I suddenly felt tired. It was exhausting keeping up this battle between us. I just wished for peace. It would kill me if I had such a tortured relationship with my daughter, or even my son down the road.

Sipping my lemonade, I ruminated for a bit, content to listen to Gaby and Ben chatter about different styles of veils and the pros and cons of white vs. cream for the knocked-up bride. Until the guilt started to creep in.

What did that say about how I was handling the situation? What if someday my daughter didn't want to talk to me? Couldn't stand to be around me? Thought I was a hypocritical bitch?

I'd be crushed.

I picked up my phone and hit voice mail.

"Brynne, I need to speak with you. It's—it's . . . an emergency. I'll try calling Ethan and see if I can reach him."

Cold fear washed over me instantly. If my mom was humbling herself to call Ethan, then it was something very bad indeed. *No! Don't let it be Daddy. Don't let it be him.* I wouldn't even go to that place in my head. I froze on the line. Her voice was *not* normal. She sounded like she was crying. My mother never cried.

My hand shook as I pressed her number on speed dial. I noticed that a text notification had just come through from Ethan, but I ignored it. And then Ben's phone lit up like a Christmas tree.

"What's wrong, Bree?" Gaby reached out to touch my arm.

"I don't know. My mom . . . said it's an emergency . . . she was crying—"

The walls started closing in fast, my heart beating so hard I could feel my body shaking. Ben answered his call. His eyes flashed to mine, and he spoke: "She's right here. Calling her mum now."

I knew Ben was talking to Ethan, and I knew it was

bad news. My head felt foggy as the call connected and I heard my mother's voice on the other end. Everything was moving so fast I couldn't do anything to stop it. I wanted to stop time. *Stop it. Please stop this . . . I don't want to know whatever she has to tell me.*

"Brynne? Sweetie, are you with anyone?" My mom never called me *sweetie* and she never sounded like she did right now.

"Mom! What's wrong? I'm with Ben and Gaby. We're shopping for my wedding dress . . ." I could hear my voice starting to break. "Why did you call Ethan?" The silence from my mother was like the blade of a knife sliding into my heart. I knew she wasn't silent because of my wedding dress comment. I wanted to believe it was the reason, but I knew better.

"Brynne . . . it's your father."

"What about Daddy? Is he . . . okay?" I could barely get the questions out. I looked back over at Benny and saw a look of sheer pain settle over his face. Then he started speaking softly into his own phone. He wouldn't look at me, just kept his eyes down. I knew what he was doing. Ben was talking to Ethan and telling him which restaurant we were in so he could come for me.

Noooooooooo! That meant something very bad had happened.

"Brynne, sweetheart, your dad—he drowned in his swimming pool—the maintenance service found him—"

My ears heard the words but my brain rebelled. I couldn't accept it. I wouldn't. "No!" I cut her off.

"Brynne . . . it's true. I wish it wasn't . . . but it's true."

"But he can't—Mom. He can't be . . . no! No, don't say that to me! Mom . . . Mom?"

"Sweetheart, he'd been in the water long time. It was probably a heart attack."

"N-n-no . . . " I whimpered. "It can't be true. Daddy's coming to London to visit me. He's coming for my wedding . . . he's giving me away. He said so. He told me he would be here . . ."

"Brynne . . . he's gone, sweetheart. I'm so sorry." She was crying. My mother was sobbing into the phone to me, and I was struck with the idea that I'd never seen or heard her cry before now.

I dropped my phone and it landed in my soup bowl with a big splash that sprayed across the front of me. I just stared and left it lying at the bottom of my chicken tortilla soup. Ethan would have to get me a new one. That phone was dust now. I'd never touch it again.

I ended up on my feet somehow, but I didn't have anywhere to go. There was nowhere good to go to—I was trapped.

So I started to float like I had that other time. Only I realized what was happening to me this time around. I welcomed the sensation. Lightness feels good when your heart is so heavy it wants to drag you down into the pits of hell. Yeah, being out of my body felt much better.

I floated higher until I could look down at myself. I saw Ben bracing me on his lap. He sat on the floor of the restaurant holding me. Gaby was beside him talking into a phone at someone. The waiter rushed over to assist.

But it was all so stupid.

Why were we all on the floor of a posh London restaurant when we should have been eating our lunches? We had to get out of there. I had a dress to find and a wedding to plan. My dad was coming to give me away at the ceremony in just seven weeks. The Queen of England had received an invitation, for Christ's sake. We didn't have time to fuck around like this!

Eventually I figured it out. The lightness that felt so nice went away and the weight of pain and grief returned to take its place.

I didn't want to come back down to Earth. I wanted to stay right where I was.

That's not true. I wanted to keep floating upward until I dissolved. That sounded really nice to me. Dissolving . . .

I felt nothing but enraged hatred for the ceiling. That goddamn motherfucking ceiling was keeping me from floating away.

Let me go! Let me float away . . .

16

♠

I sat up and looked over at Brynne. She slept. In a comfortable guest bed, in her father's modern house, in a very nice suburb of San Francisco, my girl slept. She was crushed inside her heart, but for now she rested. She was unburdened from the grief for the moment.

I couldn't let her out of my sight for more than a few hours, so leaving London and going to the States for her father's funeral without me was out of the question. What if they tried to take her on American soil? No, I couldn't risk the possibility. This was a day-by-day, hour-by-hour operation. Keeping Brynne safe was my greatest priority now, Olympics be damned. Neil was back in London stepping in for me, and between him and Frances, they'd keep the business machine running. I wasn't troubled at all about my job. No, my worries were much, much bigger and vastly more terrifying.

I hoped to shed some light on what had happened to Tom on this trip but didn't hold out much hope. Either way, I wasn't going down without a fight. They could try to get at her, but they'd have to go through me first.

Mrs. Exley had wanted us to stay with her in the home she shared with her husband, the nontalkative Frank, but Brynne wouldn't hear of it.

She said she wanted to be in her father's home, with his things, in the place where she'd last seen him talking to us on Skype. She felt grateful that the last time they'd spoken had been a happy time. She kept saying that to me. "Daddy was happy about us. He knew everything and he was happy."

"Yes he was, baby . . ." I whispered over her sleeping form. My sleeping beauty in the night with her long hair tangled in the pillows, the blanket pulled up to her throat like she was seeking comfort from the weight of the fabric against her body. She was still suffering from shock and barely eating. I feared for her health and that of our baby's. I was scared that this would change us. Change her feelings for me. Push her into an emotional tailspin.

I was well aware of her past, and that knowledge bore down impossibly heavy on me now. My girl suffered from depression. She'd even tried to kill herself at one very low and tragic point in her life. There, I said it. Didn't do me a fuck's worth of good to acknowledge it either. Yes, it was a long time ago, and she was very together and sensible now . . . but there was no guarantee she wouldn't revert back to those self-destructive behaviors again, or tell me to sod off and leave my sorry arse for good when it all became too much to deal with.

I sucked in a breath and looked over toward the

mirrored closet doors to see my reflection. Who in the motherfucking hell was I kidding? Brynne wasn't alone. Depression was a harsh mistress, and she and I had been well acquainted for quite some time now.

I resisted the urge to touch her. She needed rest and I needed a cigarette. I checked the bedside table for the time and got up carefully. I threw on some joggers and a shirt, heading outside to sit beside the pool and serve my nicotine habit. I wanted to ring Neil too.

I stared at the dark water while I waited for my call to connect. The same dark water where Tom Bennett had spent his final moments in this life.

I left the door cracked so I could hear if Brynne needed me. She'd started having nightmares again, and because she was pregnant, drugs were not a good option. There was too much risk to the baby's development. She would have refused to take them anyway. So she suffered. And I worried.

The summer moon reflected in the water's surface, and I thought about Tom dying in it. I was no homicide detective, but some scenarios were certainly running through my head. Bringing myself to voice them aloud was out of the question. If I did that, then I was damning my girl to a similar fate. I wasn't going there. No fucking way.

"Hey mate."

"Holding down the fort okay?" I replied to Neil's brusque greeting.

"Things are typically chaotic here, so you have nothing to worry over. It's business as usual, E."

"True. And I trust you too. Tell those arseholes I said that, please."

"With pleasure, boss, but you should know that every client has been very understanding. Most of them are human."

I sucked in a deep lungful of clove and held it to get maximum burn. Neil just waited for me patiently. Nothing ever seemed to rush him. Coolest bloke I've ever known. "Events like these bring out one's priorities rather quickly, you know?"

"Yeah. I bet they do. How is Brynne holding up?"

"She's . . . doing her best to be strong, but she's struggling. I haven't broached the possibilities with her yet, and I'm not sure we'll ever have that conversation. Looks like it was a massive heart attack while swimming, which it very well could have been, but I want to see the autopsy report." I sighed. "You know how long those can take. The forensics labs are just as fucked up in the States as they are at home."

"Any clues present themselves at his house?"

"Not yet. Being a solicitor for probate, wills and trusts and such, everything was in order as you would imagine, but there's something just a little too tidy about it. Like maybe he knew his time was marked. And it very well could have been his heart. Brynne knew he took blood-pressure medication and she worried about him. You'd never know to look at him. The guy was very fit."

"Hmmmm. The only people who would benefited from his death are Senator Oakley's camp."

"I know. I hate to know it, but I do. Everything goes to Brynne—the house, the cars, the investments. No surprise there, but I'm wondering if Tom left anything incriminating against Oakley."

"Like a videotaped deposition?"

"Yeah . . . exactly like that. May know tomorrow. We have a meeting with his business partner in the morning to go over the trust, then the funeral and service. It's gonna be a long fucking day."

"When are you coming home?"

"If we can wrap everything up, the red-eye tomorrow night. I want Brynne out of here. Makes me fucking nervous. I'm out of my element."

"Right. Give her our condolences, please. Ring if you need me. I'm here."

"Thanks . . . see you in twenty-four."

I ended the call and lit a second clove, the smoke curling slowing up into the still night air. I smoked and thought, my mind going back to a place I'd not been to for a long time. It terrified me, and with good reason.

Drowning is a horrific way to go out. Well, it is if you're conscious. This was something I knew from experience. The cold and desperate feeling as water invades your nose and mouth. The impossible attempt to stay calm and hold your dwindling breath. The pain of lungs utterly depleted of oxygen.

I think the Afghans experimented on me to see what all the fuss was about with waterboarding. It wasn't their preferred method, that's for sure. Winching me up by the arms and shredding my back was their favorite. That and depriving me of sleep for what seemed like weeks at a time. The mind does crazy shit when there is no rest for the cogs.

I looked up at the stars and thought of her. My mum.

She was an angel up there somewhere. I knew this. Spirituality is deeply personal and I needed no other confirmation of what I believed other than what I knew to be real inside my heart. She was up there watching over me somehow and was with me when they were going to cut off my—

Nope. Not going to that fucked-up horror right now. Later . . .

I got up quickly and stubbed out my second ciggie. I tucked the butts back in the pack and went inside my father-in-law's nice American modern house. I'd never speak to him again, but ironically, one of the most important conversations I'd ever had, when weighed against all the others in the whole of my life, had been with him. An email with a plea for my help . . . and a photograph.

As I went back in to crawl into bed with Brynne, I prayed. I did. I prayed that Tom Bennett had been unconscious when he left this world.

In a black Chanel suit with her hair pinned up, Brynne looked gorgeous. Terribly sad, but tragically beautiful. Her mother had brought the clothes over for her to wear. They were the same size, apparently, and Brynne was pretty much helpless against arguments at this point. I sensed she was merely coping to get through and hadn't really allowed herself the freedom of indulging in her grief yet.

I stayed on the fringe and kept out of discussions as much as possible. Brynne was in no shape to bear a family row, and so I held my tongue to keep the peace. Mrs.

Exely and I had a wary truce—we pretty much avoided direct contact. I never heard her ask Brynne about how she was feeling with the pregnancy once. Not one time. It was almost like she pretended it wasn't happening. What mother didn't care about her daughter being pregnant enough to even ask her about it?

I wished for this to end swiftly so I could get my girl out of here. I wanted her back on British soil. The flight home tonight couldn't come soon enough for me.

The funeral had gone off well, if a death suffered too soon could be memorialized in a good way, that is. I wanted it to be an unfortunate consequence of life, not murder. Brynne had not asked me. I don't think the idea occurred to her, and for that I was grateful.

I knew him the instant he walked into the gathering after the graveside service. I'd seen enough photos of the slimy prick to know him on sight. Bollocks must be the size of grapefruits for him to stroll in here looking entitled, as he most definitely did. He came right over and put his hands on Brynne, hugging her, and offering his fake sympathies for her terrible loss. I think she was too sad to react much to his presence. Her mum stood alongside and engaged him with demonstrative affection, which angered me. How could she do that to Brynne? This man's son had raped her child, made a public video of it, and she called him a friend? Blah, blah, bullshit. I locked eyes with Oakley and made sure my handshake was delivered overly hard.

Yeah, that's right, Senator, we're just getting acquainted. You'll meet my dick in a bit. It's huge.

I had to step away and pull myself together. I kissed my girl on the forehead and told her I'd be back shortly. The senator and I had a date.

I tracked him around and pegged his security detail immediately. I mean, we're all recognizable in the trade. All I would do was talk to the senator. Harmless, right?

When Oakley left for a piss I made sure I was a bit delayed behind him. Perfect timing. Security goon was busy filling his plate with food. The men's room had a lock, which was an added bonus. My luck seemed to have no bounds today.

I was leaned up against the wash counter when he came out of the stall adjusting his belt.

"We are alone and the door is locked, Oakley."

He stopped dead flat and assessed the situation. The senator seemed to have been blessed with some modicum of intelligence, I'll give him that. He did not panic.

"Are you threatening me, Blackstone?" he kept his voice level.

"You remember my name. Very good. And I really couldn't say . . . yet." I shrugged. "Why don't you tell me, *Senator*?"

"I'm here to honor the life of a friend of many years, that's all." He went forward to the sink and turned on the water.

"Ahh, that's what you call it. I'd say it was more of a campaign stop, wouldn't you?"

"Tom Bennett's death was a tragic shock to me, and to everyone. Brynne is a very sweet girl. She always has been. The loss of her father must be a terrible burden for her to bear. I know how much Tom loved her. She was his world."

I just stared at him, quite impressed with his dramatic dialogue. He must be in training for all the political speeches he had in his future.

"Congratulations on your upcoming nuptials and forthcoming child," he said as he washed his hands at the sink.

"So you've read the announcement already." I tilted my head in a bow and planted myself in front of the door. This motherfucker wasn't leaving until I was ready for him to go. "This is how it works, Senator. You listen, I talk."

He pulled down a hand towel and methodically began to dry his hands.

"I know everything. Montrose is dead. Fielding went missing in late May. I'll bet he's dead too and will remain missing. I know you had your son stop-lossed by the U.S. army. I can connect the dots. Everyone is disappearing. When the autopsy report is filed on Tom, I *will* read it. Wonder what it'll say?" I shrugged dramatically.

"It's not coming from me, Blackstone." His light-brown eyes bored into me. "Not me."

I stepped a little closer. "That's good to know, Oakley. Make sure it is true. I have taped depositions, documents, records . . . everything. Tom Bennett did too." Couldn't know for sure on that one, but it sounded good. "And if you think you can take me down to get to Brynne, you'll unleash a political shitstorm that will make Watergate look like an episode of *The People's Court*." I took another step forward. "My people know what to do if I disappear."

I whispered. "They pop the party balloon and it all goes . . . *poof*." I flicked my fingers out for emphasis.

He swallowed imperceptibly, but I caught it. "What do you want from me?"

I shook my head. "It's not what I want, Oakley. It's all about what *you* want." I gave him a moment to absorb. "*You* want to run for your vice-presidential office and sleep in your comfortable bed at night as opposed to a prison cell with a roommate who wants to get to *know* you better." I cracked a small grin. "*You* want to do everything in your power to make absolutely certain that Brynne Bennett, soon to be Blackstone, leads a charmed and very peaceful life with her husband and child in England, with no threats or worries about anything that went on in the past." I spoke my words more harshly. "A shameful event of which she was the victim. Of. A. Heinous. Crime."

He'd started to sweat. I could see the sheen breaking out at his temples.

"*You* want to make sure of it, Oakley. Do you understand me?"

He didn't move his face, but his eyes agreed. I know the look, and he said *yes* to me with his eyes.

"Good. I'm glad you understand because this is the only warning you'll get. If anything happens to either one of us . . . well . . . it all explodes. I'm talking British Parliament, the *Washington Post*, the *London Times*, Scotland Yard, M6, U.S. congressional inquiries, the whole enchilada, as you might say." I tilted my head and shook it slowly. "And with the Olympics in London, and all that goodwill between the U.S. and Britain?" I held my palms up. "There'll be no hole deep enough for you to hide in." I wafted one hand for emphasis. "Think . . . Saddam Hussein . . . if you will." I moved to unlock the door. "I'm sure I don't need to remind you about shit running downhill either." I went to leave the men's room and turned back one last time. "Best of luck to you in the upcoming election. I wish for you a long and successful career, *Senator*. Cheers."

Oakley's security ape pushed past me and entered the bathroom, looking a tad confused after overhearing my friendly departing comment.

I gave him a nod and went out to find Brynne. The love of my life, the mother of our unborn child, my sweet girl, had been out of my sight for too long, and I needed to get back to her side.

17

♥

I was relieved when Ethan returned to me from wherever he'd been. I needed him, and everything seemed easier to bear when he was near. It made me very weak, which I despised in myself, but I couldn't help it, and was too exhausted to care. He was the only lifeline I had here. I wanted to go back home. London—home.

He had two plates of food with him when he walked up.

"I brought you a little bit of everything," he said.

"Oh, thanks . . . but I'm not hungry at all. I can't eat that." I looked at the fruit and the croissant sandwich.

He frowned and set his jaw. I knew I was in for an argument. "You have to eat something. What've you had today besides a little tea?" He whispered. "Think of the baby . . ."

"You can't force someone to eat. Trust me, I know from experience."

My mother's disdainful voice broke into our exchange. No sentiment of "Ethan's right, Brynne, you need to eat because your baby needs food even if you don't feel hungry."

No "You're eating for two now, dear" comment. Yeah . . . what did I expect?

I saw Ethan's head turn and peg my mom. I think there was a little smoke rising from his ears too, but he didn't lose it as I thought he could have. He just turned glacial and ignored her.

"Come sit with me and have a little something," he said to me with a gentle voice paired with some serious intent to see it through.

How could I turn him down? I never could. What he did, he did out of concern for me. I *did* need to eat, even though my appetite was nonexistent. Ethan was right. I had someone else to consider besides myself. Especially now.

I looked at my mom and roamed my eyes over her perfectly coiffed and dressed presentation today for her ex-husband's funeral. Why in the hell had she even come to the service? She'd barely spoken to Daddy after I moved away to London. She certainly couldn't have any true grief for him. Could she? I had absolutely no idea. It saddened me to realize that I couldn't tell because I didn't know her well enough to tell. My mother and I weren't close like that. We didn't share deep feelings or secrets. I never knew why she suddenly divorced my dad, or if she'd ever even loved him. I didn't know why they ever got married in the first place. How had they met? Where had he proposed? Stories of them dating? I had nothing.

I turned away and went with Ethan to a table, my heart closing off from her a little more with every step I took.

"You are so very beautiful," Ethan said softly as I tried

valiantly to ingest some of the food he'd gotten for me, "on the inside as much as the outside."

I tried to swallow the honeydew melon that must surely be a hunk of wet sawdust from the way it tasted on my tongue, and told him, "I want to go home."

"I know you do, baby. I want to take you home. There's not much left to worry over now. Since your dad had everything in a trust . . . we can come back in a few months and see to things then. Mr. Murdock said it's best to wait a bit anyway . . . you don't want to make decisions about something so personal right at first." He put his hand over mine.

Yes. Pete Murdock was Daddy's business partner in his law firm. Or . . . he had been. Living trust was the way to go, Dad always said. I now controlled a house in Sausalito, all my dad's money and investments; everything of material possession he had acquired in his fifty-one years now belonged to me.

I didn't want any of it. I just wanted my dad back.

A friendly voice interrupted my thoughts. "Brynne . . . oh, honey, here you are."

I turned to find Jessica with her arms open. I went into them and hugged my friend tightly. Jess and I went back to elementary school. First grade, Mrs. Flagler's class. Nearly inseparable all the way up till our senior year of high school, Thanksgiving break, to be exact.

Yes, Jessica had been with me the night *it* happened. She had been a true friend in my time of need, but I had been too sick for friendships after the event. I'd needed to go away. A necessary component to my recovery process. We'd kept in touch over the years since I'd been in London, but hadn't seen each other in more than four years. She still looked tanned and athletic, her blond pixie haircut the perfect complement to her petite shape. I was touched she showed up here today to pay her respects to my father.

"I'm so sorry, Brynne. Your dad—he was just the sweetest man—I enjoyed our conversations every time we saw each other at the gym. He loved to talk about you."

"Oh, Jess . . ." I felt my eyes go wet and the emotions come pouring out. "Thank you for coming—it means a great deal to me to see you here. He really liked you too. Thought you were very sweet." We hugged again and I really looked at her. "It's so good to see you again." I turned to Ethan. "Jess, this is Ethan Blackstone, my fiancé." I held up my hand and showed my engagement ring. "Ethan, meet Jessica Vettner, my friend since the first grade."

"It's a pleasure, Jessica," Ethan told her as they shook hands. I wondered if he remembered that Jess was the one I went to the party with on that ill-fated night of my life. If he did remember, he didn't show any signs of it. Ethan was smooth as silk in these situations.

Jessica turned to her companion then and made introductions. Another face from my past. Karl Westman stood beside Jess. Wow . . . so many emotions there. I needed a moment to take it all in, I was so overwhelmed. Seeing Lance Oakley's father earlier had been crazy enough. I had been in such a fog, though, I barely registered whatever it was he'd said to me. My mom had spent more time talking to the senator than I had. Now Karl was here too?

"Brynne, I'm so sorry for your loss," Karl said and moved in to hug me.

"Hi, Karl. It's been a long time." It felt awkward, but I know it had to be for him as well. We had a small past together, but it wasn't really that which made my broken heart feel like it was being squeezed from the inside out. It was that all four of us standing here together knew about *it*. They had either seen the video of me or they had knowledge of its existence.

I really wanted to go home more than ever now. "Thanks for coming today. It was very kind of you."

"My pleasure." Karl ended the hug and I searched his dark eyes. I didn't see anything hurtful in them. Just some kindness and maybe a bit of curiosity. That had to be normal, right? We'd met at a track meet the season we were juniors, and then ran into each other at the beginning of my senior year. We'd gone out on dates that ended as all my dates had back in those days—covert sex in some private location. I'd liked him a lot. Karl was a cute boy then, and a handsome man now. We both shared a love of Hendrix and had had many discussions about his music. Jess was absolutely right about Karl still being "hawt" in her message on Facebook. He had always treated me well. *Not a bit like Lance Oakley had treated me.*

Lance had been away at college, and I had been young and stupid. *A long lifetime ago. Another world ago.* Did Karl know he was the reason Lance became angry enough to drug me, and then film his buddies using me on a pool table? If I'd never gone out with Karl, maybe Lance and his friends wouldn't have made the video of me at the party that night. The scenarios were endless. Woulda, coulda, shoulda . . . Yeah, did me absolutely no good to go there.

"I heard about it from Jess, of course," he said, reaching an arm around her shoulders in a familiar affectionate gesture, "and I wanted to pay my respects in person." Jessica looked up at him with stars in her eyes. It didn't take a genius to see that my old friend had fallen hard for Karl Westman. He seemed very into her as well. I sincerely hoped it worked out for the two of them. They made a great couple.

I forced a smile and did the best acting performance of my life. "I'm so happy to see you both. It's been far too long."

Ethan drew me against his side as we made small talk with the two of them. It was a possessive move on his part, and one I was well familiar with by now. He rubbed his hand slowly up and down my arm as he gave Jess and Karl his full attention. Especially when Karl told us how his company was sending him to the Olympics for a research trip and that we should get together while he was in London. *Um . . . probably not going to happen, Karl.*

Ethan made sure to mention our upcoming wedding, and the date, while linking his hand with mine, bringing it curled to his lips, and kissing the back of it. Same effect as a dog pissing on a lamppost, really, just done very elegantly, with me being the metaphorical lamppost. Ethan managed to get away with such behavior, and make it look gallant. He always had.

And again, I wondered if he'd identified my "past" with Karl. I swear he was capable of figuring it out. Ethan's Spidey sense was ultra-keen when it came to other men and me. Remembering his blowup when I'd met Paul Langley on the street in front of the coffeehouse, I recognized Ethan's vivid jealous streak in regard to my past relationships with other men. I definitely had a past, that's true. There had been more than a few men, and he had to acknowledge that fact. Nothing I could do would change anything. But Ethan had a past too, and acceptance of what couldn't be altered was part of learning to trust in a relationship. We both had to let go of some things. I wasn't going to avoid speaking to people like Paul and Karl just because Ethan was insanely jealous of any man who had been with me before him. I was not with those others now, I was with him.

I shrugged it off as best I could. Didn't matter. The past was just that: in the past . . . finished . . . over and done with. Even though I was aching inside, and desperately low from losing my dad, I still understood what was most important. My eyes were opened clearly from this experience, and they would stay that way. Loss of a loved one will shift your priorities in an instant, I had learned.

My father was gone, but my mind was intact.

I knew what mattered, and what didn't. The person holding me against his strong body in protection with loving care, and, the tiny person growing inside me were my whole world now.

Having Brynne sleeping against me on the flight home to London made me feel the best I had in days. She was ut-

terly spent and so exhausted she'd nodded off almost immediately after taking our seats. I didn't blame her either.
The send-off from her mum had been . . . painful, for lack
of a better description. I was exhausted from the experience myself. God, I really did not like that bloody woman
even a miniscule bit. I was headed for absolute fucking
my-worst-nightmare mother-in-law hell. And there was
not a thing in the world I could do about it. My sweet girl
had a gorgon for a mother. She was very beautiful in a
designer-chic way, just as I had imagined she would be,
but a hideous gorgon all the same. I envisioned Tom Bennett was now receiving his saintly wings for putting up
with her for as long as he had. I suppressed a shudder.

Mummy dearest had tried to get Brynne to extend her
trip and let me go on home alone. I ground my teeth together in remembrance. As if I would ever allow such a
thing! She would have tried to influence her to terminate
or get her to move back to the U.S. probably.

In the end, Brynne hardly reacted to her mother at all.
She just turned away and said she was going back home
to London to marry me and have our baby. I don't believe
I was ever more proud of anyone as I was of my girl when
she said those words and looked to me.

Brynne opened her eyes and I caught that moment of
innocence, the waking up blissfully unaware of all the bad
things that have been happening in your life . . . like losing
a beloved parent. It only lasts for a fraction of time, anyway. I know from lots of experience.

Her eyes were bright at first, and then they shuttered,
showing the pain of her reality, before closing off to shield

herself from the painful thoughts so she could get through the rest of this very public journey. First class was better than coach, but we were still in a cabin with strangers around us and nowhere near private. Brynne was holding it together so far. She'd not broken down yet, and I have to say it worried me more than a little, but there was nothing I could do. I couldn't grieve for her. She would have to do it in her own way, and in her own time.

The flight attendant came by to take our orders for dinner. Salmon or chicken parmesan topped the menu tonight. I looked over at Brynne and got a tiny head shake and a sad face. I ignored it and told the attendant we'd both take the salmon, remembering how much she enjoyed it for dinner that night with Dad and Marie.

"You have to eat something, baby."

She nodded and her eyes got wet. "What—w-what am I going to do now?"

I picked up her hand and pressed it to my heart. "You're going to be back in our home and take some time to rest and do whatever makes you feel better. You'll go see Dr. Roswell and talk to her. You're going to work on your research for the university when you feel up to it. You'll plan the wedding with the girls and Ben. We'll go see Dr. Burnsley for the second appointment and find out how green-olive is doing. You're going to let me take care of you and go forward with your life. With *our* life."

She listened to every word. She soaked each one up, actually, and I was glad to give her something I think she really needed to hear. Sometimes having another person tell you that everything will be okay is all you really need to get you through the toughest part. I know Brynne needed to hear it, as much as I needed to say it.

"And I will be right with you every step of the way." I brought her hand up to my lips. "Promise."

"How do you know about green-olive?" She actually smiled a little.

"I put Bump dot com in my favorites and check it religiously, just like you suggested. We have a green-olive this week, and next week we get a prune." I winked.

"I love you," she whispered very softly, and ran her hand through her hair.

"I love you too, my beauty. So very, very much."

The attendant arrived with the hot towels and drink service. I got the wine, and Brynne got cranberry juice on ice. I waited until she took a sip. I didn't want to have to force-feed her, but would resort to persuasion tactics if I had to.

To my surprise and relief she seemed to enjoy the cranberry juice.

"This tastes really, really nice." Another sip. "I'm picking up your words."

"I can assure you that you still sound like my American girl, baby."

"I know that, I mean I'm picking up the words you say, like saying 'this tastes nice' instead of saying it 'tastes good.' It's rubbing off from being around you so much," she said.

"Well, since you're never getting rid of me, then I guess that means I'll have you speaking like a native in no time."

"Well, you can certainly try." She sipped some more juice and looked a bit brighter.

"By the time green-olive is born, you'll be unrecognizable as a Yank, I'm sure."

Her face lit up. "I just realized something kinda cool."

"What's that?" I asked, intrigued but happy to see her more animated than she'd been in many days.

"Green-olive will call me Mummy instead of Mommy or Mom." She wrinkled her nose a little. "Seems a little weird . . . but I suppose I'll get used to it . . . and I like the way it sounds."

I couldn't help laughing. "You'll be the best mum green-olive has ever known."

She smiled at me briefly, but then it went away just as fast as it had appeared. "Not like mine, that's for sure." The hurt and anguish rang out loud and clear in her words.

"I'm sorry for bringing it up." I shook my head, not wanting to badmouth her mother, but finding it *very* hard not to.

"You mean bringing *her* up."

"That too," I countered. I really didn't want to get into the complexities of Brynne's relationship with her mum, but if that's what she wanted to discuss, then I could surely give my opinion. I just hoped I didn't have to.

She saved me by asking a different question. "What about your mother, Ethan?"

"Well, I barely remember her. All I have now are the memories suggested by the photographs mostly. I think I can remember things about her, but I'm probably just imagining those experiences because of the subject of the photos and the stories Dad and Hannah have shared with me."

"You said you got the wings tattooed on your back because of your mom."

No, I don't want to do this right now.

I almost sighed, but I just managed to hold it in. I knew better than to shut her out in this moment. Brynne had asked me about the tattoo before, and I know she wanted me to share with her now, but I just didn't feel ready for that yet. Not here on a public flight under tragic circumstances. This wasn't the right time, nor the right place, for me to let out those emotions.

The salmon showed up just then and reprieved me.

Brynne continued to sip her juice and avoided the food, which wasn't bad at all for airline fare.

"Here." I offered a forkful of fish, deciding if she wasn't going to eat on her own, then I would feed it to her myself.

She eyeballed the bite carefully before opening her mouth to accept it. She chewed slowly and deliberately. "The salmon is nice, but I want to know why the wings remind you of your mom."

So that's how this game would be played, huh? Emotional blackmail in exchange for eating a meal . . . I offered another bite of fish to her.

She kept her lips pursed together. "Why that tattoo, Ethan?"

I took a deep breath. "They're angel's wings and since I think of her as such, it was very fitting to have the wings across my back."

"That's a beautiful idea." She smiled.

I offered a fresh bit of salmon, which she accepted with no argument this time.

"What was your mother's name?"

"Laurel."

"It's pretty. Laurel. Laurel Blackstone . . ." she repeated.

"I think so," I told her.

"If green-olive is a girl, I think we have a perfect name for her, don't you?"

I felt my throat move as I swallowed hard. And it wasn't from eating the salmon. Her suggestion meant something to me—something deep and very personal.

"You would do that?"

"I really do love the name Laurel, and if you want it, then . . . yes, of course," she answered, her eyes a little brighter than before.

I was stunned, utterly humbled by her generosity and willingness to give to me such a beautiful gift, especially in a time of such horrible grief for herself. "I would love to name our girl Laurel after my mum," I said truthfully, before holding up a small piece of bread torn from a roll.

She took the bit of bread and chewed it slowly, never taking her eyes off mine. "Good, that's settled then," she said softly, her voice wistful and sounding rather far away.

I imagined what she might be thinking about, so I went for it. "And if our green-olive is a boy?"

"Yes, yes, yes." She started to cry. "I want to . . . name him Thom-m-mas," she managed, before breaking down right over the Atlantic Ocean, in a first-class cabin, on British Air flight 284, the red-eye, San Francisco to London Heathrow.

I pulled her to me and kissed the top of her head. I held Brynne and let her do what she finally needed to do. She was quiet about it and nobody even paid any attention to us, but still it hurt me to have to witness her going through this next step in a very normal process.

The flight attendant, wearing a badge with the name Dorothy and a soft Irish burr, clued in, though, and rushed right over to offer assistance. I asked her to take away the dinner and bring us an extra blanket. Dorothy seemed to understand that Brynne was grieving, and worked quickly to get the food removed, the lights turned out and a blanket for us to cover up. She took extra care of us for the remainder of the flight, and I made sure to thank her sincerely for her kindness when we disembarked several hours later.

For the rest of that flight, I held my girl against me until she'd exhausted her tears and fell into sleep. I slept too, but on and off. My mind was moving all over the place. I had worries galore and could only hope and pray that calling Oakley's bluff at the funeral service would work. I was prepared to do everything I'd promised if anyone made a move on Brynne. I knew how heavily guarded she would be from here on out.

I didn't know who was responsible for Montrose's and Fielding's deaths. I didn't know if Tom Bennett had been part of that mess and was murdered. I didn't know who sent the lunatic text message to Brynne's old mobile or who called in the bomb threat the night we were at the Mallerton Gala. I didn't know a lot of shit that I really needed some answers to.

I had fear inside of me.

Batshit, crazy-as-fuck, have-me-committed, I'm-petrified-out-of-my-bloody-skull, fear.

18

♥

"I slept for about three days straight once we got back to London. I needed it, and returning to my familiar surroundings did help a great deal," I told Dr. Roswell. "I'm starting the research project the university approved for me, and have good friends around me helping to plan this wedding."

"How are the night terrors now that you are off the medication?" she asked.

"It's inconsistent. I started having them again after I stopped the pills, but now that this stuff—now that my dad has died—they've stopped again. Do you think it's because my mind is now full of something worse to take the place of what I dreamed before?"

Dr. Roswell looked at me carefully and asked, "Is the death of your father worse than what happened to you when you were seventeen?"

Whoa. Heavy question, that. And one I had never pondered before. My first urge was to say that of course, the death of my father was worse, but, if I was honest with myself, I don't think it was. I was an adult now and could see things with more experience than when I was a teenager, but I had tried to kill myself over the rape video. I had no thoughts even in the same realm as that now. I wanted to live. I needed to live my life with Ethan, and especially to take care of our baby. There were no other options. As I sat there in Dr. Roswell's office, everything sort of illuminated for me all in an instant. Finally seeing the light helped me realize that I would be okay. I would get through this, and the joy would return for me—in time.

I shook my head and answered my therapist truthfully. "No. It's not worse."

She wrote that down with that turquoise fountain pen I thought was so beautiful.

"Thank you for helping me to see everything with clarity for what I think is the first time," I told her.

"Can you explain what you mean by that, Brynne?"

"I think so." I took a huge breath and gave it my best shot. "I know my dad loved me and I know he knew how much I loved him back. We had the kind of relationship where we shared our feelings all the time, so there are no regrets there. I'm heartbroken our time was cut short, but there is nothing to be done about that. It's just life. Look at Ethan, who lost his mother at the age of four. They basically had no time together and he barely remembers her. I got my wonderful loving father for almost twenty-five years."

Dr. Roswell gave me a beaming smile. "It makes me so happy to hear you talk like this. You've cracked the secret code, I'm afraid. Pretty soon I won't have any excuses to keep sending you a bill for my services."

"Um . . . no, that won't be happening, Dr. Roswell. You will be stuck with me for years yet. Just imagine all those mommy guilt trips I'll be taking soon."

She laughed in her gentle way. "I look forward to those chats very much." She closed her notebook and capped her fountain pen. "So tell me about these wedding plans. I want to hear every detail . . ."

Facebook was quite a nice tool for planning a wedding, I had discovered. Elaina had suggested it to me because she was deep into planning her own and knew what she was talking about. I sat down with my Cranberry Zinger tea and logged into my account.

I'd set up a private group for sharing photos and business links that consisted of me and my small army of foot soldiers: Gaby, Ben, Hannah, Elaina, Marie and Victoria, the official wedding planner, who actually made her living at what had to be a *very* challenging job, in my opinion. Things were coming together amazingly smoothly for what was now an impossible deadline of only five weeks. Considering I was hormonal and pregnant, and coming off a devastating personal loss, I decided I was doing pretty damn well for myself.

Ethan had been so crushed at his job we barely saw each other, and the majority of our conversations were via text message. I know he worried about me and tried to give me as much of his attention as he could, but there just wasn't any time to spare. I understood the pressure he was under, and I mostly needed time to come to terms with everything that had happened in the last weeks anyway. He came home very late, and pretty much wanted only two things once he got there. To make love, and to have me within reach while he slept. Ethan's need for physical contact was still as strong as ever. I did not mind a bit. I needed it just as much as he did, I think. We both worried about each other.

I shot off a quick message to Elaina about the pictures of floral arrangements she'd posted and joked that we talked to each other more on Facebook than we did in person. Stupid, really, especially when she lived in the same building as I did. Elaina and Neil were just as totally swamped with their jobs at Blackstone Security International as Ethan was. Nobody had much time to spare.

I left there and checked my main profile to find some new messages had been left for me. There were some donation notifications from the Meritus College Fund in San Francisco that my dad had supported for years. It was a nice charity pledged to assist disadvantaged but motivated kids to get a university education. I knew he would have wanted it, so I had announced that in lieu of flowers, donations could be sent directly to Meritus instead. The fund kindly sent me a notice whenever someone left a gift in my dad's name. Paul Langley had left a gift, as had the staff at the Rothvale Gallery, and Gaby's father, Rob Hargreave. Their thoughtfulness touched me deeply, and I told them so in my personal thank-you messages back to them.

I posted a nice photo on my Facebook profile of my dad holding me when I was a baby. I had been busy scanning pictures from the photo albums I'd taken from his house and brought home with me. In this particular one, we were both dressed in what looked like pajamas, so it was probably a morning shot. Daddy had me sitting in front of him on his desk, facing the camera, big grins on both our faces. I wondered who had taken it. My mom? Daddy was so young in the photo . . . and looked really happy. At least I had precious memories like these to hold close to my heart.

I got sad when I realized there would be no grandpa pictures of him and my baby. Not now . . . The familiar pang hit me in the chest and I had to close my eyes for a moment and just breathe.

The pain you get when you have to remind your brain that you will never see them, hug them, laugh with them, or talk to them again . . .

Sucks.

Jonathan will have grandpa pictures, though. Yes, he would. I knew that Ethan's dad would be a hands-on grandparent. It made me glad just thinking about Jonathan and Marie babysitting for us. I had my aunt to be "grandma" to my baby even if my own mother showed no interest. Ugh. Change of topic please.

A new message popped up with the little blip sound and a message box.

Karl Westman: Hi there. I just logged in and saw your green dot. I've made it to London for the Games and hope we can reconnect while I'm in town. Just got in yesterday morning, actually. Still recovering from jet lag. :/ How are you?

Karl . . . He'd found me on Facebook shortly after the funeral and we'd chatted a tiny bit since then. I remembered he said his company was sending him for the Games, and Jess had reminded me too. She was disappointed, really, that she wasn't able to come with him, as she was a huge sports fan. The Olympics were her thing far more than they were mine. Still, having the Games of the XXX Olympiad in your home city is exciting stuff, no matter how you look at it.

Brynne Bennett: Things are better . . . thanks. Where are you staying in London?

Karl Westman: In Chelsea, of course! I'm not going to miss getting in my history of Jimi while I'm here.

Brynne Bennett: Ha! I remember. It's funny because Ethan's dad is taking me to lunch later today. He used to drive a London cab and knows all the sites and history of places like that. You could meet us if you want and get in a quick history lesson??

Karl Westman: Would love that. Thx! Text me the restaurant when you get there and I'll find you guys.

I logged out of Facebook and headed for the shower. I had a lunch date with my father-in-law-to-be, and then a photo session after. No time for the sin of sloth today.

"So Ethan put you on guard duty today, didn't he?" I asked Jonathan between bites of some *really* good chicken salad. I'd have to remember the dried cherries and the dill the next time I made it. My appetite was improving slightly, but I didn't know if it was because of my pregnancy or that I was coming to terms with my father's death. Either way, I could now look at food without the urge to turn my head away so I wouldn't puke.

"I know nothing about that, my dear. I wanted to take my soon-to-be-daughter to lunch is all," he said with a shrug, brown eyes gleaming, "and Ethan told me that Len would be away today."

"Ha! Thought so," I laughed. "I know his tactics by now, Jonathan. Ethan doesn't let his guard down easily, or without very good reasons." I sipped my juice. "I know he's very protective and he does it because he loves me."

"You understand him so well. In fact, I'd say that you have transformed my son into a person I had hoped he might become someday, but feared I would never know." Jonathan smiled at me with a great deal of kindness and absolutely no judgment.

"The war?" I asked. "I know something very bad happened to him in the army, but I don't know what. He can't share with me . . . yet."

Jonathan patted my hand gently. "Well, that makes two of us then. I don't know what they did to my son either. I just know he came home with a haunted look in his eye and a very hard edge to him that wasn't present before. But I do know that he is more like the Ethan I knew when he was younger now that he's found you. You've brought it out in him, Brynne. I can see how he looks at you and how you comfort each other." He took a drink of his beer. "In short, you've made an old man very happy and greatly relieved."

"I feel the same way about him in a lot of ways. Ethan really saved me from myself."

Jonathan listened carefully and pointed at my belly. "You'll find that you never stop worrying about your children no matter how old they get."

"I've heard that said a lot." I sighed heavily. "I worry now . . . about him or her." I touched my stomach. "If something happens to me . . . well, then—I can already sort of see how it works."

"Nothing's going to happen to you, my dear. Ethan won't allow it and neither will I. The next few weeks will find you extremely busy and your schedule filled with plans and events, but soon things will settle and the two of you will be figuring out married life and I'll be awaiting the arrival of my fourth grandchild."

He smiled at me and I wholeheartedly returned it with one of my own. I was really beginning to care about Ethan's dad. He would be a loving grandpa for our baby and it made me feel good inside knowing he was rooting for our little family. It was a small thing to some, but for me, it was huge. Jonathan was giving to me something my own mother couldn't, or wouldn't give—the simple blessing for the success and happiness of starting our family.

We were heading out of the restaurant when I spotted Karl rushing in, looking somewhat harried for the easygoing guy I remembered from high school.

"Brynne! God, I'm so sorry I'm late. I got your text, and then it was one delay after another." He held up his hands. "I got held up with work business." Stepping closer to embrace me, he kissed me on the cheek affectionately.

"Karl, this is my . . . father-in-law, Jonathan Blackstone. Jonathan, Karl Westman, an old friend from my home-town. We used to compete in track and field together back in the day."

They shook hands and we all three chatted for a mo-ment. Karl seemed frustrated he'd missed our lunch and "reconnect," as he'd put it. I wasn't so sure Ethan could handle a connection of any sort between Karl and me. Honestly, I could do without it too. I had nothing against an old friendship, but in this case there was a great deal of added emotions and that made it more than slightly uncomfortable for me.

"Jess will slay me for coming all the way to London and then not making the time to catch up with you even a little," he said to me before turning to Jonathan, "and I re-gret I missed the opportunity to get valuable in-the-know tourist tips from you, Mr. Blackstone."

"If you're interested in Hendrix history and locales, I can share what I know. I drove hundreds of tourists around for more than twenty-five years in this city. I think I've seen them all." Jonathan gave Karl his card. "Email me and I'll send you what I have. You'll want the Samarkand at number twenty-two Lansdowne Crescent, in Chelsea, I imagine."

"Absolutely right." Karl took Jonathan's card and put it in his pocket. "Thank you for any suggestions you can give me. I don't have a great deal of time and I want to make the most of it." He turned to me again. "So . . . any chance we can arrange something else? I imagine you have some-where to be right now, don't you?"

"Yeah, I have a photo shoot in a little over an hour and I need time to prepare." I thought for a moment. "Well, you'll be attending the Games, right? Ethan will have tickets for just about any event you could possibly want. Why don't we plan to meet up for one of the athletics events like hurdles or the hundred meters? I'm actually starting to get excited to see some competitions now."

"Perfect," he said. "We'll be in touch, then."

Karl hugged me again and we parted ways.

Jonathan was quiet in the car while driving me to my studio shoot. He seemed to be thinking and I wondered . . . How did he feel about the nude modeling? What had Ethan told him about it? Had he ever seen any of my pictures? I guess I wouldn't know if I didn't ask him, and that was something I didn't get into with people. My modeling was personal and not open to negotiation.

In no time, it seemed, Jonathan pulled up to the address in Notting Hill and waited for me to enter the elegant white house that was hosting my photo shoot today. I waved to him as I went in, and then I was off to work, my focus shifting smoothly to what I'd been hired to do.

The inane questions people ask during conversations are so ridiculous at times I wonder how I manage not to leap on the table and shout, "How can you be so fucking stupid and manage to still be breathing?!" Alas . . . I've learned to keep my flap shut even when it has pained me greatly to do so.

I was just about to sneak in a much-needed nicotine fix after that waste of a conference call when Elaina rang through to my office. She didn't do it very often, and my curiosity was triggered immediately.

"Ethan, I think you might want to come up to reception."

"Yeah? What's going on?"

"It's Muriel . . . from the newsstand. She's up here to deliver a package to you personally, and she won't leave it with anyone but—"

I was out of my office and running to the front before Elaina could even finish her sentence.

My heart started to thump and the insta-worry flooded my system. I slid to a halt as I busted through the doors into reception. There was Muriel in all her horse-toothed, mustached glory waiting for me. She held a packet in her ink-stained hands, and leveled a green-flecked gaze over me as I rushed up to her.

"Mister, I got summat for ye." She waved the envelope. "Ye said, anyone an anythin'."

"I did. Did someone leave that at your newsstand just now?" I pointed to what she held.

She nodded and flicked her eyes around the room, taking in the décor and probably calculating her fee. "Yeah, near an hour ago now. I could'na leave t' stand. 'Tis written out 'Blackstone' an I know ye said number forty-four."

I tried not to be shocked that she could read and nodded back, the adrenaline starting to race around inside me. What was it this time? More death threats for Ivan? "You have an excellent memory, Muriel. Thank you for leaving your stall to come all the way up here to deliver it in person." I reached into my pocket to retrieve my wallet. "I appreciate your dedication."

I handed her a twenty and we switched. She gave a short nod and turned to leave. I tore open the red string, releasing the flap on the envelope—acutely aware it was identical to the one I'd received on the day of the Mallerton Gala—the same envelope that contained the photos of Ivan plus a cryptic message that read "Never attempt to murder a man who is committing suicide" or some incoherent bullshit I didn't have time for right now. Still, I couldn't take the chance on my cousin's life. He would be front and center at the Games in another week, announcing all the archery events, deep inside the media circus, being interviewed, in the public view all over. If someone was targeting him, I needed to have precautions in place.

I stuck my hand inside and pulled out photos, again, just like the last time—glossy black-and-white, eight-by-tens. I felt terrible fear slice into me. These were not pictures of my cousin at all. They were photos of Brynne . . .

Fuck no! No. NO!

The pictures were a sequence of photos shot on the street—Brynne and me on the day we went to our first appointment with Dr. Burnsley, and then afterward when we ate lunch outside before we stopped into Fountaine's Aquarium. Us hugging on the sidewalk after we came out of the doctor's offices. Me touching her belly and kissing her. Us eating our sandwiches and talking about our run-in on Christmas Eve in the snow. There was even a photo of Brynne taking a picture of me with her mobile and laughing because it had been right after I came out of the shop with the shit-smelling baby. I would have noticed someone snapping photos, though. I would have seen them. How did I miss it? How in the fuck did I miss this?!

I'd been distracted. Distraction is enemy number one in the security business and I had failed miserably. I had been distracted by the doctor's visit and then by the insanity of the aquarium shop—too unfocused on where we were and who was around us to even notice someone trailing us!

I groaned and flipped through them again. I couldn't find any message or ambiguous note on the back of any of the photos. I looked up and realized Muriel had left.

I barked at Elaina, "Get Brynne on the line and tell her to hold for me! I need to speak with her now!" Then I ran for the lifts.

"Muriel, wait!" I chased her down in the lobby as she was exiting the building. I'm sure others must have thought I was insane for all the spectacle I was giving them, but it didn't matter. They could think whatever they liked.

"Yeah, mister?"

"Who? Did you see who left the envelope?"

She flicked her eyes up and they flared a little. This was it—the moment of truth where she either helped me because she was a good person or she took advantage of me because she wasn't.

"I did as he walked away. I seen the back of him."

"What do you remember about him? Build, hair color, anything to give me at all? It's so very important," I begged.

"My—girl—my wife's pictures were in that packet. Her life

could be in danger." I lowered my voice. "Please, Muriel? Any small thing you may remember could help."

She pondered it for a moment, her eyes moving infinitesimally. "He were talkin' on a mobile an I only seen 'is back walkin' off. 'Is hair were brown an he were not as tall as ye."

Brown hair and shorter than me. Not much help in a place with millions of the same right now. I needed to get back upstairs and make sure Elaina had found Brynne. "Thanks again," I said halfheartedly and turned to go.

"There were summat I did notice, though," Muriel called out to me, "'is voice . . . he weren't native. He were a Yank."

The stalker is an American. It has to be coming from Oakley's people . . . or maybe Fielding isn't dead after all. Maybe he's here in London. Oh no! Please no!

My blood ran cold at what Muriel had told me, all the possibilities and scenarios spinning in my head in a terrifying entangled rush.

And then my legs started moving.

19

♥

My phone went off just as I was heading out of the dressing room. I could tell it was Elaina calling from work by the ringtone, so I let it go to voice mail without listening to the message. I sent her a fast text instead: **Can't talk . . . on photo shoot now. Call u later. —B**

I silenced my cell but left it powered up as Ethan had told me to—something about the GPS app he'd activated—slipped it into the pocket of my robe, and didn't give it another thought. I had a job to do and found my focus.

The hair extensions tickled my back and the floor was downright cold under my ass. I wasn't wearing any string thong today either, but I did have some really gorgeous black stockings with pink ribbons laced around the top of my thighs and tied into bows.

Simon, my photographer for this shoot, was an unconventional dresser at best, but with his electric-blue skinny jeans paired with a lime-green shirt and white patent-leather ankle boots, he not only had me in need of retina protection but attempting a shot I'd never tried before. I could only shudder at what Ethan would say when he got a look at the proofs.

He would hate them on sight, and then try to buy the images so no one else could have them.

I felt the rush of adrenaline, though—the knowledge of doing something a little scary and unfamiliar. I liked to push myself, and wanted these pictures to turn out well, to deliver the most professional services I could to the artist.

My back faced the camera, legs spread open, knees slightly bent, feet flat, my palms holding on to my inner calves to hold my legs apart. It was meant to be a provocative shot, and anyone who walked in front of me right now would see my lady parts on full pornographic display. *Ethan will definitely disapprove.* But I wasn't worried. There were rules in place, and everyone followed those rules . . . or they didn't get called back again for another job.

The ends of the hair extensions just barely brushed the floor, in effect covering my butt, which was a good thing because I didn't want ass crack to be visible in these pictures.

I told Simon and he laughed over at me. "Brynne, my luv, if anyone can do elegant bum cleavage it would be you."

"Well, thanks, Simon, but no thanks, if you get my drift. No vertical grin for me on this one, please."

"I promise you, all I see is a suggestion of curves and your long sculpted legs. You are absolutely glowing, darling. New vitamins?" he asked distractedly as the camera clicked away.

"Well, actually, yes."

"Oh, share with me, please," he gushed. "I need any beauty secrets you've got."

I snorted out a laugh. "I don't think you want what I'm taking, Simon . . . unless you desire a set of breasts."

"Oh, darling, please tell me you're not going for implants. Your tits are perfection as is!"

I laughed at the canvas drape in front of me, wishing I could see his face. "Um . . . no, not getting implants. They'll get bigger the natural way."

"Huh? What treatment does that?" I could tell he was way off base from where I was trying to lead. Gay or not, Simon was a man, and they just don't catch on to subtleties in these matters most of the time. I'm guessing it has something to do with having a penis.

"The kind where you have a baby at the end of it." I grinned and wished I could see his face now more than before.

"Oh my God! You're up the duff, aren't you?"

"That has got to be one of the most hideous terms you Brits have ever come up with, but yes indeed, I am."

"Congratulations, darling. I hope this is happy news for you?"

"It is." I was quiet for a minute, thinking about everything that had changed for me in such a short time, battling the emotions that seemed to simmer just under the surface these days. Maybe I could blame the hormones raging inside me, but it was a still a daily struggle to stay even.

Simon continued to snap pictures, directing me with subtle changes of position and then the lighting, keeping up a dialogue as was his style. He chattered constantly while he worked. "So you're getting married to your boy-friend?"

"Yeah, August the twenty-fourth is our big day. We're doing it in the country at his sister's Somerset mansion."

"Sounds very posh . . ." Simon mused over a new direction. "Can you tilt your head back and look upward for me?"

"Yeah . . . that too," I said dryly. "Do you want to come, Simon?"

"Darling, I thought you'd never ask! Perfect excuse for a new suit," he babbled, going off on a tangent about Italian silks and something about a green one he'd spotted in a shop in Milan that would be just perfect for a country wedding.

I thought about my dad and how he wouldn't be getting a new suit for my wedding. He wouldn't be there to give me away. I had nobody to do that for me now. I wasn't asking Frank either. My mom had already tried that angle with me and there was no way. I'd go down the aisle alone before I did that one. Nothing against Frank, but he was not my father in any sense of the word. He was my mother's husband, and that's all he was.

The wave of grief came upon me suddenly and I tried hard to suppress it, but my posture must have showed signs of fatigue because Simon asked, "Need a break, sweetheart?"

I nodded, but I couldn't speak. All I could manage was a deep swallow.

Sometimes when a person shows some kindness and you are in a vulnerable state, everything comes tumbling out no matter how hard you try to hold it inside you. That's what happened with Simon when he put down his camera and walked up behind me, resting his hand on my shoulder in a simple gesture of support and comfort.

"I heard about your father. I'm so sorry, luv. This must be a terribly hard time for you."

"Thank you . . . it's still very fresh. Little things remind me . . . and I miss him so mu—"

And that's the moment when Ethan busted into the room looking like a gladiator ready for the arena.

"Brynne! What in the fu—" My speech cut off. It just up and died a quick and silent death once I got a good look of my girl fully naked with her legs spread and some toff with his hands on her!

I reacted and moved. That's pretty much all I can recall. I got Brynne flying to her feet and the bloke in the green shirt flying into the canvas backdrop.

"Ethan!" she screamed, "what are you doing?!"

"Trying to find you! Why don't you answer your goddamn phone?"

"I was working!" she screeched, standing fully nude except for some black stockings and something added to make her hair appear much longer.

"You're finished here. In fact, this whole mess is finished!" I waved my hands and stalked toward her. "Get dressed, you're leaving."

"I am not leaving, Ethan. What in the hell is wrong with you? I'm working right now!"

Oh, yes, you are leaving, my beauty! In fact, I'm dead certain you are, because I'm taking you out of here myself.

The photographer wearing all the colors decided to make his move right then and pulled out his mobile. "Call security—"

"I *am* the security when it comes to her." I pointed in Brynne's direction as I relieved him of his mobile and cut the fucker off midcall. "Brynne is finished here. Ring my office if you want compensation for your trouble. I will gladly pay." I took out a business card and flicked it. It spun through the distance between us and landed at his feet on the floor. I thought I was being remarkably calm, considering...

He glanced over at Brynne, who just stood there, staring at us with her mouth hanging open. And still fucking naked!

"Don't look at her, motherfucker!" I yelled at him.

He squeaked like a girl and turned his head away, cringing.

"Simon, I am so sorry for thi—" Brynne stepped toward him.

"Oh, no you don't!" I grabbed her arm and spun her, shielding her body with mine. "Would you put something on? You're standing around here fucking naked, for fuck's sake!"

Brynne glared at me with daggers shooting from her eyes and reached for her robe. It had been on a side table the whole time, just out of the camera's view. I hadn't noticed it there a moment ago. She pulled it on and belted the waist, her arms and hands making hard, snapping movements as she squinted her eyes, searing fiery brown daggers at me. She stuck her hand up under her hair and worked it around for a moment before extracting a long wavy brown hairpiece. She set it carefully on the table. Then she turned her back on me and bent over first one leg and then the other, removing the stockings and straightening them out to drape over the table next to the hairpiece.

I could tell she was beyond enraged with what I'd done, but I simply did not care. She was okay, at least. Couldn't say that with much certainty about her photographer friend, but Brynne was safe in my sights and not in the hands of abductors. She was fucking naked and alone in a room with another man having her picture taken, but at least my worst nightmare wasn't a reality. She was here and I could see her.

The ride home was pretty silent. Just some sighing and the swishing of bodies on seats, and not much else. Brynne wasn't speaking and I was in no shape for discussion either. No telling what would come out of my mouth the way I was feeling at the moment. Best to leave it stewing for a bit.

Once we arrived and got inside the flat, she beelined it into the bathroom and locked me out. I could hear the water running, but no other sounds. I put my ear up to the door and listened. I didn't want her to cry alone if that's what she was doing, but I was still furious. This modeling thing? It had to go. I just couldn't stand the idea of it anymore, and it made me utterly irrational to think of her posing in the nude for others to see. *And fantasize about fucking her . . . or worse!*

There were a million things I needed to do at this moment. Places I should be and people I should be meeting with, but did I even consider leaving Brynne at home and going back to my office? Negative. I was going fucking nowhere right now.

I stepped out onto my balcony instead and settled onto a lounger where I could watch the city change from day into night. And smoke cigarette after cigarette after cigarette. It didn't help me much. Funny how something that used to soothe me when I felt agitated didn't really do the trick anymore. I waited for Brynne to come out of the bathroom, but she took the first round in a knockdown. It didn't look like she would be making the first move tonight.

When I couldn't bear my self-imposed solitude for another second I went back inside to try to reason with her. "Brynne?" Silence. "Let me in." I rattled the knob, and to my great surprise it turned. *Not locked out after all.*

I opened the door to find her perched on the vanity stool painting her toes, her hair pulled up in a clip, wearing the yellow silk robe that made her skin glow. She wouldn't look at me, but continued to work the dark pink nail polish as if I wasn't there.

"Can we talk?" I asked finally.

"What about? How you manhandled me in the middle of a photo shoot, which happens to be my job, and practically beat up the photographer? Not to mention the damage done to my reputation in the business." Her voice was flat.

"I don't want you in that *business* anymore."

She capped the lid on her nail polish and set it on the vanity counter. "It's all about what you want, huh?"

"I needed to know where you were and you wouldn't answer your mobile." I let a moment go for some kind of an explanation but she didn't offer one. "Fine, I admit I went in there hotheaded and lost my temper, but I was running on clues that led me into a panic situation." I dragged a hand through my hair and kept it stuck there. "And you were fucking naked, Brynne."

She stared down at the floor as she spoke, "I probably won't get any more calls after today. Nobody will want me now."

Oh, the motherfuckers will still want you. I stood in front of her and took her chin in my hand, forcing her to look up. "Good. I hope they don't call you." She still stayed silent but her eyes flashed. "I'm serious, Brynne. You're not posing naked anymore." There, I said it.

"It's my decision, Ethan. You have no right to tell me I can't do it."

"Oh, really?" I grabbed her left hand and held it up. "What's this ring mean, then? You're going to be my wife, the mother of my child—a person whom I don't want posing in the fucking nude *anymore*!" I glared right back. "I definitely have a say."

She snatched her hand away and spit up at me, "You don't get it. You just don't understand ANYTHING about me!" Screaming now, and looking utterly furious, she pushed at my chest to keep me from getting too close.

Fuck that! My temper was getting the better of me again as I struggled with how to bring us back together on the issue. One idea came to mind of how I might accomplish it, though. I could tear off that yellow silk robe she had on and fuck her into next week, and *then* we could have this conversation, or argument, or whatever the hell this shit was right here. That might work.

I pulled her up from her seat by the shoulders instead, trapping her arms to her sides so she couldn't fight me. She still struggled, though, even as I had her gripped tight against my chest, our faces an inch apart, her soft curves melting into me and making my cock rock-hard.

"I'm trying to *understand* why my girl needs to take off her clothes and let people see photographs of her like that!" I said with more anger than I wanted to . . . and then I crushed my mouth against hers.

I pushed my way inside her with my tongue first. I'd get more later, but for now I just needed inside her body in any way I could manage to get there. I needed her acceptance of me more, though. She was still spitting mad but I felt her response the instant we connected. She was still my girl, and we both knew it as I held her jaw and took her mouth hard. Lips, tongue and teeth working together to send a very specific message. *You're mine, and I know you want to be mine.*

I was just getting started on taking her. This session would conclude in one way, and only one way—with my cock buried inside her sweet cunt in an orgasmic frenzy.

There were no apologies for what I did next, either. I took her. I took what was mine and had my way with Brynne.

She stuck with me the whole distance in body for sure. The spirit part would have to be considered later. *Shag*

first, talk later had worked for us before, and I felt confident it would now.

I hauled her up and carried her to our bed. She looked
up at me with blazing eyes as I laid her out, stripping
open that silky robe and freeing her hair from the clip.
Her chest heaved and her nipples budded up tight as I
shucked off of my clothes and got naked, my cock so hard
it might shatter when the spunk erupted the first time.

I was about to find out, and more than willing to take
the risk, because there would be a second time and possibly a third. We would be at this for a while.

I covered Brynne's gorgeous naked form, which only
I should ever see, and fucked her. I fucked her hard. She
fucked me hard right back. We fucked until we both
came. And then we fucked some more, until we didn't
need to anymore. Until there was nothing left but to fall
into tangled sleep after all the orgasms, both of us spent
physically from the pleasure that had burned us with
its heat, and drugged us with its smoke . . . into utter
oblivion.

The nightmare woke me up. It was an old one where I see
the video of myself and wish I was dead. It is still such a
dreadful image that's seared into my brain, and has stayed
with me intact throughout the years. I don't think it was
even possible to remove it; I was doomed to carry that
image with me throughout my life. I wondered, not for
the first time, if the three of them ever thought about that
video after the fact. I hadn't known the other two at all,

but did Lance ever have a morsel of regret for what happened to me? For how sad my life was after they did their deed? Did he ever even think about it? *Ugly. So filthy and ugly.*

I tried to have a quiet breakdown in the middle of the night, but Ethan hears everything. We'd had some explosive sex and released some anger and frustration through our bodies, but the main crux of the problem was still flapping in the breeze like a signal flag. Nothing much had been resolved.

Ethan stirred beside me and drew me close. I felt his strong arms wrap around me and his lips kiss the top of my head. He stroked over my hair and held me as I wept.

"I love you so much. It kills me to see you sad. I'd rather have you mad at me than hurting like this, baby."

"It's okay. I know you love me," I whispered in between sobs and wiping my eyes.

"I do," he said with a sweet kiss. "And I'm sorry for how I acted with that photographer today," he paused, "but I still loathe the process and I don't want you doing it anymore."

"I know . . ."

"So you'll stop posing?" There was hope in his voice. Too bad I was going to crush it.

"I don't think I can, Ethan. I can't stop—not even for you."

He waited after those words left my lips. The words were painful to say to him but he had to hear it from me. The truth is sometimes hard to bear, and I imagined this would be so for Ethan, but I wanted him to get the uncensored version. I owed him that much.

"Why not, Brynne? Why can't you stop modeling? Why won't you do it for me?"

Those bastard tears showed up again. "Because . . ." I blubbered, "because the pictures I take n-now are so—s-so b-beautiful. They are . . . just something beautiful of me!"

Ethan held on to me while I cried. He seemed to get that this was breakthrough territory for me. I wish Dr. Roswell was around to witness it.

"They are. You're right, Brynne. Your pictures are stunningly beautiful." He kissed me softly, his tongue moving slowly against mine. "But you've always been beautiful," he murmured against my lips.

Ahhh, but he was wrong. Ethan had never seen *it* so he did not know what I absolutely knew to be the truth. "No. You don't understand me." I wiped at my tears. "It's okay, but you don't understand why I need to have those beautiful pictures of myself." I sighed heavily against his chest, my fingers starting to twirl around a pectoral muscle.

"Explain it to me so I can understand, then."

I don't know how I got the words out, but I managed it somehow. Through the tears, which grew stronger, and because of his quiet strength and patience as he held me and stroked my hair, I finally told another person my horrific truth. "Because the video of me was so very . . . ugly. The images were ugly. *I* was ugly in it! And if I have something beautiful to replace the ugliness with, I can let go of my experience a little more each time I create something new."

Ethan rolled me underneath him and propped himself above me, holding my face up to his. "There is nothing about you that is ugly," he told me.

"Yes. On that video I was."

He got quiet, his eyes flickering back and forth as he studied me. "Is that why, baby? Is that the reason you tried to . . . kill yours—"

"Yes!" I sobbed into Ethan's strong chest and let him hold on to me. He knew my truth now. My hang-up. My dysfunctional quirk. The motivation that drove me on a daily basis and that I assumed would stay with me forever. I prayed he could accept me in spite of it.

He held me for a long time without speaking. He was pondering what I'd shared. I'd learned it was his method; that Ethan was incredibly honest and blunt with his opinions and needs, and a deep thinker.

"It's not the photography process that I hate. I get that you are all professionals doing a job. The photographer is just using you as the object of his art. A breathtaking image that is you." He stroked his palm down over my hip. "I know that guy today wasn't after you. He was seeing your body as art."

"Simon is also incredibly gay as opposed to just regular gay, in case you didn't notice."

He gave a short quiet laugh. "I noticed, baby. If the clothes didn't give a clue—his girly scream confirmed it."

"Poor Simon. I invited him to the wedding, you know. He wanted to wear a new Italian suit in leaf green that he saw in a shop in Milan." I tried for the tiniest bit of teasing.

"Awesome." He sighed. "I'll ring him tomorrow and apologize."

"Thank you."

But Ethan wasn't done airing his feelings. He had more

he wanted to say. "What I hate is people seeing your body in the photographs. Men see you. Men like me see you naked and they want to fuck you. Brynne, that is the part I hate, because I don't want anyone to look at you like that and think those thoughts about you. I want you all for myself. It's selfish, but that's how it is for me."

"Oh . . ."

"So now you know my feelings on the matter," he said quietly, his voice carrying his honest truth straight to my heart.

"I hear you, Ethan, and I hope you heard me when I told you how I felt, and why I do the modeling."

He reached for me with his lips, caressing soft and slow, telling me with touch, if not with words, that he understood. After some time well spent thoroughly kissing me, he finally pulled back and brushed my cheek with his thumb. He'd been doing that to me since the beginning of us. He'd done it the first time he ever kissed me. I loved the gesture.

I wondered what Ethan was thinking about now. Studying me carefully with those deep blue eyes of his, he settled on his side propped on an elbow so he could look down over me. I imagined he wasn't done talking yet. I waited. I could wait all night if he was the view. Ethan naked in the bed was a sight I never tired of. He was male beauty personified. His arms, his chest, the washboard abs and V-cut hips, all of him—a delicious feast for my eyes.

Funny how he said the same thing about me sometimes. But my body would change as the baby grew. I would get big as all pregnant women do. Would Ethan still want me then the way he did now?

"I need to tell you something that happened today. It

really shook me up and was mostly to blame for what happened at your photo shoot . . . and with me." He smoothed my hair back behind my ear.

That makes more sense. I should have known there was something driving Ethan's off-the-charts irrationality. Something had happened to trigger his behavior. "Okay . . . tell me."

In the dark of our bed, he shared with me the latest events: the stalker photos he'd received earlier in the day, and the knowledge that the person was American and had been here the whole time watching me. Watching us and taking pictures of our daily movements. I was really scared now . . . and I understood better why Ethan had been so panicked and unreasonable at the shoot. This situation was not getting better. It was getting worse. Who knew what would stop them? Or if I'd even get through this alive? All I could do was think about my baby and about Ethan and knowing that whatever it took, or sacrifices I had to make in order to see us all through, I would do it.

We talked about security and GPS and guards and precautions. All the ways to ensure my safety in the next weeks until the wedding could happen and Ethan's full attention could focus on me solely. He explained things clearly and I listened to him. We both ended up on the same page, and when I finally slept again it was up against his chest with his strong arms wrapped around me. I knew I was in the best possible hands I could be in, and that the man who held me did indeed love me. Ethan needed me as much as I needed him.

We figured out that much, at least.

20

♠

"How does it feel to breathe, son?" Dad raised his glass with an ecstatic grin.

"Like the three-ton elephant has moved off my chest and now just sits on my feet," I answered truthfully and toasted him back.

"I bet you do. But really, the ceremonies were the most magnificent feat of organization. Absolutely brilliant show, that. Bravo, I say." I guess we could all assume my dad had been thoroughly impressed with the opening ceremonies because he couldn't seem to stop talking about them over our midnight dinner. I just felt immense relief that they had gone off without a hitch.

Even if I was exhausted and longed for my bed with Brynne in my arms, I found I was actually enjoying the celebratory evening tonight at Gladstone's. Ivan had got us a reservation somehow, despite the insanity of the city, but then everyone loved Lord Ivan, Britain's golden arrow, with his good looks and celebrity name. It'd had been a long time since we'd gone out for anything nice together and I knew that Dad and Neil and Elaina appreciated his connections even if I could take it or leave it. Brynne looked like she was having fun, and that was enough for me.

The whole city was in celebration mode, as the Games were now underway. I could actually start to see some light at the end of the tunnel for us. We'd made it through another week and the start of the Olympics with no problems, threats or messages. Just regular life.

I brought my hand up Brynne's back and caressed between her shoulders. "Yeah, the hard part is done. Opening ceremonies went off smoothly. No crazies interrupting the show. The perfect end to all the months of planning. Now it's just getting the various VIPs to the separate events and venues, but they're much smaller and easier to manage, plus I have excellent staff to see to most of it." I nodded to Neil and raised my glass again.

"If we can just keep the psychos back from Ivan, this thing's a wrap," Neil said with a smirk.

"Yes, please. I'd very much appreciate a wide berth between the psychos and anything to do with me," Ivan retorted.

There was still that . . . Some lunatic Korean rival had it out for Ivan over a grudge stemming back three Olympics ago in a judgment dispute that got him disqualified and Ivan the gold. The mess had never gone away. Rather like messes often do. Once you step in shit, it sticks to your shoe for a long, long time, and it's a wicked bitch to get all traces of it off.

"You look tired, baby," Brynne said softly, her hand brushing over my arm.

"I feel tired," I said, glancing at my watch, "just think—if we leave now we can be in bed in half an hour." I winked at her, thinking all I really needed tonight was her close enough to touch, and a few hours' sleep. Those two things really would top off this night for me in the most perfect way.

I was teasing about leaving the party, but my girl surprised me, as she often does. "Then what are we waiting for?" she asked in a quiet voice. "I think I could pass out in my soup."

Looking her over, I could see the signs of fatigue and felt guilty for not noticing earlier. She was pregnant and needed rest for two people. I saw my window of opportunity and grabbed it.

"Goodnight, everyone. Time for us to be off. My woman is begging me to take her to bed." Brynne gasped and thumped me in the arm. "And seeing as I'm a semi-intelligent bloke, I think it's best if I let her have her way just now." I rubbed my arm where she'd busted me and spoke with exaggerated emphasis to the group: "Pregnant women—insatiable all the time."

I grunted when she kicked me in the foot, but the laughs I'd gotten were worth it.

"You are so dead, Blackstone," she told me on the way out to the car.

"Hey now, it got us out of there, didn't it?" I snaked my arm around her and leaned down to steal a kiss. "And everything I said about you was true."

She turned her lips away to avoid mine and laughed. "You're an idiot and you won't be so smug in about five months."

"What happens in five months?" I asked, confused.

"The insatiable pregnant female thing?" She cocked her head and shook slowly from side to side. "That goes away. Completely." She made a cutting motion with her hands. "Think *no sex*. At all. For months."

Well now, that's a very unpleasant thought . . . "Wait. Are you joking? You are, aren't you?"

"You should see your face right now!" She laughed some more at me, giddy at having had the last word. Yeah, my girl was competitive and she didn't go down without a fight.

"That bad, huh?" Praying she was indeed winding me up about the dry spell because that would truly be torture.

"Yep," she said, snaking her hand back around to grab my arse. "And you totally deserved it, even though I love you, Blackstone."

And what a lucky, lucky bastard am I. "You were baiting me with the five-more-months thing, right?"

She laughed again, looking very smug and sexy as hell, but she never answered my question.

"No, you cocksucker! I said no video! No fucking video!"

Ethan woke me with his shouting. He was dreaming again. No—definitely make that nightmaring.

The stuff he shouted really scared me. He'd said the

same sort of thing before on other occasions. The words "no video" over and over in a begging voice. It frightened me because he was so out of himself when he had these nightmares. He became like another person—a complete stranger.

I knew his nightmares were related to something from his time in the war when the Afghans held him prisoner. He would never talk about it with me, though. It was something terribly horrible. That much was clearly evident.

"Ethan, you need to wake up." I shook him as gently as I could but he was moving erratically all over the place, in another world and very unreachable.

"He's gone . . . awww Christ! A baby! Just a little fucking baby, you medieval fucks!"

"Ethan?" I shook him again, rubbing harder up his arm and to his neck.

"No! You can't do this . . . No . . . no . . . no . . . please no . . . don't—don't—they can't see me die in a video—"

"Ethan!" I smacked him a little on the jaw, hoping the sting would bring him out of his nightmare.

His eyes flew open, wild and terrified, and he lunged up in the bed. He hung there bent over, heaving in great breaths of air, his head at his knees. I laid my hand on his back. He flinched from my touch but I left my palm there. His breathing grew more ragged and he didn't say anything to me. I didn't know what to say to him.

"Talk to me," I whispered to his back.

He left the bed and started dressing—throwing on some sweatpants and a shirt.

"What are you doing?"

"I have to go outside now," he said weakly.

"Outside? But it's cold out there. Ethan, stay here with me and talk about this. You have to talk to me!" I begged him.

He acted like he didn't even hear me, but I think he did because he came over to where I was sitting up in the bed and touched my head. Very gently and for just a moment, but I felt him shaking. His hand was shaking violently, and he looked so lost. I reached my hand up to take ahold of his but he pulled it away out of my reach. Then he walked out of the bedroom.

"Ethan!" I called after him. "Where are you going? Come back here and talk to me!"

I got silence.

I laid there for a moment and tried to decide what to do. Part of me wanted to confront him and force him to share with me, but another part of me was scared to death of doing that. What if I caused him more pain and suffering, or made things worse for him? Ethan needed some professional help to deal with this. If he'd been captured and tortured while in the army, then he was most likely suffering from a full-blown post-traumatic stress situation. I should know about that.

I made my decision and dressed myself in some leggings and a sweater to go and find him. I shouldn't have been surprised to see where he was. He'd told me the truth. He was outside. Smoking his clove cigarettes.

I stood behind the glass and watched him for a moment. Stretched out in the lounger, his bare feet hanging off the end because he was so tall, the curl of smoke twisting and floating above him, the bright city lights in the foreground creating a glow around his body.

The smoking didn't bother me, really; it never had. I loved the way his brand smelled, and Ethan rarely tasted like cigarettes. He was a fanatic brusher and always tasted minty and good to me, but the spicy scent would cling to him and I could tell when he'd been having a clove. His brand of cigarette wasn't typical, though—Djarum Black. Clove-spiced tobacco, imported from Indonesia. I still didn't know even why he smoked cloves. Ethan wouldn't talk about his smoking much—or his dark place with me.

My Ethan was certainly in his dark place right now, and it utterly broke my heart to see him this way. I slid the door open and stepped outside.

He didn't acknowledge me until I sat beside him on the other lounger.

"Go back to bed, Brynne."

"But I want to be with you."

"No. Go back in the house. The smoke isn't good for you or the baby." His voice was eerily detached and scared the shit out of me.

"It's not good for you either," I said firmly. "If you won't let me be here with you, then put out the cigarette and come back inside and talk to me. We need to talk about this, Ethan."

"No." He shook his head in denial and took another deep drag on his clove.

A cord snapped inside me and I got angry, but I needed to do something to get a reaction out of him, he was so separated from me right now. "This is such bullshit,

Ethan! You need some help with these nightmares. Look what it's doing to you!"

He didn't say anything, and the silence between us screamed out against the city's night sounds.

"If you won't talk to me about it, then you need to find a therapist or a group or something to get you some help in dealing with this." No reaction, just more smoking. The red tip of the black cigarette burned in the dark and still I got nothing back from Ethan.

"Why won't you answer me? I love you, and I'm here for you and you won't even tell me why you smoke cloves, let alone what they did to you in Afghanistan." I leaned closer to him. "What happened to you over there, Ethan?"

I could hear the panic in my voice and knew I was close to another crying spell. His behavior hurt me terribly and made me feel like I wasn't important enough to share in working through his biggest fear. Ethan knew all my deep shit and said none of it mattered to him. Didn't he know I'd walk through fire for him? I'd do anything to help him when he needed me.

He carefully stubbed out the cigarette he'd been smoking, using the ashtray next to the lounger. He folded his hands in his lap and stared out at the city. He never looked at me once as he started to speak in a soft voice.

"I smoke them because all my guards had cloves. Hand-rolls of spiced tobacco that smelled so fucking good I nearly lost my mind. I craved to have one. I nearly went insane with craving them."

I froze in the chilled night air, listening to Ethan, my heart breaking with each word he gave me.

"Then . . . on—on th-the day they were going to execute me, a miracle happened . . . and I was spared. I lived. Their wicked blade did not find my neck." His voice cracked.

"Blade?" I had an idea where this was going, but was afraid to even think about what Ethan might be trying to explain to me.

"Yeah. They were going to videotape my beheading and show it all over the world," he spoke so softly but the words were brutally loud.

Jesus Christ! No wonder he had nightmares. I couldn't even imagine what he'd endured physically as they tortured him, but the emotional torture of believing what they would do to him must have been worse. I couldn't hold back the gasp that escaped, wanting so badly to hold him, but he continued speaking.

"You want to know what the first thing was that I asked for?"

"Tell me."

"I walked out of my prison, not completely sure if I was really alive, or dead in hell. A U.S. marine got to me, shocked I'd walked out of the rubble still breathing. He asked me if I was okay. I told him I wanted a clove cigarette."

"Oh, baby . . ."

"I was alive, you see. I lived and was finally able to smoke one of those lovely clove hand-rolleds I'd gone mad over for weeks. I smoke them now . . . because . . . I guess it helps me to know I'm really alive that way." He swallowed hard. "It's such a load of shit . . ."

"Oh, Ethan . . ." I moved up from the lounger and over to put my arms around him but he held me back.

"No," he said, holding his hand up to keep me at a distance. He seemed so very distant from me right now—unreachable. I wanted to cry, but I knew that would just make it harder on him, and I didn't want to cause him any more stress than he already had.

"Go back inside, Brynne. I don't want you out here with me right now. It's bad for you. I'm not . . . good . . . to be around. I need to be alone."

"You're sending me away?"

He slowly lit up another clove, the flame of his lighter glowing bright as the tobacco ignited. "Just go back to bed, baby. I love you, but I need some time by myself right now."

I felt something from him. I couldn't believe it, but I could swear I was reading him correctly. Ethan was terrified of doing something to harm me somehow and that was the reason he asked me to leave him alone.

I granted Ethan his wish even though it broke my heart to do it.

21

♠

I caressed Brynne's photograph in its frame on my desk. The one I'd taken of her with my mobile when she showed me Lady Percival for the first time at the Rothvale. She looked so happy and beautiful. *Last night she wasn't happy.* No, I'd scared her and then made things worse by sending her away when she tried to reach out to me.

. . . God in heaven, I fucked up with her. I tried to imagine switching places. What if it had been she who had sent me away after a nightmare and refused my comfort? I've been on the receiving end of that before, and it sucked. It had felt awful, just like I'd made her feel.

Still, I had been afraid last night of what I might do to her if she touched me any more than she did. The other times I woke up from one of those nightmares? Yeah . . . not nice. I'd gone off on fucking tangents—literally. Using sex, and Brynne, to level me out to a place where I could come back down from that horrible place I'd found myself in my dreams. She didn't understand how much I was walking the razor's edge in those moments. I didn't trust myself with her. What if I hurt her or went too far with the sex? She was pregnant and vulnerable now. I just couldn't take the risk of what I might do.

It had been the hardest thing to send her back inside last night when she wanted to stay with me and listen to my story. She'd tried to hold me, but I'd kept her back. I hadn't even looked at her face, because if I'd done it I would have caved. I had no willpower when it came to Brynne.

To keep myself from taking her after I came back inside, I'd slept the remainder of the night on the couch. I didn't trust myself to get back into bed with her. All it would take was her scent up my nose and the sound of her breathing next to me, and I would've been on her and buried deep, trying to get lost inside her. Brynne was my heaven. I'd seek out my heaven endlessly. I knew myself well.

She was right, though. About so many things, but about last night's fuckup she was completely right. I needed some help. There were places I could go for it. Lots of soldiers came home from the war with issues and baggage. I was just another in a long fucking line of others before me. I got that. I didn't want to face the demons, but I knew I needed to. More important priorities were in the canvas that was my life. I had Brynne now. We had a child on the way. Neither needed me having psycho dreams and terrorizing their peaceful nights.

I had to ask myself why. Why was I suddenly back to that time so vividly in my subconscious? Could Brynne's situation be triggering the long-shelved memories of my time as prisoner and bringing them back to life? Fucking hell . . . It was a painful thought, but probably spot-on accurate.

I'd make it up to her tonight. Flowers, dinner, romance— complete honesty about the hell I'd been in and how I'd made it out. She deserved to know everything, and was strong enough to handle it. The bonus was having her support on some of the emotional burden. This was one of the aspects of a deep relationship. She shared her stuff with me. Why wasn't I doing the same? *Because you are a thoughtless arsehole a lot of the time and you need to work on that.*

Brynne hated when I shielded her from things. I'd learned firsthand that she was incredibly strong, with the will to fight ingrained deeply inside her. She was no coward, and wouldn't go down without giving it her all. My girl faced her fears head on. I should take her example and do the same. I accepted the time had come for me to seek out some professional help and to trust someone else with the burden of my demons. Brynne would be there to help me through it, and I couldn't be in better hands than hers.

Brynne would also serve my arse to me on a silver platter, and I should be prepared for that when I got home. She would never let this issue go, regardless. I had to grin at the thought of her reaction to me tonight. She'd looked gorgeous as usual with her eyes blazing, hands on her hips, battle-ready and full of fire. I looked forward to seeing the change in her when I came in bearing gifts and humbled, ready to finally share with her the darkest demons inhabiting the unmentionable places in my soul. And how she might reward me for all that, afterward . . .

I had some phone calls to make and plans to be put into motion. Life was speeding by at a reckless clip and there was no time for sitting around woolgathering over regrets that couldn't be remedied. I sent Brynne a text first: **I love u. Sorry 4 last nite. xx I'm going 2 fix things ok?**

I dialed my sister in Somerset and waited for the call to connect.

"Brother, you have impeccable timing. I just had a visit from Mr. Simms, and he's got some papers for you that need signatures."

"That is very welcome news then. Let me have Frances get you an overnight slip and we'll do it that way."

"Sure. I do think it's the most marvelous idea, E."

I grinned in my seat. "I do too. After having a look, do you think it's possible in such a short time?"

"Well, it'll be close, but I think it can be done—not everything, mind you, but for your purposes, yes."

"Good. I mean, I trust you implicitly, Han. Just do your best."

"When can you come here? At some point you need to see it with your own eyes."

"Right. I won't be able to manage anything until the closing ceremonies, but the moment that's all behind me I'll slip in a quick trip . . . somehow."

I kissed Benny on the cheek and hugged him tight. Then I went right back to looking at the image proofs on the screen. "Oh my God. I love them all, Ben. I can't choose."

He laughed softly. "He'll think they're beautiful, Bree. They are. They're breathtaking."

"Thank you so much for doing this for me on the spur of the moment. The idea just came to me after . . . something that happened . . . and I wanted to do these pictures for Ethan. Nobody will ever see them but us." I touched his cheek. "Thank you for making that possible, my dear, amazing friend."

Ben smiled down at me with such kindness—I could tell he was touched I had asked him to take special pictures of me. Very special pictures indeed. Just me and my wedding veil. And only ever for Ethan's eyes to see.

Ethan . . . yeah. We had yet to talk about last night. He'd never come back to bed and when I woke up this morning he was already gone from the flat. That bullshit wasn't going to fly with me tonight, though. I would be sitting him down when he arrived home and he would talk to me—or else.

Or else what? I didn't have all the answers, but I'd think of something. He was in bad shape emotionally with those nightmares and I had absolutely no intention of allowing him to continue suffering without some professional help to deal with them. And the part he *had* shared with me last night just shredded my heart into pieces. His torturers were going to behead him and taunted him with the fact. I couldn't imagine how he had endured it all and wasn't stark raving mad. It made me want to wrap my arms around him and shower him in my love. Ethan was going to get it from me whether he wanted it or not, I vowed.

"Hey, is everything all right with you two? You look a little worried there, luv."

I nodded and began folding up my veil carefully and repacking it. "We are fine. Just some relationship stuff that needs to be aired out." I put my hands on my hips. "But I've got it covered. Men can be so damn stubborn, you know?"

Ben laughed at me. "Riiiiight. Just the men. You're talking to the right guy on that topic, Bree. I agree with you completely." Ben winked at me and packed up his equipment. "Come on, beautiful girl, let me get you back home before Blackstone starts looking for you, thinking you've gone on the lam. I take it this is a surprise and he has no idea you're with me, doing this."

"Nope. No idea whatsoever. This was a spur-of-the-moment decision and I've kept my phone turned off all morning so he couldn't track me with GPS. I'll turn it back on when I get home and he'll see that I'm safe and sound, and be none the wiser."

Ben shook his head at me and looked up at the ceiling.

"You're a wicked sneak and I don't have any idea what you are talking about."

I snorted at Ben.

"I'm dead serious, Bree. Don't involve me in your plans to deceive your man. I want to live to see thirty, thank you."

"Don't worry so much," I teased as we went out to his car, "it's giving you frown lines."

Ben frowned at me then caught himself, smoothing out his forehead and trying to be sly about it. Ben was hilarious a lot of the time, and it felt good to laugh.

Annabelle was at the flat when Ben dropped me at the

door. He had to head off for another appointment, but we made plans for dinner on the weekend. I had a favor I wanted to ask of him and had even already discussed the idea with Ethan, but I wanted Ethan and I to ask him together. No rushing a good thing, and this was something really important to me.

Annabelle interrupted my thoughts with her usual greeting. "Hello, missus."

"Oh, hi, Annabelle. Any messages while I was out?" I asked carefully, really hoping that Ethan had not been frantically looking for me and getting everyone upset.

"No, missus. It's been a very quiet day. The mail arrived for you and some packages."

"Oh, good. I hope it's the sample wedding favors." I wished she would call me Brynne, but Annabelle was very old-school in her ways and it seemed that anything more familiar than "missus" was out of the question. Still, I liked her a lot. Annabelle came here twice a week, on Mondays and Thursdays, mostly to clean and do the laundry. She cooked for us, but only on those days. She used to make things and freeze them for Ethan to heat up whenever he made it home, but I stopped that practice when I moved in.

Ethan had me to take care of him now on the other days of the week, and cooking was something I enjoyed.

This had caused a bit of a flare from Annabelle at first, mostly because she had been his housekeeper for five years and liked things to be very organized and planned out. Since my arrival, though, we'd all had to get comfortable with each other and figure out our various roles and routines. We fixed it by having her do the cooking only on the Mondays and Thursdays she worked, and planned around her schedule.

"I set them on the desk in the office as usual for you."

"Thanks, Annabelle, I'll open them later." I peered around her into the kitchen, surprised there didn't seem to be anything started for dinner. Annabelle always had something nice simmering or baking on her days.

"Miss Frances called and said Mr. Blackstone would be taking you out for dinner this evening." Annabelle could read minds too it seemed.

"Oh, is that right?" I raised a brow. "I love how he has Frances deliver that information."

"Yes, missus." Annabelle smiled at me.

"Well, I should have a shower, then, and start getting ready," I said, checking my watch.

"Oh, I nearly forgot to tell you before I go, the aquarium service will be coming at four o'clock for the fish tank. Mr. Blackstone scheduled it a few weeks ago and made sure it fell on one of my days. They called to confirm, but I've an appointment this afternoon, and will have to leave early," she barely paused to take a breath, "but you needn't worry, missus, I've let Mr. Len know the time and he will let them into Mr. Blackstone's office once they arrive."

"Thank you, Annabelle. I'm sure Simba will be thrilled."

She laughed at my comment and shook her head. "That fish is something else, he is."

The shower felt good, and I was glad Ethan had plans for me this evening. It meant he was trying to make amends

for last night and I really hoped he would finally be opening up to me about his past. It was time for me to know.
And honestly it felt really nice to be the one to take care of
him for a change. Our whole relationship had been built
on Ethan protecting me, taking care of me, and recently
with the pregnancy bomb, ready to marry me. I'd like to be
the one driving the boat once in a while, but to do that he
had to allow me to. I was glad that finally seemed about
to happen. Tonight I'd get to be his strength.

As I was blow-drying my hair I realized I'd forgotten
to turn on my phone when I returned home. Ethan would
have something to say about that, I was sure. *Shit.* I hated
being scolded by him, but reasoned that if he was really
panicked about me, he would call Len and talk to him.
Len would confirm where I was. I just hoped Len wouldn't
also mention the part about Ben taking me away and
dropping me off back home. I wanted the photographs
to be a complete surprise. They were my wedding gift to
Ethan.

I hurried to finish so I could go down and find my phone
to check for messages, really hoping that Ethan had been
so busy with the event venues he hadn't noticed my absence. *Fat chance of that happening. He notices everything.*

I got my purse off the kitchen counter and dug out
my phone, but when I tried to turn it on, the battery was
totally dead. It needed a charge in order to even check my
messages.

The charger cords for everything were in Ethan's office. I started for the hall and remembered the aquarium
service appointment. They were probably already set up

and working by now. I checked the clock on the micro-wave; it read 4:38. Yep, they were here. I decided to bust in on them anyway. I needed my phone.

I knocked before I went in. "Sorry to interrupt, but I need my phone charger."

The guy bent over the tank had his hands full with tubing and buckets. He gave me a nod from the back with a "yeah" and kept on doing his thing. He didn't seem to mind me, so after I plugged in my phone and turned it on I started to look through the mail on the desk.

I was opening the first box when arms slammed around me and pinned me from behind.

"What the hell—" My speech was stopped by a hand over my mouth.

"Brynne . . . I've waited so long for this moment. So long . . ." he murmured in a voice that sounded familiar but I couldn't place it.

My mind was racing; whoever this person was, they'd come to kill me. My time was at an end. I would die to-night and Ethan would find my body. We wouldn't have a life together after all. Our baby wouldn't be born in Feb-ruary, because killing me would kill our baby too. There wouldn't be a wedding at Hallborough, and I'd never give Ethan my gift of the photos . . .

I would have begged for my life if I'd been able to. But there was no air for speaking, or crying, or even for breathing.

But knowing I was going to die wasn't the worst part. The worst feeling in all of this was that I would never get to see Ethan again, or touch him, or tell him how much

I loved him. My final moment with him had been last night when he sent me back inside so he could be alone. Oh, God, this would destroy my Ethan. He'd never forgive himself for this.

My captor kept me pinned up tight against his body and his mouth at my ear. I struggled, but my strength was waning. He gripped the back of my neck and squeezed, my nose and mouth covered, my lungs screaming for air, I felt a haze begin to surround me as my vision clouded. I was going down. It was finally happening. Everything Ethan had tried to prevent was going to happen anyway . . . and I couldn't stop it.

Oh, Ethan . . . I'm so sorry. I love you so much and I'm so terribly sorry . . .

22

♠

I checked my watch, wishing I could leave Lord's Cricket Ground right now, but I knew I had at least another hour here. Ivan had just finished announcing the archery and the media crew was done with their telecast, but the stands were still being cleared, and I knew that would take some time. I was giving my cousin the personal treatment, the same as I did for members of the royal family, and so far, so good. The men's individual elimination had proved no great surprise, and I could think of nothing I wanted more than to get home to my girl, and back into her good graces. I had some humble pie being served to me this evening and I was good with that.

Ivan was making his way over to me when my mobile went off. I hoped it was Brynne. She'd never replied to my text from earlier. I smiled when I saw her name . . . but I read what she had typed in her message.

And then my whole world collapsed.

I can't do this anymore with u. Ethan, u killed us last nite. My Old life is what I want back now . . . I don't love u

anymore . . . and not having ur baby either. I'm goin home where I want to be left alone . . . don't come after me an don't Phone me! Get some help, ethan, I think u need It desperately. —Brynne

I don't remember how I got out of there. I know Ivan was with me so he must have helped. My dad showed up later too. I wanted to get home because the GPS told me that Brynne was at home. The last signal from her mobile registered from my flat. Our flat.

She wasn't at the flat, though.

When I discovered her engagement ring and her mobile lying at the bottom of Simba's tank, I wanted to curl up and die. It was a message loud and clear. A brutally painful and cruel one, but one I understood implicitly.

Our first meeting had been in the aquarium shop, even though neither one of us knew it at the time. Brynne had seen Simba before she'd ever met me. We had started with Simba. And we would end with Simba as well. How fitting.

The situation made absolutely no sense, though. My emotional side wanted to give up, but my pragmatic side still fought for reason in what was a colossal clusterfuck. Last night had been bad, sure, but worthy of a breakup? Hardly. Brynne was not cruel. If anything, she was softer-hearted than most people. And she was very honest. If she wanted out, she would have told me in person, never in something so impersonal as a text message. The text was not her style at all. She also told me she'd never give me another "Waterloo." True, she hadn't actually written the word in her text, but she promised she would never take off and leave like that ever again.

Len didn't even know Brynne was gone from the flat. He told me he let the bloke from Fountaine's into my office to service the tank at four o'clock as scheduled. At about five-thirty, Brynne texted him and asked him to run down to Hot Java and get her the special masala chai she liked to have now that she was pregnant. Len left for the coffee shop, but while he was queued up she rang him and told him not to bother with the tea, since I was on my way home and had already picked something up for her. Len told us that when he returned to the flat, the bloke from Fountaine's appeared to have finished the job and let himself out. He could hear the water running in the bathroom and assumed Brynne was in having a shower.

I got ahold of Annabelle, and she relayed an account of a perfectly normal Brynne excited to look at some wedding-favor samples that had arrived. I found her wedding veil folded carefully in a bag. That didn't make sense to me. Why would she be excited to look at wedding favors if she was leaving me? Why did she have her veil out? I'd even found her periwinkle dress laid out on the bed as if she was choosing what to wear for dinner. Why would she lay out clothing for a date if she was planning to leave? The part about how she wasn't going to have my baby was all wrong too. Brynne wanted it. She wouldn't get rid of our child. She already loved our baby as a mother does. I knew this in my heart, no matter what her text said.

The other thing that got me really suspicious was that the security cam at the door had glitched out during the time Len was down at the coffee shop. During the same window of time in which Brynne had to have exited the flat, and when the aquarium service had supposedly let themselves out. Those kind of coincidences just didn't occur in real life. They only happened on television.

I rang up Fountaine's and asked who they had sent out to do the service call on Simba's tank.

Their reply turned the blood in my veins to ice, stopped it dead on its way to my heart.

"Mr. Blackstone rang us this morning to reschedule his service, sir."

That is when I knew that the person who'd sent the photos of Brynne and me in front of Fountaine's had been in the fucking shop. He had followed us around London and stood there in the shop and listened to me make the servicing appointment. I had given them the time, and the place, so he could take my girl from her own home, in broad daylight, right under my fucking nose.

Goddamn me to motherfucking hell . . .

A bell rang. The deep, sonorous clang of a bell tower, somewhere in London, was making its scheduled performance. I counted seven rings before I opened my eyes, finding myself waking in a strange room and praying it was from a nightmare.

It wasn't.

My head was fuzzy from not one but two blackouts. The first time had not been a complete job—just enough for my captor to get my attention and tell me what I had to do.

He'd made me do terrible, cruel things to people I care about—to people I love. But I'd done those things hoping and praying it might save their lives. My captor was no stranger to me. I had known him for many years, and in every sense of the word. He was no stranger to murder either. He had murdered people to get to where he was now. I had no reason to believe he wouldn't murder me as well. I had nothing more to lose.

"My pretty awakens," he whispered from beside me, his hands moving over my body purposefully, his breath at my neck.

"No . . . please don't do this, Karl. Please . . ." I begged him, trying to push him back with my hands.

"But why not? We've fucked lots of times in the past. You loved it back then. I know I did," he crooned, "and I was just a kid before. I know what I'm doing now." He slid his hand up my top and over a breast and squeezed. He slathered his mouth over my neck and tried to kiss me, but I curled my lips and turned my head.

He gripped my chin roughly and pinched, turning me back to him. "Don't think you can play hard to get with me, Brynne," he said in a cruel voice, before he slammed his mouth over mine, his tongue pressing in and trying to invade me.

"Karl, I'm pregnant—no, please—stop, please!" I begged between gasps for air.

"Ugh . . . that bastard's spawn growing inside you is not the nicest thought, my dear, especially when I'm trying to fuck you. You really know how to cock block, you know," he complained, "but fine, have it your way. I can wait."

Karl heaved himself off me and leaned on the wall, his eyes roving over my body with lust. He adjusted himself at the crotch and sneered at me.

"Are—are you going to kill me?" I tried not to think about his motives and what would happen if he succeeded. I fought to stay calm and not run. I needed Karl to trust me a little for what I hoped I could manage to do. Not running from him would be the first step.

"I don't know yet. Maybe I will and maybe I won't." He grinned evilly. "If you decide you want to fuck sooner rather than later, let me know. That just might work in your favor, babe."

I tried to ignore his comment. "Did Senator Oakley hire you to kill me?" My heart was thumping so hard it hurt under my ribs.

He tipped his head back at the wall and laughed. "The senator is a sock monkey who couldn't find his way out of a paper bag if the thing was torn in half. Um . . . no, my dear, Senator Oakley didn't hire me."

"Then why? Why do this, Karl? You were always so . . . nice to me."

"Fuck you to hell and back, you little slut. In seven years you've never known anything about me," he snapped, looking half insane. Make that wholly insane. "I'm not the *nice* guy you remember from high school," he told me smugly, grinning now as he talked, his demeanor completely changing from crazy to cheerful in a matter of seconds.

"So tell me what changed you, Karl. How come you're not the nice guy I remember?" I asked the question and then stayed quiet. I studied my surroundings the best I could, and tried not to think about Ethan, or what he was doing at that moment. Had he figured out my text message yet? Or was he still reeling from the pain of the words, and believing I no longer loved him.

As if that could *ever* happen!

If Ethan had decoded my hidden message, would I ever have opportunity to act on the only clue I could think to give him at the time?

Karl started talking; rambling, really. Going off on a rant about how he'd killed Eric Montrose and made it look like a bar fight. I barely listened. I was trying to find a way to get to his phone, and knew what I'd do with it the moment I did. I would only need one. One moment of time. I could do it in one small minute if the opportunity arose.

"Nobody else had to die, you know, after Montrose," he said.

"What do you mean?" I asked.

"It's your fault that more people had to die. I'm not loving the killing part here, Brynne. It's very distasteful to me." He frowned and looked over my body again, no doubt thinking about something to pass the time alone in this bedroom he'd locked me in.

"Karl, no . . . you're not like them. You wouldn't have done what those boys did to me at that party."

He narrowed his eyes a fraction and said, "You're right. They were pigs to do that to you. Raping a girl who is out cold is not my style." He got off the bed and went to the window and looked at the darkening sky. "You'll come around in time and be begging me for it eventually."

Umm . . . no I won't, you maniacal motherfucker.

"What do you mean about nobody else had to die after Montrose?"

He turned and looked at me like I was an idiot. "I was here—in London. I had everything planned out. We would meet again and start back up right where we left off all those years ago. We'd make a pact to bring Oakley down with the story of that sex video his piece-of-shit son made," he explained as if he were speaking to a small child. "Then sell out to Oakley's team, or if he wasn't interested, then the other side's team, and go off to live a happy life somewhere nice and quiet."

"So what happened to change your mind?" I asked in a soft voice.

"Your fucking boyfriend happened!" he snarled. "Out of all the guys you could have hooked up with, you had to pick security with connections to the fucking royal family and British military intelligence! Thanks for that, Brynne. Nice one!"

"But I didn't find him, he found me. My dad hired Ethan to protect me from . . ." The instant the words left my lips, the fog began to dissipate and the truth of my father's passing became revealed to me.

"I know," Karl said simply, his dark eyes showing just how deep his madness was rooted.

"You murdered my father, didn't you?" I grappled with my hold on any shred of rational thought and action.

I lost.

"Where is she?! WHERE IN THE FUCK IS SHE?!" I yelled to no one in particular. I had Ivan, Neil, Len, and my dad all standing around looking to me for guidance. I didn't know where to begin, though. It took everything I had not to fall apart and turn to quivering mush in fear and desperation.

"Son, look at this. I think Brynne left you a hidden message in this text." Dad was holding my mobile and studying it.

"What? Tell me!!" I grabbed my phone from out of his hands and read it again.

"The capitalization," Dad said over my shoulder, "it's only certain words excepting the *I*'s. Look at the others."

The words: Ethan, My, Old, Phone, Get, It, were the only ones with capital letters . . . except for the *I*'s. Dad was right. I couldn't believe it. My girl had successfully delivered a message to me in code under duress of kidnapping. I closed my eyes and prayed for another miracle.

"And other words that should be capital are left lower-case, like your name—"

"Yeah, Dad, I get it!" I cut him off and ran for my desk drawer, fumbling around until I located her original mobile phone. I plugged it in with the charger and turned it on. The wait was torture while it powered up.

There was nothing new on it. My excitement plummeted, but now there was some hope, at least. Some small odds for me to bet on. A layer I could start peeling back to guess at the cards held underneath. I understood those kind of odds. A message meant hope. A message meant she was alive. And if I had to bet on Brynne, I was confident she would fight to her last breath to win. My girl was like that, and there was nobody I had more faith in right now than her.

"She sent me a coded message," I said again, to no one in particular, still in amazement at her quick thinking during a terrible situation.

I raised the volume settings and left her precious mobile plugged in on my office desk. I sat down and watched its light flash normally. I had to. My girl was going to ring me on it and tell me where she was, so I could go to her and bring her back. *Come on, baby . . .*

What felt like aeons of time passed painfully slow. I recalled later that I never once desired a smoke while I waited for my girl to message me from wherever she was. I didn't think about having one, or imagine the taste, or even feel the sting of nicotine deprivation. None of it. I'd never touch another ciggie in my life if doing so would bring Brynne safely back to me. Not much of a vow, I know. Pathetic, really. But it was all I had to wager with.

I prayed to my angel for another miracle, and hoped she would hear me for the second time in my life. *Mum, I need your help again . . .*

Then the picture came through in a media message with the most wonderful sounding blip I'd ever heard. I opened the message and stared, my eyes absorbing what she'd just sent.

Brynne was playing her hand in a kill-game situation, and had just upped the ante by betting huge stakes that could go either way. I loved her so much for doing it, I thought my heart could burst right on the spot. My girl played her cards with the instincts of an experienced ace. *Of course she does, she's my girl.*

"Dad?" I held the mobile out to him with a shaking hand. "Where is that bell tower? You must know where it is; take me there right now. Brynne can see it from where she just took that photo."

23

♥

My first instinct was to rip the lamp out of the wall and start bashing Karl on the back of the head with it. I don't know how I didn't. I wanted to hurt him, make him suffer in agony for a long, long time before he died. The evil my mind imagined for him was not fit for anyone to ever know. I'd have to keep it buried inside me forever. No problems there.

It took some time, but we got there eventually. Karl got bored in our small prison and started texting someone or playing a game, I couldn't tell. That's how I knew he had his phone and where it was. I would have to get it from him at some point and use it to call the only phone number I could remember—the phone number I'd had since my move to London four years ago. I did not know any other numbers by heart but I knew that one.

I thought about how I could get to Karl's iPhone. In time I realized the only way was for me to dig deep into my psyche to where I was willing to go all in, as Ethan would say. To bet everything. To carefully leverage the risks—or the consequences. To try to win, or be willing to lose everything.

Anger would be the vehicle to get me there.

"You murdered my dad, you evil motherfucker," I said quietly.

He looked up from his texting and stared at me. "He deserved it. Even way back I hated him for not letting me see you after it happened. He kept you secreted away from your friends, and from me. I wanted to help you and to be there for you. Your prick of a father shut me down every time I tried to talk to you."

"He was protecting me by shielding me from further hurt. He was being a parent, you asshole!" I let my emotions build up inside me. "He loved me!"

"Yeah, well he was in the way. Killing him made my plan work better. Oakley was shitting a brick at the funeral. Did you see him sweating?"

"No," I answered, "I was grieving for my father, you soulless shit."

Karl smirked at me and I wanted to gouge his eyes out with a dull spoon. "Not like your dad when I took him out. He was one cool son of a bitch, even when he knew what was happening." Karl looked me over dismissively. "He said your name right at the last . . ."

I couldn't hold in the gasp, the agonized cry that poured out from my heart as I heard his nonchalant words, spoken almost as an afterthought. It was too much for me to accept. My father had died knowing what Karl intended for me.

"Don't look so upset, Brynne. I told your dad I'd take care of you," he said in a cocky voice, and then he turned his back on me.

Thank you, you fucking monster!

They say that under the influence of an adrenaline surge, humans are capable of extreme feats of strength. Mothers lift cars to free their children and stuff like that. I didn't know if the effect could apply to me, but I didn't care. It was lamp-bashing time—my very best option for the choices within my grasp. A nice solid stone-component base that would do the trick if it didn't shatter from the force I was going to use when I hurled it at him.

Right. Fucking. Now!

I took ahold of the damn thing and launched it with all my strength at the back of Karl's head.

I had done the shot put in high school, and I did it now. Contact coupled with perfect precision and brutal force. Karl went down like a rock in a pond. Maybe the stories about mothers lifting cars did apply to me.

I was a mother, and Karl just got reminded of that very important fact.

I grabbed his phone off the floor and did the first thing I could think of. I held it up to the window and took a picture of the skyline. Then I sent it to my old phone number.

I hoped I'd killed Karl, because it was precisely what he deserved, but I couldn't be sure and I didn't want to stick around to find out. I was getting out of here.

The door ate up a precious minute of time because he'd finagled a chain lock on the inside that took me a few tries to undo, my hands were shaking so badly. I knew we were up three or four stories, and that I had to get down to the street to find safety, but when I exited the attached flat, I found myself in a corridor. This place was a mess of architectural planning. Make that complete unplanning. I looked around for the best way out. The fastest way.

The corners and stairwells reminded me of the Mission Inn in Riverside that I'd visited with my parents as a kid. You could follow different paths and end up going in crazy loops, up and down stairs and around secluded alcoves that turned you right back where you had been before. Where were the elevators in this place?

I thought about Ethan and wondered again if he understood my message in the text, and how he would ever find me. Then I thought about the GPS stuff we'd discussed, and it came to me in a flash. *Facebook!* With Facebook you could check into places and post your location status with a built-in GPS application.

I flicked through Karl's phone and found the Facebook app. I logged into my account and clicked Places. I let the app do its thing and selected the first location that popped up on the list of possibilities. I almost had to laugh at what showed. Number 22-23 Lansdowne Crescent. The Samarkand Hotel. I typed on my Facebook status, **I'm here, Ethan, come get me.** I tagged Karl Westman in "Who are you with?" and pressed Post, continuing my desperate search for the elevators, needing to gain distance from this place.

After what seemed like forever, I found the lifts and stabbed the down button, looking around for signs of Karl approaching, or of anyone for that matter. Why was this place so dead, and where were all the people? The doors opened for me and in I hopped. I pressed G for ground and didn't take another breath until the doors shut me in and the lift began its lumbering descent.

Freedom was in my grasp. *Almost out.* Ethan would see my messages on my old phone and on Facebook and know where to come for me. I could call him as soon as I found a safe place like a restaurant or a shop.

The doors opened smoothly, and I stepped out into a dim courtyard sort of service entrance. This was obviously the rear entry of the hotel, not the front as I had hoped. I went out anyway, and that is when I heard Ethan call out my name: "Brynne!" The sweetest sound my ears could ever know.

I went toward the sound, focusing only on him. I could hear the urgency in his call, and I felt such relief. Ethan had found me; I was alive and everything was going to be okay.

"Ethan!"

I was running toward Ethan, to my love, and my whole heart, when I was snatched from behind by arms that grappled first, and then secured me tightly, entangling me like a fly in a sticky web.

"Nooooo!" I screamed in devastation.

"You didn't think you could get away from me, did you, Brynne?" Karl's disgusting drawl panted in my ear.

My attempt at killing him had obviously failed, because he now had a sharp blade pressed up against my neck, shocking me with its coldness, forcing me to stop struggling. The disappointment I felt was a bitter pill to swallow, but even worse was the heartbreaking sight of Ethan's face in the twilight. He stood not less than ten yards away from me. *So close, but not close enough.*

Ethan's flat-out run had come to a screeching halt, his arms splayed out in surrender, his head shaking back and forth in a silent plea to Karl not to cut me.

This . . . would be Ethan's undoing. His fear of the blade would propel him into any kind of negotiation to free me. I knew it. Ethan would sacrifice himself to keep me from having my throat slashed. Karl could not have chosen a better trigger for Ethan's fear in all the world.

Events and sequences had come together in near-perfect harmony, but *near* was not enough for my needs right now and wouldn't be until I had her safe in my hands again.

My dad had known exactly where to find the bell tower the second I showed him the photo from Brynne, as I knew he would. Nobody knew the city of London better than my father. St. John's Notting Hill parish church held the tower she could see from the window. Dad said she had to have taken the photo from Lansdowne Crescent.

Elaina called Neil in the car as we raced through side streets, confirming Brynne's location at Lansdowne Crescent in Notting Hill . . . and who had taken her. *Karl Westman?* I did not see that one coming, and had to fight the panic that rose up inside me. The only thing helping me to function at the moment was knowing that Westman had once felt an attraction to Brynne. If he wanted her for himself, then there was a better chance she would remain alive. At least that's what I now prayed for with everything I had.

Elaina also relayed the message Brynne typed out

on her Facebook post to me, and I had to dig deep in order to hold myself together. *I'm coming to get you, baby.* Again, Brynne's brilliance in problem solving blew me away. Talk about grace under pressure. Maybe she'd missed her calling and should be working for MI6 instead of conserving art.

I even spotted her coming out of the building as we skidded up. She ran toward me and called out my name. My girl was alive and running into my arms. I was about to have her back where I could touch her again, and kiss her, and tell her how she was *everything* to me.

But that piece-of-shit cocksucker stepped in and put his hands on her. He snatched her up and stretched a blade across her beautiful, innocent neck. There was no worse horror for me than seeing the sight of my girl with a knife threatening her throat. Threatening her life.

Karl Westman was a walking corpse. My mission in life was to see that become a reality, even if I had to become a corpse along with him to accomplish it. As long as Brynne was spared I could live with my decision. Or die with it.

"You know you cannot hurt her, Westman. Whatever you want, you can have. Money? Safe passage out of Britain? Both of those things? I can make it happen for you, but you have to let Brynne go." *Too bad I'm lying and planning your death, motherfucker.*

"I don't have to do anything you say, Blackstone!" he screeched.

"The world is not big enough for you to hide in if you harm her. She's out of your reach already, Westman. She's untouchable to you. If you kill her you'll be joining her within seconds. Don't think my threats aren't real. Look around you. You are marked all over the place. They're on you—everywhere . . ."

Westman panicked just as I hoped he would, frantically stretching his neck out to turn his head and look around for any marksmen ready to take him down. It was the opening I needed, a distraction just long enough to shift the balance of power.

My opportunity presented itself, and hesitation was out of the question. My eyes were on Brynne's as I lunged forward to take him down. If this was it for me, I wanted my last view on this earth to be of her.

I felt a whoosh of air slide right by my cheek. A flash of light radiated outward in my lefthand peripheral vision. I had an idea what the first one was. I didn't want to imagine what the second thing was. Or from whom.

There was the metallic clang of the blade falling to the courtyard stones. The thud of an impact on flesh. An involuntary groan. A scream. Then the three of us were on the ground in a mess of bodies. I had only one purpose, and that was to get my hands on my girl, and it didn't take me more than an instant to do it. I rolled us away and looked around and up. I couldn't see a shooter up on any of the walkways, but if they were professional I shouldn't be able to.

Westman lay on the cobblestones on his back, dark blood pooling from the side of his head. I hoped the bullet he'd just taken to the skull had been painful, but he probably never knew what hit him. *Too bad I can't thank the person who'd delivered it.*

"You okay, baby?"

"Yes!"

It was enough. I took Brynne with me as I scrambled away and out of the courtyard. I just ran with her, not bothering to wonder how it was possible I wasn't hit or why my body still worked. I was fairly confident I had just dodged a bullet and narrowly missed the arrow shot from Ivan's bow. But where had the bullet come from? Did the Secret Service just take Westman out in an undercover hit? Now was not the time to speculate—that could come later, and I knew my lads would find out anything there was to know. I had precious cargo in my arms and she was all I cared about.

I ran us to my car, put Brynne in the back and got in after her. My dad was there, ready and waiting for us, thank God. *No, thank Mum.* I told Dad to drive us out and get us home.

I looked her over in the backseat. I checked her neck, gripping her face in my two hands, and saw no blood.

"You're okay . . . you really are okay, aren't you?" I babbled like an idiot, and made little sense, probably. I wanted to stare at her forever and never let go of her eyes. Her eyes told me she was alive. Brynne was alive!

She nodded with my hands still cupping her cheeks, her eyes wet with glassy, beautiful tears looking up at me. "You f-f-found me," she stuttered, "I'm okay, Ethan . . ."

"I told you I would always find you . . . and tonight you made it possible," I whispered against her lips. "*You* did it."

I thanked my angel up in heaven first, and then I crushed Brynne to me and held her against my heart. Her heart and my heart both beating together, in the backseat of my Rover, the very same place where we'd started on the night we'd met at the beginning of May when I convinced her to let me give her a ride. And what a ride the last months had been. Very bumpy and full of unexpected twists and turns, but in the end, worth it because of this moment—and where we were going right now—forward into a future together.

I held on to her the entire drive home. My greatest love, and my greatest potential loss, was safe in my arms and I just couldn't let her go.

I didn't speak much during the ride. When Dad drove into the lot of the building, I thanked him for his help and said I'd ring him later. I carried Brynne up through the garage lift entrance.

"I can walk," she said against my chest.

"I know." I kissed the top of her head and told her, "But I need to carry you right now."

"I know you do," she whispered, and then rubbed her cheek against me and closed her eyes, inhaling deeply. She was breathing me in. I understood her need for that too.

The part about holding her, holding me up, still held true. I would have to do this for her always—for as long as my body would allow me the strength to lift her. Holding Brynne to my heart was necessary for me to . . . exist. Talk about needing another person. It didn't get any stronger for me. If things had been different, if outcomes had turned tragic, then my time in this life would be at an end . . . and other things wouldn't matter anymore. And I wouldn't want it any other way. With Brynne it was my truth. Wherever she went, I needed to be right there with her.

We still hadn't spoken much, but it didn't bother either of us a bit. I carried her into the bathroom and turned on the shower. I set her up on the counter and removed her shoes first, and then her shirt, and then the rest of her clothes, piece by piece, until she was perfectly and beautifully naked. I looked her over carefully and saw nothing but her perfect skin, gratefully unmarred by signs of abuse. Then I did the same with my clothes, and carried her into the shower.

We just stood under the spray and held on to each other . . . and let the water wash us clean.

24

Four weeks later . . .

"So I hear that congratulations are in order for the two of you." Dr. Burnsley looked up from between Brynne's legs, where he was using the banana probe on her again. I realized I was definitely jealous of the probe. That fucking thing was seeing more action than my cock lately. Brynne wanted to keep things chaste in the bedroom for the previous couple of weeks to make our wedding night a little more special. The most goddamn ridiculous notion I'd ever heard of, but hell, I just did what I was told. Mostly.

"That's right. By our next visit she'll be Miss Bennett no more. It'll be Mrs. Blackstone from here on out." I gave Brynne a slow wink.

She mouthed the words *Love you.*

I love you too, my beauty. I thought my words.

"Lovely news, then," Dr. Burnsley said, now looking at the monitor as he found the black blob on the white blob with the beating heart, except our blob had grown considerably and didn't look even remotely blob-ish anymore. My eyes were transfixed—I could see arms, legs, hands, and feet, moving all over the place. Our baby was in there becoming a little person. "Everything looks to be progressing very well. Baby is growing strong and about the size of a—"

"—peach," I informed the good doctor.

He turned his head in disbelief and surprise.

Brynne laughed softly but kept her eyes on the screen, watching all the gymnastics our little one was performing so brilliantly for us.

"Yeah, weighs around eight ounces and already growing teeth and vocal chords." I grinned at the doc. "And Brynne is one-third through the pregnancy now and officially in her second trimester."

"Someone has been reading," Dr. B said with a bemused gray eyebrow quirk.

"Bump dot com, doctor—brilliant resource." I winked at him too, but I don't think he liked that too much.

Three hours later . . .

We were officially on vacation.

Bags packed and loaded? Check.

Rover crammed to the roof with everything we could possibly need for our wedding trip up to Hallborough, and then some? Check.

Bride? Check—most fucking definitely.

My girl looked as mouthwatering as always in her flowery purple dress and her hair pinned up in a messy knot. I liked when she wore it like that because it made me think about taking it down and dragging my hands through it when we were naked in bed together. *Soon* . . .

"So, are you ready to go get shackled, Miss Bennett? Last chance to ditch this celebrity bash and elope with me," I teased, dragging her up against my chest and tucking a wisp of hair behind her ear.

"Hmmm, whose idea was that again?" she asked quizzically.

"Just say the word and we don't have to do it, baby." I was serious, and would pull out of the whole thing if it was truly what Brynne wanted, but man, my sister would kill me over and over again for it.

"No, no, no, Mr. Blackstone. You ordered this posh event with royalty and dignitaries coming to eat the gourmet food, and drink the expensive champagne in your sister's historic country manor house." She raised an eyebrow. "And now you must deliver all those goods." She plucked at my shirt. "We reap what we sow."

"True that."

"Besides, I want to see you standing at the end of the aisle waiting for me, looking handsome with those blue eyes of yours only for me."

"You've got that fucking right—only for you." I kissed her thoroughly, tasting her deliciousness and thinking I had the rest of my life to enjoy it.

She grinned and shook her head a little at me. "Your filthy mouth . . ."

"You love the things I do to you with this filthy mouth."

"Mmmm, I so do." She grinned. "You're right, Mr. Blackstone." She smoothed the spot on my shirt she'd just been plucking at, making me smile. Brynne did that a lot when she was explaining her feelings as she was right now. I thought it incredibly sexy, but then everything about her was sexy to me. Especially since it had been far too many days since I'd been inside her. Only forty-eight hours more of this no-sex nonsense—thank fucking Christ. And then? Well, it'd be HoneymoonLand, here we fucking come! Lots and lots of coming would definitely be happening on that trip too. Italian villa along the coast, secluded, private—nothing but time to make love, eat, sleep, swim in the ocean and make more love. I could probably do that for the rest of my li—

"Plus, I got a pretty new dress and a veil for this hoedown." She looked up at me and winked. "You paid for it."

"Hoedown? What kind of Yank word is that?"

"An appropriate one, actually. It means a country party with dancing and fiddles." She did a quick air violin gesture for me. "I know this thing is most definitely happening in the country, *and* you've got David Garrett coming—there is no fiddle player hotter than him, by the way—and I'm not merely talking about his musical ability here, Blackstone, so yeah, we got us a big ole hoedown to get to. You'd better start moving your sexy British *arse* and get us on the road."

"So you've got some fancy for David Garrett, now do you?"

She pretended to consider, giving me a wicked gleam and tapping her chin with a finger. "A lady never tells."

"Fucking fabulous! My wife is about to throw me over for the fiddler at my own wedding! Absolutely brill." I pulled out my mobile. "Excuse me, I need to call David Garrett and uninvite him to our wed—"

"Don't even think about it, buster," she told me sternly. "If we're having all these celebrities at the wedding I should get to choose at least a few of them! It's only fair."

I pretended to be jealous. "So you're going through with this whole high-profile nonsense because of the fiddle player?" My question was in jest, but there was some definite truth to it.

Ironic how the plan I'd set into motion only for her protection and safety had turned out to be unnecessary in the end. Brynne didn't need the high-profile celebrity status anymore because her stalker was dead, taking the eternal punishment he so richly deserved.

To date, I hadn't found out exactly what happened to Karl Westman, but I had a really good theory. After my dad had driven us away from the scene, Neil, Ivan and Len stayed back to investigate. My first priority was to get Brynne to safety above all else, and I'd seen plenty of dead bodies to recognize one when I see one. Westman was killed instantly by a high caliber bullet to the head. But by whom?

What happened there was strange, though. I'd worked it out for the most part and highly doubted there would ever

EYES WIDE OPEN | 325

be confirmation from the senator, but Ivan had told me that when he went looking to retrieve the arrow he'd fired, somebody had taken the body away. It was just gone in a matter of moments. Only professionals are capable of that kind of operation. Neil and Len sniffed around again the next morning when it was light and there was nothing there. Even the blood was washed away. No trace of anything.

Brynne had mentioned how the whole place was eerily quiet and that she'd never seen another person at the hotel, which made no sense with the Games happening. So that pretty much confirmed there were people involved at the highest levels. U.S. Secret Service, most likely. Westman was a dead man before he ever took Brynne from the flat. The senator had protectors in high places apparently. Westman had overstepped in his attempt at blackmail, and paid the ultimate price.

Disaster averted, but still, far too fucking close for my comfort. This whole mess had happened for a reason. Very strange, but true. If Westman hadn't started stalking her, we wouldn't have met, or ever gotten together, or be about to marry and have a baby. It was all just a bit much to rationalize sometimes, even if it was our reality. I tried not to think about that part. Brynne was free to live a regular life now, with nobody out there plotting to take her away, or harm her, or bother with any aspect of her, and this was my greatest gift. *Thank the heavenly angels . . . and one very special angel in particular.*

"Ethan!" She was frowning at me.

"Yeah?" I asked, rubbing my thumb between her brows to smooth out the lines of her frown.

"You're not listening to me. I answered you and you were off in a dream somewhere."

"I'm sorry. What did you say?"

She gave me a look and then started in with the shirt plucking and smoothing again. "What I was saying was that . . . I would go through a hundred of these ridiculous celebrity weddings if it meant I was marrying you." She lifted her brown/green/gray eyes up to mine. "You're so worth it, Mr. Blackstone."

It was a good while before we got on the road up to Hallborough.

Two days later . . .

Ben and I watched Simon from the rose garden and hoped he didn't spot us. In his very green Milanese bespoke suit, he arranged guests for candid shots in all sorts of crazy avant-garde positions.

"God help us if these pictures he's taking get out to the general public. We'll all be royally fucked—quite literally!" Ben said dryly, nodding his head toward the naughty antics of a certain ginger-haired prince and his unidentified date. "Why on earth did Ethan hire Simon Carstairs to do the wedding pictures?"

"Ahhh . . . well, that would be a situation where Ethan found himself having a slice of humble pie, or as we say in the states, eating crow, in regards to our dear Simon.

Ethan called him to apologize for his blowup, and by the end of the conversation had secured the photographic services of the most flaming gay photographer in all of London, if not all of Europe." I shrugged. "He takes beautiful pictures and it all worked out in the end." I nudged Ben. "Simon really had his heart set on that freaky green suit."

Ben and I laughed together and continued watching the revelry. Simon really looked like the train wreck you couldn't tear your eyes away from in his leaf green suit. He had Gaby and Ivan together in a few shots. I wondered how they were getting along since they'd been thrown together in this as maid of honor and best man. Gaby looked beautiful, as always, and Ivan looked at her like he thought so too. I'd have to corner her later and get the scoop. I could see the potential for the two of them just in their body language and how they moved in relation to each other. There was some chemistry brewing, I was sure.

"I would have taken your wedding pictures, you know," Ben said.

I looked up into his handsome face. "I know. But I needed my friend, that I love so dearly, for something much more important today."

"I know," Ben whispered back and grabbed my hands, "and it was my very great honor to walk you down the aisle at your wedding. I—I'm pretty speechless right now, Bree. You are so beautiful, my darling friend, on the inside and on the outside." He squeezed my hands. "And seeing you happy, standing up there with Ethan, was just something so breathtaking I don't really have the words to tell you properly, except that I love you." He brought my hands up to his mouth for a kiss.

"Okay . . . I'm crying now, Benny." I laughed through a sob. "Got a handkerchief for the blubbering, hormonal bride?"

"I'm sorry, luv," he said sheepishly, handing over his handkerchief.

"You're fine," I told him, dabbing at my eyes carefully. "There really wasn't anyone else I could ask. I didn't want to walk alone. I don't know why, but I knew that Daddy would have wanted me to have you there. He thought the world of you and our friendship, Benny. And you were there at the gallery that night—you told me to look over at the hot guy in the gray suit with the wide-open eyes that burned me from across the room. You were there right at the first of Ethan and me."

"Yeah, I was." Ben was looking pretty watery himself right now.

"Here." I handed him back his handkerchief.

We both laughed and pulled ourselves together. "Thanks for inviting my mum today," he said.

"Of course! I love your mom. She's so adorable when she's had a few drinks, and she loves to see you all prettied up. I'm so glad you brought her with you."

"Well, she loves you too, and if I wasn't gay she'd have made me marry you years ago. She wants to be a granny, and she's going to be all over that baby when it gets here, so you'd better be prepared." Ben nodded down at my bump, which was just beginning to make its appearance.

"That's so sweet," I said, looking out in the gathering

to find my mother and Frank chatting with some Italian diplomat at their table. Things were somewhat better between my mom and me, but I didn't know if there was much hope for the future of the relationship. And that was okay. It really was. I had a family now that needed me as much as I needed them. All of those people lived in England. This was my place in the world now.

There were plenty others around me that counted. My baby, for one. Ethan's dad and my aunt Marie would be the grandparents my mom and dad never would be. Hannah, Freddy, Gaby, Ivan, Ben, Neil and Elaina would be the aunts and uncles. Jordan and Colin and Zara would be the cousins. So much love surrounding me.

Strong arms wrapped around me from behind and familiar whiskers brushed at my neck. "Mrs. Blackstone, are you hiding in the garden at your own wedding party?"

"Pretty much," I said leaning back into him in deep contentment.

"Awww, Christ in heaven! Not my mum too!" Ben growled at the dance floor where Simon was now doing a very lewd rumba with Mrs. Clarkson for a cheering crowd.

"Go get 'em, Ben." Ethan and I laughed at Ben's retreating back as he went off to rescue his mother from Simon's undulating hips.

"As insane as Simon looks right now, that crazy boy can dance," I said, still laughing. "I am not quite over the fact that you hired him to do our photos."

Ethan snuggled into me a little deeper. "Don't remind me, please. He blackmailed me, you know. Said he would forgive the whole mess if he could secure the wedding photography for us. I figured that would be okay, so I agreed. Then he sent me the contract. Trust me when I say that your friend Simon has been well compensated for his services today. He even sent me the bill for a fucking bespoke suit made in Milan!"

I nearly choked from laughing. "Oh my God!" I pointed at Simon slithering behind Ben's mom in his shiny green silk. "There you go, baby. Money well spent, I say. Simon looks soooo happy." I laughed some more.

"They'd better be fucking museum-quality photographs," Ethan muttered.

"I saw you dancing with the local beauty with the penchant for ice cream a little while ago," I said, hoping to divert attention to something more pleasant.

Ethan's whole face changed immediately. "She's so amazing. I hope our little peach is just like her if we have a girl." He put his hands over my stomach. "I can feel peaches now. Your belly is hard, and it wasn't before."

"Yep. Peaches is in there, all right." I put my hands over his.

"I love your dress. It's perfect. You're perfect."

"You're pretty hot yourself in that tux. You got a purple vest just for me. I love it. We are very matchy-matchy, Mr. Blackstone." And we were indeed. My cream lace dress had a purple belt that tied in the back, and I wore the amethyst and pearl heart pendant around my neck. Ethan had his violet striped vest and a deep purple lily on his jacket. My veil was long and simple, but I loved it because of the pictures I had taken wearing it. Pictures only for Ethan's eyes. I wanted him to see. "I have a gift for you," I said.

"That sounds very nice," he said with another nuzzle against my neck, "but everything about you is my gift." He held my face with both of his hands as I loved him to do. "How does Mrs. Blackstone feel about leaving here and getting started on the wedding night?"

One second later . . .

"Mrs. Blackstone is so onboard with that plan."

He held out his arm for me. "My lady, shall we?"

"Did I ever tell you how much I enjoy your gentlemanly manners? Such a contrast with that filthy mouth you've got, but man, it really works for me."

Ethan got a very pleased look in his eyes. "Well, that's really good to know, baby. I think I can walk that line for you." His eyes hooded, he drew my hand up to his lips. "I'll make sure of it tonight."

Thank sweet baby Jesus. "I have to run upstairs to our room and get my gift for you, okay? I'll just be a moment."

He kissed my hand and swirled his tongue in a circle, just above where my ring sat next to the wedding band he'd slipped on my finger during our vows, before letting me go. "I'll be waiting for you at the bottom of the stairs when you come down. I just have to tell Hannah that we're escaping," he purred at me.

"God, I love you so much," I said to him.

He gave me a rare Ethan smile and said, "I love you more."

"Highly doubtful," I called over my shoulder, "but I'll take it!"

I hurried to get the package from our bedroom and was coming back down when I sensed a warmth of feeling. It touched me, wrapping around my body like a cloak in a comforting way. I stopped on the landing where the magnificent Mallerton of Sir Jeremy and Georgina hung on the wall. I loved looking at this painting, and it wasn't just the subject matter or the execution, which was stunning, it was the emotion expressed in it. There was great love in this family. Sir Jeremy with his blue eyes and sandy hair looked to his lovely, fair Georgina with an expression that just exuded his deep love for her. I don't know how Tristan Mallerton managed to get it down in paint, but he most certainly had captured the moment between these lovers from so long ago. And it just took my breath away in its pureness.

And then there were the children—an older boy and a younger girl. The little girl sat on her mother's lap, but she had eyes only for her father. I imagined how he must have entertained her during the long hours of sittings for such a portrait as this. My art training gave me an understanding of the time involved to create a painting of this scale; it would have been immense. A child didn't look like that unless she felt it. This little girl had loved her daddy, and been loved very much by him in return. *Just like me.*

I love you so much, Daddy . . .

As I turned away from the painting to go down the rest of the way, I could see Ethan waiting for me at the bottom of the staircase. Just waiting patiently as if he understood I was having a moment and needed my privacy.

Ethan seemed to recognize my moods at times like this. And if I really thought about it, Ethan had been the greatest gift my dad had ever given to me.

Thomas Bennett, my precious and loving father, had sent Ethan Blackstone to find me in London so he could rescue me. I now had the rest of my life to be thankful for that fact.

Thank you, Daddy. I looked at the little girl in the painting and felt the connection with her, even with centuries between us. I hoped that Sir Jeremy Greymont's daughter had enjoyed many long years of knowing her father. Twenty-five years was the amount of time I had been given with mine, and I must accept it with grace for the priceless gift it was.

I refused to be sad in thinking of my dad on my wedding day. He was only a happy thought for me now. He loved me, and I loved him. He was still with me somehow, and I was still with him, and nothing could ever take that away from either of us.

"Keep your eyes closed until I tell you to open them, okay?" I parked the car and went over to Brynne's side to help her out. "No peeking, Mrs. Blackstone, I want to do this right."

"Eyes are closed, Mr. Blackstone," she said, standing before me. "My package. Give it to me, please."

I retrieved it from the seat and placed it carefully in her hands. It was light, just a flat black box tied with a silver ribbon. "Ready?"

"I am," she said.

"Okay, keep them closed, and I'm going to pick you up and carry you."

"Sounds very traditional," she said.

"I like to think of myself as a traditional guy, baby." I scooped her up, careful to arrange her dress so it wouldn't drag, and started walking up the gravel drive of Stonewell Court. The rocks crunched under my feet and you could hear the sound of the waves on the rocks far below us. It looked amazing and I hoped she liked it. The whole place was lit with torches in old urns and candles glowing inside glass luminaria on the ground. Even the upper suite was lit up from the inside. Our wedding-night suite.

"I can hear the ocean," she said up against me, one hand on the back of my neck lightly caressing back and forth.

"Mmm-hmm." I stopped at what I felt was the perfect place for the unveiling. "Okay, we have arrived at our nuptial destination, Mrs. Blackstone. I'm going to set you down so you can get the full effect," I warned before tilting her down to stand on her own. I faced her toward the house and covered her eyes gently with my hands.

"I want to look. Are we sleeping here?"

"Not sure how much *sleeping* we'll be doing . . . but we will be here tonight." I kissed her on the back of the neck and took my hands away. "For you, my beauty. You can open your eyes now."

"Stonewell Court. I thought this is where we were. I remember the smell of the sea and the sound of the gravel when we walked here. It's so beautiful I—I can't believe all this." She opened her arms. "Who did this for us?"

She still doesn't understand. I brought my hands to her shoulders and kissed her neck from behind. "Hannah, mostly. She's been trying to work a miracle for me."

"Well, I think she has succeeded. It takes my breath away." She turned to face me. "It's the perfect place for us to spend our wedding night," she said, leaning into my body.

I took her face in my hands and kissed her softly, surrounded by the glow of torches and the ocean breeze. "Do you like it?"

"I more than like it. I love that we get to be here." She turned back around and leaned into me again and looked at the house some more.

"I'm very glad about that, Mrs. Blackstone, because after we were here together I couldn't get this place out of my head. I wanted to bring you back here. The inside needs some attention, but the bones are good and the foundation stone-solid, perched up here on the rocks. This house has been here a long time and hopefully it will still be here a long time from now."

I slipped the small envelope from my pocket and brought it around to hold in front of her so she could see it.

"What's this?" she asked.

"It's your wedding present. Open it."

She opened the flap and tipped the odd assortment into her hand—some modern, some very old. "Keys?" She turned around, her eyes wide with shock. "You *bought* the house?!"

I couldn't hold back my grin. "Not exactly." I turned her to face the house again, drawing my arms around her from behind and resting my chin on the top of her head. "I bought us a home. For you and me, and for peaches, and any other raspberries or blueberries that might come along later. This place has plenty of rooms to put them in."

"How many blueberries are we talking here? Because I'm looking at a really big house that must have a lot of rooms to fill."

"That, Mrs. Blackstone, remains to be seen, but I can assure you that I will give you my very best efforts at filling a few."

"Ahh, then what are you standing out here for? Hadn't you better get cracking?" She asked smugly.

I swooped her up, and started walking. Fast. If she was ready for HoneymoonLand then I was not the fool to be delaying matters. Again, not a moron.

My legs swallowed up the rest of the path quickly, and then the stone steps of our new country house. "And the bride goes over the threshold," I said, pushing the heavy oaken door with my shoulder.

"You're getting more and more traditional all the time, Mr. Blackstone."

"I know. I kind of like it."

"Oh, wait, my package! I want you to open your gift too. Set me down. The lighted foyer will be perfect for you to see them with."

She handed me the black box tied with silver ribbon, looking very happy, and very lovely in her wedding lace and the heart pendant sitting at her throat. I had a small flash of the memory of what she'd endured that night with Westman, but I pushed it down and far away. There was no place in this moment for anything ugly. This was a time for joy.

I lifted the lid and pulled back some black tissue paper. The photographs revealed underneath stopped my heart. Brynne beautifully naked in many artistic poses, wearing nothing but her wedding veil.

"For you, Ethan. For your eyes only," she whispered. "I love you with all of my heart, and all of my mind, and with all of my body. It all belongs to you now."

I had trouble speaking at first, so I just stared at her for a moment and counted my blessings.

"The pictures are beautiful," I told her finally when I could get the words out. "They're beautiful, baby, and I . . . understand why now." Brynne needed to make beautiful pictures with her body. It was her reality. I needed to possess her—to take care of her in order to fulfill some dominant requirement within my psyche—my reality.

"I wanted you to have these pictures. They're for you only, Ethan. Only you will ever see them. They are my gift to you."

"I hardly have words." I looked through the poses slowly, soaking up the images and savoring them. "I like this one where you're looking over your shoulder, and your veil is down your back." I studied the photograph some more. "Your eyes are open . . . and you are looking at me."

She held my gaze with her beautiful multicolored eyes, which surprised me all the time with their changing hues, and said, "They are looking at you, but my eyes have really only been opened since you came into my world. You gave me everything. You made me really want to see what was around me, for the first time in my adult life. You made me want *you*. You made me want . . . a life. *You* were my greatest gift of all, Ethan James Blackstone." She reached up to touch my face and held her palm there, her eyes showing me so much of what she felt.

I covered her palm on my cheek with my hand. "As you were for me, my beautiful American girl."

I kissed my lovely bride in the foyer of our new old stone house for a long time. I wasn't in a hurry and neither was she. We had the luxury of forever right now and we would take it for the precious gift that it was.

When we were ready, I picked her up again, loving her soft weight resting against my body, and the tensing of my muscles as I carried her up the stairs to our awaiting suite where I would hold her all night long. *Holding on to her in order to hold me up.* The concept just made sense to me. I couldn't explain it to anyone else, but I didn't need to explain anything. I knew what we meant to each other.

Brynne *was* my greatest gift. She was the first person to really see inside me. Only her eyes seemed even capable of doing it. *Only my Brynne's eyes.*

A Gift for the Reader

A Christmas Story—
Ethan and Brynne's
Very First Meeting

24 December 2011
London

The street was remarkably sparse considering it was Christmas Eve. Probably because it was so damn freezing cold outside people were smart enough to stay in. It was totally clichéd to be shopping for a gift at this late minute, but here I was pushing my way through the doors of Harrods in hopes of something really perfect for my aunt Marie. I knew I'd better get my ass in gear too, because I would be spending the day with her tomorrow and had nothing to show up with!

Marie was hard to buy for because she was so unique and unconventional; it was ridiculously difficult to top her lifestyle. She also had money enough to get anything she desired. She reminded me of Auntie Mame from the movie in a lot of ways. From the exotic travels to the rich dead husbands to the fantastic dresses in her wardrobe.

After three quarters of an hour I gave up and started to head outside, stopping for a mocha coffee in the food court first. I needed the caffeine and the warmth.

I strolled down the street and sipped as I looked into shop windows for anything of interest. The bite from the cold air was going to put some color in my cheeks for sure. At least I had hot coffee, and the Christmas carols piped out from somewhere sounded nice. Very *Christmas Carol*-ish. I'm sure Dickens would have loved to know that 168 years later, some of the same songs were still playing. I loved history, and it made me smile to think that some traditions had changed hardly at all in those long years. Change isn't always a good thing. It takes a strong character to withstand the changes of time. I wish I could be strong like that.

Some days I wondered if I would last a long time. Despite my determination to be on my own in London, I missed my parents during the holidays. The decorating, and the baking, and the parties . . .

Well, maybe not the parties. Parties were not really my thing anymore. And I seriously wondered if I'd ever step foot in San Francisco again.

Move on—change of subject, please.

I came up to a shop window that looked intriguing. Like an antiques shop or secondhand store. The name on the door was etched in the glass: TUCKED AWAY. And it certainly was. There were tons of these small shops in London, and some of them were beautifully arranged. This was one of them. I stepped inside and heard a bell jingle at the top of the door.

"Happy Christmas," a cheerful voice called out.

"Happy Christmas," I returned to the smiling face of an older gentleman wearing the Brit uniform of sweater vest and tweed jacket.

The shop smelled good. Like cinnamon. I would bake at Aunt Marie's tomorrow, and I looked forward to that. I loved to cook, but it lost something when there was nobody to cook for. I felt a sigh coming and suppressed it.

I gravitated toward a section of soft knits. These were obviously a consignment of some sort. Not antiques. Scarf-and-hat combos in so many colors. I pulled out a dark-purple set and fingered the scarf. It felt like cashmere, it was that soft. Probably lamb's wool, though. I checked the price and raised a brow. But I wanted it. Hell, I needed it on a day like today. I looked at the price again and decided it was okay to splurge on myself. It was Christmas, after all.

Who in the hell are you kidding, foolish woman? You still have nothing for Marie.

I think I was starting to panic a bit. I sighed and kept looking.

I drifted around and found nothing and decided it was time to leave. I stepped up to the counter to pay for my hat and scarf and saw the display of costume jewelry under the glass. Now this caught my eye. It was very pretty stuff, for one thing—vintage bohemian fit Marie's personality like a leather glove. *Score!*

One piece stood out clearly to me and it was perfect. A dove pin. Silver with seed pearls on the wing and tail, a black crystal eye and a tiny heart charm dangling from its beak with a blue crystal in the center. A dove symbolized peace, and God knows the world could certainly use some of that. The best part was that I could picture my aunt wearing this pin. I knew she'd love it.

I paid in a rush, almost giddy to have struck gold in my labors of gift-buying angst. Checking my watch, I knew I needed to get going and saw it was a bit of a walk to my Tube station.

It was cold.

Frickin' frigid.

Cold enough that I pulled on the new hat and wrapped the scarf around my neck right then and there on the street. I checked my face quickly in the window of a parked car, just to make sure there wasn't something stupid-looking in my appearance—not that I cared too much when it was so freezing.

I walked another couple of blocks until I couldn't stand the cold another second, and pushed into the first place that had a door with a WE'RE OPEN sign. FOUNTAINE'S AQUARIUM. I was in a pet store. Or more correctly, a tropical fish shop. Worked for me. It was warm and quite dim inside, the humidity rising from the tanks making it a pleasant change from where I'd just been. I unwound my scarf and wandered around, stopping by each tank to observe and read the names of the fish.

The saltwater section reminded me of a trip I took to Maui when I was fourteen. I'd gotten to snorkel and see some of the same fish that were in these tanks. I didn't know it at the time, but that vacation had been the last one I'd take with both of my parents. My mom and dad separated soon afterward, and there would never be another trip for all of us as a family unit. *Sad.* They had to fight to be civil to each other now. *Well, isn't that the perfect oxymoron . . . "fight to be civil."*

I stopped at one particularly interesting fellow. A lionfish. Lionfish are something else up close, with all their spiky colored fins making them look unreal. This guy seemed curious, and came right up to the glass and fluttered at me as if he wanted to have a conversation. He was cute. I knew they were poisonous to touch, but still captivating to watch. I imagined that a saltwater aquarium was a great deal of work to maintain.

"Hey, handsome," I whispered to the fish.

"Can I help you with anything?" a young guy asked behind me.

"Just admiring. He's really a beautiful fish," I told the store clerk.

"Yeah, he's been sold, actually. The owner is coming to pick him up today and take him home."

"Ahhh, well, I hope you're happy at your new home then, handsome." I spoke to the fish again: "Hopefully it's someone who'll spoil you with treats."

The clerk agreed with me and chuckled.

I turned away from the tank, deciding it was time to brave the outside cold yet again and head home to my flat. I still needed to wrap Marie's gift, and I had plans to bake tonight—some sugar cookies that I would take over there tomorrow. It was a little tradition we'd started, and it was really fun piping on the frosting and adding sprinkles to decorate them. My favorites were the snowflake ones.

I headed for the door to leave, adjusting my hat and re-wrapping my scarf around my neck and halfway up my face, when someone entered the shop. I stepped aside to let him pass and was impressed with what looked like a tall person and a nice coat, but I didn't look up at him. My eyes were focused on what lay beyond the open door of the shop.

Snowflakes.

It was snowing on Christmas Eve in London!

"It's snowing?" I muttered in amazement.

"Yeah . . . it is," he said.

I stepped out into the white and caught the most appealing scent on him as we passed each other. Like some exotic spice mixed with an indulgent mix of soap and cologne. *It was nice when a man smelled so good,* I thought. Lucky girl, whoever was getting to smell that all the time.

I went up to the window of a black Range Rover HSE parked on the street and checked my hat in the window's reflection as I'd done before when I'd started out. I didn't want to look like a dork on my walk home.

The snow had started falling more heavily now, and I could see some flakes beginning to settle on my new purple hat, even just in the reflection in the Rover's window. I smiled under my scarf as I turned to go.

I was cold on my walk home. Cold . . . but strangely content. Snow for Christmas, for a California girl, all on her own in London at the holidays. Totally unexpected. But I realized something on my way home. The small things in life are sometimes the most precious gifts we are given, and if you recognize them when they arrive, then you are truly blessed.